How long 1
closed? Ten min.

Too long. If that door didn't open within two minutes… She felt for the flashlight next to the rolled-up jeans she used for a pillow, and she began to count.

When she reached seventy-four, something sharp and human cut into the howl of the wind, the way a rodent might shriek at the sudden squeeze of an owl's talons.

She stopped counting and rose up sitting.

No, God, no.

The door opened and even before the wind's entrance, Susan screamed a name…

Cooper's Loot

by

Rick E. George

Cooper's Loot

Cover Art by *Debbie Taylor*

The Wild Rose Press, Inc.
PO Box 708
Adams Basin, NY 14410-0708
Visit us at www.thewildrosepress.com

Publishing History
First Mainstream Historical Edition, 2019
Print ISBN 978-1-5092-2614-6
Digital ISBN 978-1-5092-2615-3

Published in the United States of America

Dedication

To my wife April and my daughter Emily,
who embody what it means to be strong women

Acknowledgements

I'm so lucky. I've got an awesome critique group. Thanks to Renae Canon, Janelle Childs, Glenn Harris, Jennie Mansfield, Jackie McManus, and Vernon Wade for telling it like it is and making me work harder. You see stuff that I don't.

Also thanks to Nan Swanson, my editor at The Wild Rose Press—you've got a heap of patience to put up with me.

Chapter One

On a drizzly November night in 1972, Bev Wikowski drove her VW Beetle onto a gravel lot, where *Beer Here* in frosty blue letters blinked like a beacon. Although she didn't want a beer or any other drink, she parked near the entrance and peered at the Spar Pole Saloon, so weathered it looked like it had been built shortly after Lewis and Clark paddled by on the Columbia River.

Brown planks pocked with paint blisters and spots of bare wood glistened beneath the buzzing neon sign. Rain dribbled off the roof over the entry. From nearby pulp mills, an odor like rotting asparagus climbed into her car.

She picked up her yellow notepad and squinted through four pages of notes from her interview with June Harrison, a Kelso High School basketball player who'd scored forty-three points two nights ago. After flipping to a blank page, she hung a Pentax 35mm camera on a strap around her neck and stepped out of the car into an ankle-deep puddle. Cold water sloshed over the top of her black platform shoe and drenched her sock.

"Shit!" She hopped backward.

The puddle spread in front of her like a small pond, and she giant-stepped to the far side. It was only twelve feet from her VW to the Spar Pole's boot-scuffed white door, but if it kept raining, she'd have to snorkel to get back to her car. She looked again at the notepad, already damp. Did she really need it? Would it get in the way of what she wanted to do?

She leaned forward, tossed the notepad back inside, and hid the camera under the front seat. She closed the door, almost losing her grip and falling face first into the water.

Inside the Spar Pole, a tinge of whiskey wafted through fumes of beer and cigarettes. The only man sitting at a bar that stretched left to right made no effort to assess who'd walked in as Waylon Jennings sang on the jukebox.

Opposite the bar, a thirty-something cocktail waitress with slightly Asian features and shaggy brown hair raised an eyebrow at Bev before lifting a tray of beers and walking out to the right side of the room. She stopped at a cluster of people leaning toward someone sitting in a chair with his back to the wall. Out the left side of the bar in an adjoining room, two pool tables stood, one empty and the other abandoned with eight balls remaining.

Bev tapped a finger against the side of her skirt. If she was going to finagle the quote she wanted for her story, the man at the bar was her only option. She could park next to him, bat her eyes, show a little leg. *Hey, mister. You heard about what June Harrison did, right? What do you think, a girl scoring like that? Bumping and sweating and breathing hard like she was a boy?*

She'd get her lascivious quote. Instead of a news article, she'd write a little commentary in her weekly column. Her readers would understand exactly what she was saying.

Or she could drop her idiotic idea and write the story straight up and it would be fine. What a girl, this June Harrison. Forty-three points in a game. Wow.

Over at the group, the waitress had squeezed next to a middle-aged man wearing a black cowboy hat with a gold band. Someone in the huddle shifted, opening a gap through which Bev could better see the speaker, a man with dark hair hanging to his shoulders and a black beard thick with corkscrew curls that obscured most of his face and drooped to his chest. He noticed her through the same gap and nodded while continuing to talk. At the same moment, Waylon's hollered lamentations ended in a fade-out, revealing the speaker's voice—low-pitched, calm, like a captain addressing his crew.

The waitress must have noticed the man's nod, because she turned from the group and locked her eyes onto Bev, and before Bev could escape, she called out to her.

"Pardon me, honey." She strode toward Bev. "I just got hooked into what that man was saying."

Bev tapped on her leg again. "Who is he?"

The waitress came closer, glanced at the man at the bar and lowered her voice. "He says he knows DB Cooper."

Bev's whole body lit up like the *Beer Here* neon sign—and just as quickly faded dark.

Yeah, sure. Cooper's buddy. Along with a thousand other crackpots.

"I never seen him before, but he seems to know a lot about the…" The waitress stopped herself, pressed her lips together.

"The hijacking?" offered Bev.

"Yeah, and more than that."

Bev suppressed a guffaw. The waitress seemed so earnest, so gullible.

And yet…

What if…

"What're you drinking tonight?" asked the waitress.

"I'm not sure." Her right foot soaked and her sock squishy, Bev walked to the group and filled the gap close to Beard-Face. One step behind her, the waitress squeezed next to Cowboy-Man again.

Beard-Face eyed a short thin man with a cleft chin and thick eyelashes. "It's not even close to where the FBI's been looking." He exhaled smoke onto the table, where a large Forest Service map lay partially open, with a smaller topographic map next to it.

Cleft-Chin placed his index finger in the middle of a large circle drawn on the Forest Service map. "I'm not jumping out the door tomorrow morning to go bushwhacking with the likes of you after a bunch of money no one else could find. What a load of horse shit."

He put a half-smoked cigarette in his mouth and walked away.

"Suit yourself," said Beard-Face. "I can't take all of you with me anyway. All I need is a half dozen volunteers."

Bev shifted to the spot left by the vacating man. "For what?" she asked.

The others diverted attention her way, annoyance in their eyes.

Beard-Face stood, set his cigarette on an ashtray, and offered a hand. His eyes suggested the goodwill of

4

a man comfortable in his ability to whup anyone's ass. He had crow's feet off the sides of his eyes and puffy skin below them, and the wrinkles across his forehead suggested a forty-year-old accountant more than a flower child. Bev shook his hand.

"Name's Andy O'Brien," he said. "I'm here on behalf of the man people call DB Cooper. I know him, and I know approximately where he hid the money, because he told me."

The neon sign flashed again. That would be a hell of a story. Front page. Not just her newspaper, the *Portland Morning Chronicle*, but *The New York Times*.

On the other hand…this guy was probably a nut job.

"You're saying the money's still out there?" She tried to keep the cynicism from her voice.

"Exactly."

"The army, the cops, the FBI, and everybody's uncle combed the woods, and none of them found a trace."

"That's because they were looking in the wrong places. Cooper—we might as well call him that—had quite a few chuckles hearing where they put all their manpower. I had no clue, because I didn't know he was him, not until a week ago. He fooled them in every way. Fooled me, too."

"Why doesn't he just go get it himself?" Bev asked.

"We already asked that." A man with crewcut blond hair spat tobacco juice into a Styrofoam cup. Garbed in blue jeans with red suspenders over a long-sleeved blue shirt, he looked far too young to be in a bar. "He said DB figures he'd get busted. But the feds won't bother with a bunch of loonies pokin' around."

O'Brien sat down and continued relating what he claimed DB Cooper had told him.

"It was dark and it was raining when he hit the ground. Everyone knows that. He built a small fire and waited out the night. It was cold, but nothing like what he and I endured in Korea. He wasn't sure exactly where he was, just that it was in the mountains south of where they'd think he landed, and he was damn lucky he didn't have to cut himself loose from the top of a tree.

"In the morning he walked south. When he hit a logging road, he followed it to a bigger dirt road that eventually connected to another road pointing south. He spent another night in the woods, and the next day he hit a gravel road, and a Forest Service sign told him where he was."

"He must have been hungry," said Bev.

"He had C-rats," said Under-Ager impatiently, his eyes still fixed on Andy.

"Tanya," a male voice called from behind them. The waitress stepped back, picked up her tray, and moved toward the bar.

"What, he just stuffed them in his pockets?" asked Bev.

Under-Ager rolled his eyes. "He had a knapsack."

"A knapsack?" Bev didn't remember reading anything about DB Cooper having a knapsack. The reports—the whole nation had been fascinated—depicted him having a briefcase with a bomb that was probably fake. Dressed in a white shirt and a black clip-on tie, he was polite, paying for his bourbon and water and offering a tip. They landed in Seattle and after several hours, the airline's owner personally delivered a duffel bag containing $200,000 in a hundred bundles of twenty-dollar bills. They gave him a choice of parachutes.

"Let me go backwards for a second." O'Brien took a drag from the half-smoked cigarette. "Cooper had a knapsack. It was in an overhead bin several rows in front of him."

"And I suppose he told you that, too?" Bev pressed her lips together to rein what would have been a mocking grin.

"He did," said O'Brien, his voice unruffled.

Under-Ager spun toward her so fast she thought the spittle might slosh from his cup. "Ma'am, some of us want to hear the story. You don't want to listen, you go back to wherever you come from."

She met his glare with an impassive face. At least she didn't need a fake ID to get inside. At least she knew how to ask questions, instead of swallowing whatever load of crap some too-old hippy decided to blather.

O'Brien's beard widened with a half smile, and his eyes gleamed.

What if he were right, and he knew how to find the money, and she wasn't there when she could have been?

She reached into her jacket pocket and retrieved a cigarette from her pack of Salem 100s.

"Once he knew where he was," O'Brien resumed, "he backtracked the dirt road what he guessed to be about three miles. He came to a smaller road that cut into the woods, overgrown, like a logging road that hadn't been used in years. He cut a certain mark on a tree, and he took the road and walked a while, switchbacking up a mountain. When he came to a creek that crossed under the road, he marked a tree, and then he went off the road, going uphill and marking trees along the way. He found a spot he liked, marked three trees to form a triangle, and he used a folding spade to bury almost all the money. Buried the clothes he wore on the plane, too."

"*Most* all the money?" asked the man in the black cowboy hat.

Behind them, on the other side of the saloon, a thwack indicated that the rack of balls on the second pool table was now broken.

"Later that winter, he buried a couple of bundles in a place where he figured someone would find them. I have no idea where that was. Fact is, he never told me anything 'til last week, and I was just like you, miss"— he nodded toward Bev—"thinking he was bullshitting me. By the way, you want a beer or whatever, just let Tanya know. Everything's on my tab."

"Well, hell," said Under-Ager. "If it's all marked and you know which road, you could find it yourself."

"That's what he thought, and that's what I meant to do yesterday. But I ran into some difficulty. First off, the bigger logging road ended up very, very rocky. It reached the point where I had to get out and walk. The mark's not easy to find, and there are several logging roads with green gates. Once I found the right one, I didn't get more than a quarter mile up it, and guess what I ran into?"

He paused. Bev leaned forward to flick her cigarette over an ashtray next to the maps. She glanced at the circle someone had drawn—it encompassed a lake and a town named Ariel in tiny lettering. When she leaned back she noticed O'Brien watching her.

"Don't go tellin' us Bigfoot," said Under-Ager.

O'Brien shook his head. "A fucking clear-cut."

Cowboy-Man chuckled until a coughing fit choked away the amusement.

"No shit. When I got back last night, I called Cooper, and he started laughing, too. All that planning he did, risking his neck to pull it off, staying the hell away for a solid year, and for what? A bunch of loggers cut most all the trees that marked the path. But it looked to me like the back end of the clear-cut wasn't as far as he said he'd hiked before he buried everything, and so I kept going on the little logging road. I crossed four culverts beneath the road from one side of the clear-cut to the other."

"And any one of them could've been where he marked the next tree," said Under-Ager.

O'Brien took another drag from his cigarette. "Now you know why I'm here. Cooper said to find myself a down-to-earth tavern and see who I could round up. Said to split twenty-five percent among our little search party, and I'm supposed to bring him back seventy-five percent. *If* we find it. First big snow of the season is supposed to hit Saturday night, so we'll have Thursday and Friday and then maybe that's the last anyone's going to be digging around in there 'til spring. Cooper—you know that's not his name, right?"

Bev and the others nodded.

"Cooper said he knows for a fact that he walked at least half a mile off the logging road into the woods, so it wouldn't be in the place they clear-cut."

"People think they're walkin' a straight line when

they're in the trees, but they're not," said Under-Ager.

"I suppose that's right," said O'Brien. "Anyway, this morning I called the company that owns it, the Cowlitz Lumber Company, and they told me they're going to start logging next spring where they left off."

"Not if I buy it." Cowboy-Man removed his hat and wiped a hand across the top of his head as though he'd forgotten he'd lost almost all his hair. Wide-shouldered, with a slight paunch, he wore one of those black cowboy shirts with snaps instead of buttons, and swirly lines below the shoulders.

O'Brien gave Cowboy-Man a questioning look and waited.

"Ted Martin." He extended a hand, which O'Brien shook.

Martin returned the hat to his head. "I'm in town to negotiate the purchase of the Cowlitz Lumber Company. I'm meeting with the owners on Monday. I've been scouting their land for three days."

"Best of luck to you," said O'Brien.

"Two hundred Gs. That'd help pay for the purchase. And it'd be my land it's buried in. Maybe I'd let the rest of *you* split twenty-five percent. How 'bout that, Andy?"

O'Brien nodded. "How many miles of logging road you figure you're buying? I'd guess pretty near all of it's on a hillside. How much of it have they logged in the last year?"

"So good luck to me, huh? I've got a question for you, too, Andy. Suppose my brother's a county sheriff?"

O'Brien made a show of considering the possibility, then nodded. "I suppose we could let him join us, anyway."

Under-Ager laughed.

Tanya stepped next to Bev. "What can I get you?" she asked.

"A screwdriver, and tell your bartender not to water it down."

"You're going to have to show me some ID, honey."

"I'm twenty-three years old."

"You're going to have to show me."

Bev sighed. Her wet toes were freezing, and she wanted a drink. She *deserved* a drink. The others eyed her as she extracted her license from the wallet in her purse. Tanya peered at it and nodded, but she stayed with the group.

Under-Ager, whom Bev guessed would never pass the ID test, broke the silence. "You're goin' to be my new boss. I'll be one of your worker bees. I'm a choker. Jim Rossi."

Martin kept his eyes on O'Brien. "Well, Jim, everybody's got to start somewhere. Both my boys worked as chokers. Even now they don't set foot in the office. As for my brother, his jurisdiction is two states away. None of this is his business."

"Then why'd you bring it up?" asked Andy.

"I don't like con artists."

Andy showed no anger. "How smart would it be for a man to lead folks into the woods looking for marked trees and digging holes, and all of it's a scam? All he'd get is a bunch of pissed-off people."

"Maybe you do think you know where the loot is, but maybe you're a crackpot and all this talk about knowing DB Cooper is just your way of finding a bunch of fools to help you out."

"No one's twisting your arm, Ted. You're free to go. I'll still pick up the tab for your beer. Hell, have another one and go shoot some pool."

"Now, wait a minute. Who said I'm not interested?"

"What a riot," said the woman by the wall. Bev's age or maybe younger, she had a narrow face and a pointed chin, flaxen blonde hair that flowed halfway down her back, a necklace of polished wood beads, and a lavender turtleneck sweater. She wore the kind of knee-high glossy brown boots that Bev would never ever buy even if she could afford them. The man she had her arm around towered above the rest of the group, at least six foot four, with tightly coiled dust-colored hair and a close-trimmed beard. He wore the de rigueur blue paisley bandanna headband above a pair of bloodshot eyes that pronounced him a bona fide Hippie Guy.

Bev and the others eyed Blondie.

"Suppose we do find the money. We split it evenly—even our barmaid here. Fifty thousand divided by seven, a hair over seven grand per person. Sounds pretty good—more than most of you earn in a year, I'll bet. And we'll all be nice, a bunch of thieves who don't know each other, flush with cash. Assuming we're still fuzzy-wuzzy friends when we get back to civilization, none of us will turn around and go to the cops and sell our story to the *National Enquirer*."

Now everyone looked at O'Brien, who took a draw from his cigarette and let out a slow exhale of smoke.

"I tried telling Cooper it'll be complicated to round up a crew. You want to sell the story? We talked about that, too. We decided we don't care who you tell, as long as you wait until the next day after we get back, so we can implement our exit plan. Just know that if you do that, you'll have the rest of the group mighty displeased, and even if they wind up in jail, you never know what their friends might do to get back at you."

Bev let the smoke ease out her mouth.

For her, telling someone would be the whole point. It would be the biggest scoop of the year. Put that on her résumé. She'd say adios to the *Chronicle* and move up to a real newspaper like the *Oregonian*. She'd cover real news with real impact.

Jim held up a hand as though he were in a classroom.

"I ain't saying I'm going," he said, "but if I do, I'd want everyone in the group to make a pledge."

"I hear you, man," said Hippie-Guy. "Like we won't narc each other out, no matter what. We'll look out for each other, you know, all for one and one for all."

Blondie laughed, her derision obvious.

"Son," said Ted, "Whatever you're smoking, I'd like to try it."

O'Brien flicked his cigarette onto a tray set atop the topo map. He moved his gaze around the group. "Since we're talking about agreements, there's something else you'd better understand. Assuming we find the money, which I believe we will, you can't spend it and you can't put it in a bank. Every financial institution in America is looking for those twenties. You have to hold onto the money until this whole DB Cooper thing blows over. Cooper says that's at least two years, and I agree."

Two years? Hell, Bev wouldn't wait two days. Maybe this story would be her ticket to someplace even bigger, *The New York Times* or the *Washington Post.* She and her daughter Sandra would have to move out of her parents' home, but with the salary she'd be making, she could hire an au pair, maybe a French girl, and Sandra could learn another language. She wouldn't have to grow up in a backwater burg that fancied itself a city. In a year she'd start kindergarten, and she'd be with kids from all around the world.

And Billy—her heart felt squeezed at the thought of her deceased husband—he'd be proud of the little daughter he'd never met. If there were an afterlife and he was watching them, he'd be pleased to watch her grow into a sophisticated young woman.

"Wow, man," said Hippie-Guy. "You think you can walk in here and round up a posse, no problem. I'll bet you everyone here has somewhere to be on Thanksgiving besides some logging company's land."

O'Brien put the cigarette back in his mouth and moved the ashtray. He picked up one of the maps and rolled it. "This wasn't my idea. I've got somewhere to be tomorrow, too. Tell you what. We all go to our families for Thanksgiving. Friday morning, five a.m., anyone wanting a share of fifty thousand dollars, show up in front of the Best Western next door. You won't see me, but I'll be watching to see who shows up. With enough people, we'll find a tree with one of Cooper's marks. Like this young lady said, if there's six of us, that's over eight grand. If there's four, that's over twelve grand, and I'm guessing that's three years' wages for most of you. If it's just me, I'll do my damnedest to find one of those trees on my own."

He put a rubber band around the topo map and picked up the other one. "Don't be blabbing about this, and don't bring anyone else with you. If I see someone different with any of you, I'll leave all of you in front of the hotel and go looking on my own. Don't bring any kind of weapon. People can get a little funny when they're carrying large quantities of cash."

"How about weed?" asked Hippie-Guy. "I scored some Maui Wowie yesterday."

Jim guffawed and only partially hit the cup when he spat. "I knew it."

O'Brien stood. "Just don't bring any hard drugs. I'll be driving, and there will be no smoking dope in the vehicle. Now, let me ask."

He scanned the faces of everyone around him.

"Anyone here know for sure that you *won't* be here Friday morning?"

Bev scanned the others, who were busy scanning everyone else, too. Nobody raised a hand. She wanted to raise hers—the whole proposition was ridiculous—but for some reason, she couldn't.

Chapter Two

Bev tapped the handle of her fork onto her placemat and stole a glance at the plates of the rest of her family. More than halfway through the Thanksgiving meal—and she still hadn't revealed what she wanted them to think she'd be doing tomorrow.

"Hey, Mommy! Look!"

At the children's card table, Sandra brushed aside a barrette hanging from her hair over her face, but it swiveled back in front of her again. Pea-sized red globs leaked from her mouth onto the white paper tablecloth. "My lips are bleeding."

Bev put a hand to her chest and raised her eyebrows. "My goodness, Little Goose! That's a lot of blood. Would you like me to collect it in a cup?"

Sandra squirmed atop an unabridged dictionary that served as a booster chair, and her cousins giggled. "It's cranberry sauce, silly," she said.

Bev's mother turned in her chair to examine her granddaughter. She pushed back the sleeve of her floral-print dress and dabbed her mouth with a napkin. ""I'm so relieved. I thought we were going to have to bandage your lips shut."

"We can still do that," said Pops from the head of the table. "But let's use duct tape."

Sandra licked cranberry sauce from the back of her hand. "What's duck tape?"

16

"It's big wide silver tape," said Bev. "You use it on ducks, but it will work for a little goose, too."

"On my mouth?" Sandra widened her eyes and covered her mouth, a gesture her cousin Monica, also four years old, copied. Thirteen-month-old Paul, perched in a high chair, and six-year-old Tony observed the girls with curiosity.

"On your bill," said Bev.

"I don't have a bill."

"Yes, you will. For the cost of cleaning the tablecloth."

Sandra puckered her lips and mimicked Bev's raised eyebrows. "Goofy Town!"

"That's where we found you," said Pops. "Hiding with the other goslings."

Sandra turned to her cousins. "Where am I from?"

"Goofy Town," answered Monica and Tony, for perhaps the hundredth time, though it was only two o'clock.

Bev glanced at her brothers Justin and Alex, their wives Joann and Cathy, and finally at Pops. Goofy Town?

Justin, the oldest of the siblings, had a dark brown beard and hair so long it was amazing it had missed a dip in the gravy so far, while Alex, two months a civilian since the Army had honorably discharged him, kept his face clean-shaven and his walnut-brown hair military short. Justin wore a beige smock with a beaded necklace. Alex was in a neatly-pressed white dress shirt.

At Bev's left, Justin's wife Joann had straight brown hair draped over a peasant blouse, while to Bev's right, Alex's wife Cathy had probably spent an hour curling her medium-length blonde hair. She wore strawberry-red lipstick, a blue dress, and a faux-pearl necklace. Meanwhile, Pops sported an enormous handlebar moustache and a Thanksgiving clip-on bowtie over a plaid flannel shirt.

If Goofy Town meant odd combinations, then that described Bev's family. But if they knew what she intended to do the next day, the Goofy Town residents would unite to oppose the plan.

And maybe they were right.

Pops stood up and sliced more turkey. "You got chains, Alex?"

"Won't need them."

"What makes you so sure?"

"We're leaving Saturday morning instead of Sunday."

Bev paused, half-chewed turkey still in her mouth. They were talking about the storm Andy O'Brien had mentioned.

"Look, Mommy! I got a fat finger." At the card table, Sandra held up her hand, sporting a pitted black olive on the tip of her pinkie.

"Let's not play with our food," said Bev, before noticing Monica had four fat fingers as well as black front teeth.

Bev passed Cathy's plate to Joann. Pops put a slab of breast meat on it and passed it back. "Try to outrun the storm, huh?" he said to Alex.

"That's the plan. I've got chains. I'd rather not have to put them on."

"We'll miss you," said Bev's mother. "You, too, Cathy. And Monica and Paul. Your old church friends are expecting you."

"Sorry, Mom. Maybe next time." Alex lifted a glass of white wine toward his mother. "This beats the hell..." He looked over at the children's table. "...the *heck* out of last Thanksgiving. They had turkey at base camp, but my unit was on patrol. We had C-rations."

"Well, we're glad you made it back," said Bev's mother.

"Here, here!" Pops raised his glass. "Home without a scratch."

They all joined in the toast. Sandra and her cousins also raised their cups.

Relief and gratitude filled Bev, and then a dull ache consumed her.

Billy hadn't come home. Even now, almost five years later, the vacancy of it was like a pit into which she had never stopped falling. She felt a hand on her own hand and looked up to see Alex had reached across the table for her.

"I'm sorry," he said.

"I'm okay."

He nodded quietly.

"Mommy, can I have some more potatoes?" Sandra called.

"Come over here, Little Goose," said Bev. "You can sit on my lap and have the rest of mine."

"I want to sit with my cousins!"

"If you want more potatoes, you have to come here. It's your choice."

Keeping her spoon, Sandra abandoned her cousins. Bev scooted back her chair and pulled her daughter onto her lap. She pressed her cheek on Sandra's back and the pain of loss softened.

The plates were almost empty now. Bev was

running out of time. She didn't want to tell the same lie six different times to six different people, but that's what would happen if she didn't get it done before her family broke away from the meal.

"Hey, everyone," she began.

The adults stopped. Little Goose continued eating Bev's potatoes.

"If you all don't mind looking after Sandra, I'll be going into the mountains overnight tomorrow for a newspaper story."

Mirth disappeared from Alex's face. "You've seen the forecast?"

"Storm on the way Saturday night into Sunday. But I'll be back by then."

"Cold this time of year," said Pops.

"I'll stay warm. Can I borrow one of our tents? And maybe some other stuff?"

"Mommy, are you leaving?" Sandra had stopped chewing.

"Just for one night. Tomorrow night. And then I'll be back."

"I don't want you to go."

"One night. That's all. And you'll have your cousins with you."

"What's the news story?" asked Bev's mother, worry in her eyes and voice.

"We'll be seeking the elusive chanterelle."

"Is that like Bigfoot?" asked Justin.

"It's a kind of mushroom," Joann answered before Bev.

"Who's *we*?" asked Justin, using the same big brother voice he'd used six years ago when Bev was still in high school.

"What do you mean?" she asked.

"You said *we* are searching for the…for the whatever you call it."

"I'm going with an expert mycologist," said Bev.

Alex set down his wine. "My-what?"

"Mycologist. An expert on mushrooms."

"What's his name? Or her?"

"Andrew."

"Who else is going?" asked Bev's mother.

"A few others. It's not going to be dangerous. If we're going to find the mushrooms, we need to do it before it freezes. And then I'll do a big recipe page and write about collecting them."

"Whereabouts in the mountains?" asked Justin.

"We're not really sure yet. Maybe above Stevenson or Cascade Locks."

Sandra no longer wiggled or ate. Bev knew her daughter was listening to every word, trying to understand why everyone seemed upset at her mommy.

"You don't know where you're going to be? What if something happens?" Bev's mother scooted her chair back and set her napkin on the table.

"Nothing's going to happen."

"How can you know that?"

"There will be others. Someone could always get help, but we're not going to need it."

"I don't mind watching Sandra, honey. It's your safety I'm worried about. Camping in the mountains? With a storm about to hit?"

"Justin and Alex went winter camping when they were with the Scouts." Bev felt like a child as soon as the words escaped her mouth—*you let my brothers go…what about me?*

"It's not the same situation," said Justin.

"We could at least tell Pops and Mom where we were going," said Alex.

They were all against her—because they were right. This was stupid.

On the other hand, she wasn't going to let them get between her and a possible Pulitzer Prize. Sometimes reporters—at least the good ones—took chances. Besides, it wasn't like she was going to Vietnam.

Sandra twisted around so she could look at Bev. "Mommy, are you going to be okay?"

"I'll be fine. Your grandma and grandpa and your uncles and aunts are just a little worried. Like I worry about you when you're climbing the bars at the playground."

Bev's mother glanced at Sandra, then back at Bev. "Why do you have to be there overnight? Couldn't you go with them for the day and then come home?"

"That's…I suppose I could. But that's not how it was arranged. Everyone's going in the same van. It's hard to find chanterelles. Andrew said we might not find them at all. It's late in the year, and for sure if it snows Sunday that will be the end of the season for them. But I don't have to go. I could tell them I'm not going."

No one said a word.

Go ahead. Tell us you're not going. That's what their silence said.

"Think about this," said Bev. "If it were Justin or Alex going into the woods with some buddies for a night, it wouldn't be as big a deal, would it? It's because I'm a woman. I'm the only woman in that newsroom, so what do they assign me? The Women's

22

Pages. And they put me at the desk by the door so I can greet visitors and lead them to the right reporter. I'm surprised they haven't asked me to make coffee."

Sandra had turned toward the table again, but she wasn't eating. Bev kissed the back of her head.

"I've been thinking," continued Bev. "Maybe I can do a series of pages that feature recipes with foods you can gather in the wild. Put a little adventure into the pages. I want to do something different, because writing about fashion shows and garden clubs is boring me to death."

She looked at her mother. "No offense, Mom. I think your garden is fantastic."

"Okay, Bev," said Pops. "You know I've supported your career. I'm proud of you. We all are. But that's not what we're talking about."

Bev took a breath. "I know, I know. Look, if I get a chance to use a pay phone when we know for sure where we're going, I'll give you a call."

Pops nodded. "Please do that. It looks like we're not going to be able to talk you out of it. Same as always. At least give us all the information you can."

"You bet, Pops."

The air was thick with conflict. She felt like she'd ruined the whole meal. She was sure Sandra could sense it—the mashed potatoes on Bev's plate had grown cold.

If she did end up with a DB Cooper story, she would tell them she'd had to keep it secret. She'd say she was sorry she'd misled them. But now look, she'd say—*one of the biggest stories of the year!*

The mood remained quiet as Bev and her mother brought out two pumpkin pies, an apple pie, and whipped cream. She threw herself full-bore into the cleanup, as if that could atone for her foolishness.

Later, in the garage, she gathered her backpack and camping gear, and she fished out some freeze-dried camper meals left over from a family trip in August, the one she couldn't go on because she'd begun her job at the *Chronicle.* She'd been thrilled to get hired right out of college on a newspaper close to home, but it had been agonizing to spend nine days without Sandra, who'd gone on the camping trip.

She rolled a folded tarp over the tent bag, strapped it to the top of her pack, and examined her supply list one last time. Outside, a mild wind blew, and a branch from their apple tree tapped the garage window. She smiled. For years, Pops had been saying he was going to prune that tree.

She put the box of camping supplies back on a shelf and hoisted her pack on one shoulder. Maybe this trip wouldn't amount to anything—but it if did, the world would know what Bev Wikowski was capable of doing.

After three hours of fitful sleep, at two in the morning she kissed Sandra, who shared a bed with cousin Monica. She drove to the *Chronicle* newsroom in order to research year-old newspapers about the infamous DB Cooper hijacking, and then she left for Kelso.

Chapter Three

Bev parked her Volkswagen near Kelso High School on a street where it wouldn't be noticed or towed. She hoisted her backpack and hiked a quarter mile past a gas station, a McDonalds, and a Denny's until she reached the motel parking lot next to the Spar Pole.

Ted, the young couple, and the waitress stood beneath a Douglas fir in the fringe of a street lamp thirty yards away. Pre-dawn air bit through her apricot-colored parka, and fog streamed from the others' lips when they greeted her.

An evergreen scent mixed with the cigarette smoke Blondie exhaled. She had a name now, Susan Taylor, her trim body cocooned in a luxurious white coat that hung halfway down her thighs, with black fur lining the collar and hood. Hippie-Guy, garbed in an army surplus coat and the same blue paisley headband he'd worn two nights ago, identified himself as Will Garfield. Both were students at Willamette University, Susan a senior English major from Malibu, California, and Will a psychology major from Astoria, Oregon. Bev introduced herself, too—as a secretary for Rose City Heating and Air Conditioning.

"What'd you tell your people you're doing today?" Ted asked Bev in his gruff voice. He wore a burgundy down jacket, the kind she'd seen in magazine photos

25

depicting genteel Northeasterners, but he paired it with the same black cowboy hat he'd worn in the bar.

"Told my parents I'd be dropping trees with a chainsaw," she said.

Ted laughed, open-mouthed and loud.

"Truth is," said Bev, "I told them I was joining a mycology expedition."

Even at the edge of the street lamp's circle, she could see puzzlement in their eyes.

"Mushrooms," she said.

"Oh, hey, that's groovy," said Will. "Psilocybins. Do you really know how to find them?"

"If I did, do you think I'd tell my parents? Besides, I don't do magic mushrooms."

She brought her eyes back to Ted. What the hell was he doing here? That talk of his two nights ago about using the loot to help with his purchase—that had to have been bullshit. He wouldn't be scheduling meetings to finalize a purchase while at the same time hoping to stumble upon a cache of money to finance it.

"What about you?" she asked. "What'd you tell your people?"

"Me? I don't have to tell nobody anything. Cut my second wife loose four years ago. I go where I want, when I want. If you want to tag along, I'm heading to Mexico after my meetings next week. Acapulco. Warm sun. Beach."

He winked at her. Bev turned away, feeling squeamish, as though faced with a plate of millipedes.

"Sounds like you don't need any extra cash," said Susan.

"No indeed. You want to come with us? Your boyfriend won't mind. It's free love these days, ain't it?"

Susan turned to Will and stroked his cheek. "That's what *he* says," she replied, a tease—or was it mockery?—in her voice. She turned her head to exhale smoke before looking back at her boyfriend. "What do you think, Will? Should I go to Mexico? I might have a little spending money pretty soon."

Before Will could respond, a white Chevy pickup with a rattling engine stopped on the empty road beside the tree. Jim Rossi rolled down the driver's window, the instrument lights in the cab faintly illuminating his gray flannel shirt and green suspenders.

"You folks ready for mud?" he asked. An ample quantity of the same substance was spattered across the side of his truck.

Bev glanced down at her boots. Mud. When was the last time she'd waterproofed those boots? Maybe never? She couldn't remember. Two nights ago, before they left the Spar Pole, O'Brien had emphasized the importance of winter gear—covers for their packs, rainflies for their tents, warm clothes. At least she had all of that.

Jim parked his truck across the street on the edge of a field.

When Bev turned to Will and Susan to ask them what they'd concocted for a cover story, she spotted a big brown suitcase upright on the ground behind them. Both students held rolled-up sleeping bags beneath their arms.

"You two don't have backpacks, do you?" she said.

"We were lucky to score a tent," said Will. "Have you tried shopping on Thanksgiving? Only place open is a gas station."

"Oh. Right," she said. "Where is it?"

"The gas station?"

"The tent."

"In the suitcase. I practiced setting it up last night."

Susan examined the tip of her cigarette. "It's my suitcase. I picked one big enough for us to bring back some extra cash."

Bev could guess why those two were here—a year ago at this time she herself had been in college, one of the editors of Portland State's newspaper, *The Vanguard*. She remembered what it was like to be a near-penniless student. As for Tanya, money would motivate her, too. Tips probably didn't add up to much in a dive like the Spar Pole.

On the other side of the road, Jim donned a blue parka over his suspenders and hauled a backpack out from the bed of his pickup before crossing to join them. He looked to be about average height but skinny for someone who hauled a chainsaw up and down mountains all day.

"You bring a permission note with your momma's signature?" Susan asked. He shook his head and took a tin of Copenhagen from his shirt pocket.

"Now, Susan, be nice," said Ted. "He's gonna be working for me. How long you been workin' in the woods, son?"

"Three years." He fixed his eyes on Will. "What you doin' with a suitcase?"

"It's all I've got."

"Where's your tent?"

"In the suitcase."

Jim spat, shook his head, and crossed the road to his pickup. In a few moments he returned, a large garbage bag in one hand and a green rucksack with a single compartment and no pockets in the other.

He handed both items to Will. "Put them bags in the rucksack. Put 'em in the trash bag first."

Will nodded. "Thanks, man."

Jim looked both directions on the road, then scanned the hotel parking lot behind them. "No sign of our fearless leader?" he asked.

"What if it's all a gag?" asked Will. "He'll show up with a camera crew and call out, 'Smile, you're on Candid Camera.'"

Jim looked up the road again to the north, where a vast parking area surrounded the McDonalds and other businesses Bev had walked by. "Bet you he's somewhere over there watchin' us."

"What did you tell your people, Jim?" asked Ted.

"Told my fiancée I was huntin' turkey. Guess I already found them."

No one reacted.

Jim spat on a spot in front of his boots. "That was s'posed to be a joke. Guess I'm one of 'em, too. What the hell we doin' out here, anyway?"

"You don't seek, you don't reap," said Will.

"A poet philosopher," said Susan, her voice unimpressed.

"If this all turns out, I'm gonna buy me some land," said Jim. "Maybe not as much as you"—he gestured toward Ted—"but good enough to raise a family."

Tanya smiled at him. "That's wonderful, Jim. Marriage is a good thing. Young people these days don't know how to make a commitment."

Bev couldn't quite identify Tanya's ethnicity.

Perhaps it wasn't Asian. Perhaps it was American Indian of some kind. It looked as though she had come prepared—a backpack with a yellow rain cover, a dark green jacket with plenty of insulation, an aviator hat with thick lining.

"How about open marriage?" Will put his sleeping bag in the garbage bag. "I could commit to that."

"A commitment between one man and one woman," said Tanya, not amused. She kept her eyes on Jim. "Anyway, land's a good investment. It will always hold its value."

"Why don't you buy it from Ted?" asked Susan. "That way he can afford to take me to Mexico."

Ted laughed. "There's my girl. I had you pegged, didn't I? You like a man with sophistication."

Bev took a step back from the group and fished beneath her parka for the pack of Salems in her shirt pocket. They'd been together ten minutes at most, and what did they have? Susan and Will, not getting along so well. Ted hitting on both Susan and her. A damned suitcase. And no sign of DB Cooper's pal.

No one in the group would object if she walked away. In fact, they'd probably calculate, hey, one less person, more loot for the rest of us. She could spend the day with Sandra, like she ought to. Like she wanted to. Monica was still there, and she could take them both to that new movie the kids had been asking to see.

The headlights of a white van in the Denny's parking lot lit up. Soon afterward, Andy O'Brien, more hair than face, parked on the side of the road next to the group. Bev put the cigarettes back in her pocket and lifted her pack.

Chapter Four

Ten miles south of Kelso, small red lights blinked atop a storage facility next to the Columbia River on Bev's side of the van. Beyond it, deck lights lit a long container ship creeping through thin mist toward Portland. It would be two hours until dawn.

A mirror on the windshield visor provided a view of the shadowy figures in the middle and back seats. Who were these people?

"Let's all answer a question," she said. "Why are you here—money or adventure? How about you, Tanya?"

Seated in the back, the waitress turned to the window. "I don't know." Bev could barely hear her.

"Somebody else?" she asked.

"What about you, darlin'?" asked Ted. "It's your question. Money or adventure?"

Neither reason—that was the real answer, but she didn't dare say it. Instead, she belted out lines from the song "Money (That's What I Want)."

From the middle seat Susan and Will joined her, and the drab morning took on a rhythm-and-blues vibe.

"Who's next?" she asked.

Susan switched to a German accent to sing the refrain of *Cabaret's* version of "Money." This time Andy joined the three of them, and the atmosphere changed to a rollicking musical of bad accents.

"I watched the movie in March," said Bev afterward.

"I watched it on stage," replied Susan. "Twice. On Broadway four years ago and in Los Angeles. Liza Minnelli is good, but the actress in the musical…Jill something-or-other, wow, she was bitch'n'."

"Her old man's loaded," said Will.

Susan sighed. "Dear Daddy. I'm sick of depending on Daddy."

"So, money more than adventure, plus a thirst for independence," said Bev. "Who's next?"

"Gonna buy me some land." In the back seat between Ted and Tanya, Jim spat into a soda can. "Always wanted land. Grow your own food. Hunt and fish. Place for the kids to run around. A dog, too. Couple of horses."

Susan twisted in her seat to look at Jim. "You've got it all figured out. Maybe I'll come visit, when I want out of the city. We'll take a pony ride together."

"Ooo-ooo-ooo," moaned Ted, taking off his hat and fanning his face.

Bev tapped her foot against the floorboard. What was this woman's game? Was it more than teasing when she said Will was into free love?

"Just don't go buying land or anything else for a couple of years," said Andy. "Remember what I said. Keep it out of the bank, too, unless you want to explain to the police how you came up with DB Cooper's money."

Susan turned back into her seat. Behind her, the waitress looked uneasy, or maybe she was simply tired. "How about you, Tanya?" asked Bev. "Money or adventure? Can you tell us now?"

"I honestly don't know," she said.

"You seen a clear-cut after it starts raining?" asked Jim.

Tanya turned her eyes toward the window—probably, Bev guessed, to avoid the can of spittle Jim held chest-high inches away from her. "I know," she said. "It's muddy."

"Sink-to-your-shins muddy. Better have a good reason to go slogging around in that stuff."

Tanya leaned her head back against the seat.

"Looks like you're wearin' good boots," said Jim. "You got all the gear you're gonna need?"

"Food, water, sleeping bag, tent." The engine noise and the hum of tires made it difficult for Bev to hear the waitress's quiet reply.

"You can sleep in my tent," said Ted. "I'll keep it nice and warm."

"No, thanks," said Tanya.

"Two bodies generate a lot more heat."

She eyed him askance. "Maybe you can find yourself a coyote."

Laughter followed.

"I like a softer skin—whoooo-wee!" Ted mimed a caress.

"Did you bring a razor?" asked Tanya.

"Not for overnight."

"That's too bad, because if you want soft skin you could shave the coyote."

More laughter.

"What about you?" he asked. "Did you bring a razor?"

"Lucky for you I didn't."

"How's that lucky?"

"Because I keep my blades sharp."

Bev added her voice to the *whoa!* chorus. Ted raised both arms. "I surrender."

Only then did Tanya offer a reason. She wanted a house on the Oregon coast, where she could paint seascapes. She said she used to be a painter.

By the time they reached Washougal, beyond Vancouver at the western end of the Columbia River Gorge, everyone had shared. In a year Will would be in graduate school, on his way to becoming a doctor of psychiatry. Ted said he wasn't about to pass up a chance to find a bundle of cash on land he aimed to make his own.

As for Andy—"I get the same share as all of you. My plan is to disappear, just like Cooper, only he won't end up anywhere near the U.S.A. Why he wants the money, I'm not going to say, but it's part of the reason I agreed to help. That, plus he saved my ass in 'Nam. We've been watching out for each other for a long time. If I had to, I'd go to prison for him."

Chapter Five

Waiting outside the donut shop, Bev put a cigarette in her mouth while holding a sixteen-ounce black coffee in one hand and a small paper bag in the other. She exhaled tobacco smoke, masking the smell of Camas-Washougal paper mills, kissin' cousins with unwashed armpits to their counterparts fifty miles downriver in Longview-Kelso.

There was nothing like donuts and coffee to bring a group together. Even Will had forgiven Ted's attempted raid on his girlfriend, or so it seemed by the way they bumped shoulders hurrying back to the van before everyone else.

The hand holding her bag of donuts began to complain to the other hand that it wasn't fair only one of them got to hold the hot coffee when it was so cold outside. She raised the bag-holding hand and exhaled cigarette smoke onto the fingers, just as the others emerged from the shop.

"You can't just jump on a horse and start ridin'," Jim was saying. Bev joined them as they strode toward the van, parked sideways against an undeveloped tangle of trees and brush. "You got to get them used to the idea. Brush 'em, talk to 'em, walk 'em around the corral."

"Someone ought to explain that to Ted," said Tanya.

Susan laughed, her long blonde hair hatless and hoodless despite the temperature. "He thinks all he's got to do is talk up his money," she said, "although I need to tell you, Christmas in Acapulco sounds good to me."

"What about your family?" asked Tanya as they neared the van.

"I have no idea where they'll be. They could be anywhere in the world."

Andy opened the driver's door while Bev and the others rounded the front, where they froze when they saw what Ted and Will were doing. Squatting low against the van, Ted leaned over a square of cardboard that Will held. With a rolled-up dollar bill, the middle-aged timber baron snorted a three-inch line of cocaine as though he'd done it many times before.

Will looked toward them and grinned. "Better blast than donuts."

Ted raised his head away from the cardboard. "Yabba dabba doo!"

The front passenger door opened. Andy leaned out and shook his head.

"Hey, man, you said nothing *in* the van," said Will. "We're not *in* the van."

Andy stepped out onto the asphalt.

"Cool," said Will. "I've got enough for you, Andy. I've got enough for everybody."

"Look," said Andy. "I know it's a stereotype, but what goes with a donut shop?"

"Coffee, which is, like, caffeine, man, and this'll blast you off better than that."

Andy took a step and stood a foot in front of Will. "Not *what* goes with it. *Who.*" The grins on both men's faces disappeared, replaced by puzzlement.

"Cops," said Andy.

Will bolted up, as did Ted, a tubed dollar bill still in hand. A metal screw-top container clanged to the ground. With the cardboard still flat on his hand and a ruffled line of white powder mostly still in place, Will peered through the windows toward the shop.

Tall and cornstalk thin, Will turned to their short, bushy-faced leader. "There's no…" he began before looking down as the container rolled beneath the van. He bent at the knees to retrieve it, then stopped, eyeing the cardboard in his hand.

Andy snatched the cardboard and flung it like a Frisbee into the woods at the edge of the lot.

Oh, shit, thought Bev, backing up half a step. She'd seen plenty of coke on the Portland State campus before she'd graduated, although she'd never touched it, not with Sandra in her life. But she knew enough to know the cocaine had to have traveled far to reach Will's fried-up nose. The processing and the freight jacked up the price much higher than weed.

"Get your container," said Andy.

Will dropped to the ground, the cheek of his face against the damp asphalt. He reached beneath the van, stood again, and with a triumphant look kissed the container.

Andy snatched the jar right from in front of Will's lips. He had to reach up to do it, but he made the move in a microsecond, like a magician palming a card.

"You want it back?" said Andy. "I'll give it to you and you can walk home, see what kind of blastoff pounding the pavement gives you."

"This is bullshit." Will stared toward Andy without

meeting his eyes. His grin was long gone.

"Will."

The voice came from Susan, just behind Bev. She hummed the "Money" song from *Cabaret.*

Ted raised the still-rolled dollar bill. "You should've had your line first. Mighty nice of you to make a peace offering. That's what he was doing, Andy. That's what he called it. A happy crew's an effective crew, ain't that right?"

Container in hand, Andy walked off the edge of the blacktop before turning to face the group. "We don't have time for this. Are you with us, Will, or are you walking?"

Will looked at Susan. "You know how much this means to me," she said.

He pushed the bandanna headband farther above his eyes. Hanging at his side, his other hand formed a fist. "I'm in. And I won't touch the coke."

"No, you won't." Andy unscrewed the lid. Will's eyes widened and his jaw dropped. He reached out an arm and took half a step forward, but it was too late. Andy turned over the container, and white powder flowed onto the ground to mingle with sodden leaves, pale yellows and greens, some the color of dark wine.

"You son of a…" Will stopped and pressed his lips together. Both hands were fists.

Bev resisted the impulse to retreat. This was the story, too. She'd covered the Park Blocks Riot back in 1970, a week after the Kent State killings, and she hadn't fled when Portland cops with three-foot batons stormed the students. She could deal with this.

Although people sometimes killed each other over drugs.

She hoped Will hadn't brought a gun despite Andy's edict against it.

With his black work boots, Andy lifted a clump of the leafy duff and mixed it into the cocaine.

"You poor thing." Susan stepped to Will and kissed his cheek. He looked like a child contemplating a toy action figure after his mother had backed a car over it.

Andy screwed the lid back on the container and tossed it to Will, who caught it mutely.

"What else you got?" he asked.

"Dope. You know, grass. Nothing else."

"All right. You can keep that." He swept a gaze across the eyes of everyone in the group. "Last call. No pay phones where we're going. You want to bail, now's the time."

The little doubt that had been tickling Bev below the back of her neck spread up into her brain. It was as though a yellow traffic light slowly blinked, not enough to slam to a stop but enough to put her foot on the brake pedal.

So maybe there was a little bickering. Maybe DB Cooper's pal was a little hard-nosed, but that could be a good thing, could make them safer—that is, if he knew DB Cooper like he claimed.

Either way, she'd have a story.

Bev glanced at the others, sensed similar calculations firing in their mental and emotional synapses. But none of them stepped away. None raised a hand.

"Let's go," said Andy.

****

The narrow road meandered alongside the languid Washougal River, fringed by alders and Douglas firs.

The hillside above it wore the uniform green of second growth timber, interspersed with the brown gashes of recent clear-cuts. Lone vehicles occupied occasional turnouts. Twenty minutes out of town, two men with fishing poles stood in a boat.

"This ain't the area that was circled on the map you brought to the Spar Pole," called Jim from the back of the van.

"Cooper gave me those maps," said Andy. "The circled area is where the FBI calculated he'd landed."

Jim chuckled. "That's rich. Clint got a peek at that map. Wouldn't that be something if he decided to go it alone?"

"Who's Clint?" asked Will.

"The guy that walked away at the Spar Pole," said Jim. "I don't hardly know him. It'd be funny if he's sittin' in his rig outside Woodland waitin' for us to go by."

"He'll be waiting a long time," said Andy.

Bev glanced at the sideview mirror but saw no vehicle behind them.

Jim peered out the window. "Got me a steelhead last winter on this river. Lost one, too. You got to let 'em fight a while before you land 'em. I know a guy, he's got a place right on the Coweeman River fifteen miles out of Kelso. Fishes off his deck. That'd be the kind of place I want to own."

Ted took off his cowboy hat, propped it on a finger, then twirled it like a Frisbee. "Oh, yes." He stared at the spinning hat. "Land can tie you down. The more you've got, the stronger the knots. You think you're putting roots down, but the roots are growing over the top of you like jail bars, and there's so damn many of them you can't squeeze your way out."

"And here you are wanting to buy more," said Susan.

"You look at those bars, and they're somebody's expectations. You think you own the land, but you're a prisoner."

"Whoa, dude," said Will. "You need any help unloading some of that burden, I'm available."

"Ha-ha. I'll bet you are." Ted lifted the finger-propped hat until it was at most two inches from his eyes. "Well, fuck it. We're on an adventure now."

He jammed the hat upside-down on his head and thrust an arm forward, landing his hand on the backrest next to Susan.

"Charge, baby!" he called. "Treasure hunters of America, step aside. Let the Kelso Crushers through, 'cause we've got Andy-Man leading the way."

He broke into song.

"Who can take the sunrise? Sprinkle it with doo-doo. The Andy Man can!"

Bev made a show of covering her ears. "'The Candy Man'—I hate that song. I can't believe it was number one."

Susan and Will turned their heads and laughed when they saw Ted's upside-down hat. With the money he must have spent on that hat, Bev figured she could buy enough clothes for a week.

He pointed both forefingers at Will. "You're the real Candy Man, my hippie friend. A bona fide actual Nose Candy Man. Ha-ha. Helluva rush."

"Call me Doctor Snow," said Will. "But the Andy Man fucked up the Candy Man's medical supplies."

Andy glanced toward Bev. "How long's he going

to be buzzing like that?"

"I wouldn't know," said Bev. "Couple of hours, maybe."

"Andy versus Candy, Round One to the Andy Man," said Ted. "Roll the dice for Round Two. Hey, what do Monte Carlo, Macau, and Aruba have in common?"

"Monte Carlo I've heard of," said Susan, back to facing forward, a smile on her lips. "I don't know. They're in the Mediterranean?"

"Far apart, far apart." Ted restored the hat to its proper shape and put it back on. "How 'bout if I add Vegas to the list?"

"Blackjack and women, none of it free," said Susan.

"They'll take your shirt, your pants, your underwear. They'll take your soul, and you can't wait to come back and give them more."

"So you're a gambler, huh?"

"Two hours," muttered Andy. "We'll be hoofing it by then. If he's still blabbing like that, we'll tie him to a tree."

Pavement gave way to gravel and dirt. Tatters of cloud draped themselves halfway up steep slopes thick with firs. Andy zigged and zagged from one side of the road to the other, but he still hit potholes brimming with rainwater. Coffee sloshed out of Bev's lidded cup. Andy turned up the heater.

Bev tried to picture what it must have been like for DB Cooper to tromp through the woods until he found a beat-up road like this, rain pouring onto him, the stash of money weighing on him literally and figuratively. A guy in a suit jacket, white dress shirt, black loafer shoes. Maybe he had other clothes, if she could trust what Andy claimed Cooper told him, but Bev's brain depicted Cooper in formal garb, more like a desk jockey than a soldier, short dark hair and big sunglasses, the way he looked on the Wanted poster drawings.

Somehow Ted had rambled over to the topic of his house.

"…four thousand seven hundred square feet, all logs, exterior and interior, big windows looking down over a pretty little valley, only thing missing is a woman's touch…"

Susan still wore a smile, but next to her, staring straight ahead, Will's face seemed to have grown sour.

Chapter Six

Andy dodged one rock and steered the van right over another. A grinding noise bellowed down the length of the chassis, and Andy hit the brakes. He threw his nearly smoked cigarette on the floorboard and stamped it out. They sat idling on the single-track road, nobody, not even Ted, daring to say a word.

"Fucking A," muttered Andy. He drove another twenty yards to a pull-out and parked the van. "This is where we stop. Twelve miles from pavement."

Rocks the size of anvils cluttered the road ahead, which likely served as a streambed during heavy rains and snowmelt.

Bev stepped out into a walk-in freezer. Droplets of ice clung to the needles of Douglas firs and Pacific hemlock. She put on her parka, lifted the hood, and slipped on black ski gloves. She stomped on a frozen puddle but couldn't put a crack in it.

Wearing only his orange-hued plaid shirt with his jeans and boots, Andy dropped to the ground and peered beneath the van.

"Helluva rock," said Jim, a black wool cap snug on his head and a thick black jacket unzipped over his suspenders. "I thought it was gonna pop right up through the floorboard."

Andy rose from the ground. "Don't see any leaks." Fog spilled out with his words.

The smokers smoked and Jim spat, and then they marched up the road, Andy and Jim each with a mattock, while Bev and Jim carried shovels. The weight of her pack pressed at Bev's hips and shoulders, and the climbing strained her calves and thighs. She'd done enough backpacking to know that after a few days the discomfort would diminish, but she wouldn't be out that long this time.

Twenty minutes brought them breathing heavily to a logging road, barred by a green iron gate.

Andy pointed toward the trees next to the gate. "See it?" he asked.

"See what?" Ted wheezed.

"The mark."

"You ain't showed us what it looks like." Jim breathed no harder than if he'd been sitting in a recliner reaching for a beer.

Bev stared but saw nothing on the gray-trunked conifers.

Susan walked around the right side of the gate and stopped next to a fir. "I'm standing right next to it," she said.

Bev edged closer and peered at the jagged ridges and deep furrows before finally noticing a faint shape the diameter of a shot glass with dribbles of frozen pitch beneath it. It looked like a turkey's footprint, or a peace sign without the circle, a lighter brown than the trunk.

"How did you see that?" asked Bev.

"Susan'll see the needle in the haystack from a hundred yards," said Will, "and that's if it's buried in the middle. If it's on the outside, she'll see it from a quarter mile away."

"That way nobody can prick me with it," said Susan.

Andy took a folded piece of paper from his back pocket. "I walked right by that tree the first time. Saw a few more logging roads but none with a green gate. Finally, I backtracked, and then I noticed the mark right away."

Jim walked to the tree and stared at the scratches. "Looks like all he had was a pocketknife. Spray paint'll work better. You sure that's his mark?"

Andy unfolded the paper to reveal a symbol drawn in black ink.

"Look the same to you?"

Jim nodded. "Yep."

A breeze iced the perspiration on Bev's neck and worked its way to the dampened T-shirt she wore against her skin.

Ted unscrewed the lid of his canteen. "If this ain't bullshit, we're standing within a mile of two hundred thousand dollars in cash."

Tanya stepped closer to Andy. "He's not bullshitting," she said.

"Whoa there, honey." Ted took a sip from whatever he had—probably some sort of vodka mix, thought Bev. "I ain't saying Andy-Man's putting the con on us. He seems like the real McCoy. It's his buddy claiming to be DB Cooper without no proof. He could've put those marks up a couple of months ago, for all we know."

"He wouldn't bullshit me," said Andy. "Not about this. We've been through too much together. He's about as sane a man as I know, even if he did do a crazy damn thing. But he didn't do it just for personal gain."

"So what is he?" asked Bev. "Robin Hood with a clip-on tie?"

Andy gave her a long look. "You've been doing some research," he said.

"He left it on the plane. I've got access to old newspapers."

"At the heating and air conditioning company?"

Andy wasn't the only one eyeing her. The skin on her neck danced the twist and shout. Couldn't she keep her damned mouth shut?

"At the library," she said in her best ho-hum matter-of-fact voice.

"On Thanksgiving?"

"My mom works there." She rolled out the words, no hesitation.

Andy looked as convinced as he would have been had she told him she was Tinker Bell without the wand. He put the paper in his pocket and walked around the gate. Tanya hurried next to him, and Bev and the others followed.

"Far fucking out," said Will. "We're going on a treasure hunt."

Knee-high yellow grass brushed against Bev's rain pants. Evergreen boughs stretched across the path, sometimes forcing her to hunch low to keep her pack from snagging. She climbed over several fallen trees.

"This can't be the access road," said Jim.

"You mean for the clear-cut?" Bev asked.

"They sure as hell didn't run any logging trucks on this one."

Ahead, beyond the tops of the trees, a swath of pale blue appeared. Were they close to the clear-cut? She quickened her pace, matching Andy and Tanya.

Her right foot landed on a rock, and her ankle bent sideways. Pain shot up her leg. She collapsed, thrusting out a hand to cushion the impact, and a new pain yelped from her palm when she landed. She rose to a sitting position, yanked the hand to her eyes. A thorny vine had pierced her glove.

"Shit! Shit! Shit!" Her face in a grimace, she breathed hard against the pain. Blood leaked out of the bottom of her glove.

She had to get up. She couldn't look like a damn fool in front of these people.

Jim hunched down, his eyes showing concern. "Let's get that pack off your back," he said. She unsnapped the buckle, and he eased it off.

"Ankle?" he asked.

"I…I think I broke it." It felt as though she'd jammed in an ice pick near her ankle and then shoved it straight up her leg.

Susan knelt next to her, stroked a hand across Bev's hood. "I'll stay with you." She looked up at the others. "Or I would, if I could trust anyone."

"What do you mean by that?" asked Will.

"Like you haven't already thought of it, darling. Find the money. Go back a different way. Leave us here."

"Susan! Why would I—"

"Take your squabbling somewhere else," said Jim.

"Sorry." Susan resumed massaging Bev's head.

"Might just be twisted," said Jim.

Andy sat on the ground next to her, a first aid kit in his hands.

"See if you can get up," said Susan.

"No," said Andy. "Not yet. Bev, we're going to

have to remove your boot."

She sucked back a breath. She hadn't felt this much pain since Sandra's birth. If someone pulled on her boot, she might pass out.

She nodded her head.

While Jim unlaced the boot, Andy took off her glove and pressed an antiseptic pad to the puncture in her palm. Dizzy with pain, she pressed her lips together and suppressed a cry when Jim removed the boot. Andy rolled down her sock and placed both hands around her foot, her Achilles tendon, and finally her ankle.

"I don't feel anything broken. We're going to have to wrap it, before it starts to swell."

He gave her two aspirin and wound an elastic band multiple times around her ankle and foot, leaving the heel bare. Jim put the sock and the boot back on, laced it, and tied it tight.

The pain eased from nonstop scream to pulsating throbs.

"We'll help you up," said Andy.

"Give me a second." Bev closed her eyes to muster the strength.

I'm not turning around—that's what Andy said in the van. If she didn't get up, they'd leave her there. Susan called it right—there was no loyalty in the group.

Pitch your tent, Bev. We think we'll come back this way. Can't guarantee it, though.

"Okay," she said, opening her eyes.

She took control of her breath and tried to banish from her mind the throbbing ankle and the hole in her palm. Leaning on Jim's and Andy's arms, she rose on her left leg, set her right foot to the ground, and shifted her weight.

It hurt. Sweet mother of God, it hurt. But she kept her breath steady.

Depending on their luck, she'd be home this night or tomorrow night at the latest. That's what she'd promised Sandra.

"Hold on a sec," said Jim. "I got an idea."

He unfastened a hatchet from the back of his pack and walked down the path to a dead tree over which they had climbed. Soon afterward, he returned with a branch he'd stripped.

"One deluxe walking stick," he said. "Only $3.99, plus shipping."

With the help of the stick, she hobbled forward.

"You carry my mattock, I'll carry her pack," Jim told Andy.

"We'll take turns," said Andy.

They moved on, ducking beneath a thick branch that leaned four feet high across the road.

"I twisted my ankle playing basketball in high school," said Will. "Came down on somebody's foot."

"You're tall enough, son," said Ted. "You play college ball?"

"Just high school. It hurt like hell. Coach told me to walk it off. It sort of worked. Wasn't much on the fast break, but I got a few rebounds."

Bev recalled her interview with the Kelso girl, less than forty-eight hours ago, both of them standing on a basketball court. Its surface was smooth, a lot easier on a wounded ankle than a forest.

She was on a different story now, one that lay ahead of her, not behind. She took another step, and another.

****

The clear-cut climbed with the hillside, a rolling expanse of bare earth strewn with charred branches, downed trees devoid of needles, and blackened stumps. Leafless willows and tangled brush formed islands littered with bright yellow leaves. The carnage reached the top of one hill and halfway up another, until the forest resumed. It looked like a quarter mile to where the trees began again, and left to right, more than half a mile wide.

Jim stepped off the rocked road onto the mud, but he didn't sink. "It's all froze. They cut fireline around this and then they burned it. I've done it before, back in high school. Cut line for ten cents a foot."

Andy stared up the mountain. "Somewhere up in those trees, my buddy marked another tree."

"Bet you there's a dozen culverts between here and them trees. He might've stepped off at any one of 'em."

Andy picked up Bev's pack. "Good thing he said I could bring some help."

He resumed the trek. Bev gimped right behind him, like an old woman quick-stepping with a cane. By the time they reached the tree line it was 12:30.

"Look behind us," said Susan.

From the west, a thick quilt of clouds had edged over a line of ridge tops. When that blanket overtook them, any precipitation that fell would come in the form of snow. But perhaps that would be better—they wouldn't get as wet.

Andy lit a cigarette. "Four hours 'til sunset. I'm going to walk us over to the northeast edge. I'll drop you off one at a time every hundred yards, close enough to be shouting distance from one another. Bev, you'll be in the middle, so we can keep an eye on that ankle.

We'll go into the woods fifty feet at a time, and we'll check every tree. Every five minutes, I'm going to holler. People on either side of me, holler back, and then the next people after that. If you don't hear from the person in the next area, walk that way and holler until you do and reel them back closer. If you can't make contact with them, walk back toward the middle until you get the next person's attention, and get the word passed on to me. You can eat your lunches while you're looking."

Susan blew out a cloud of cigarette smoke. "If someone gets lost, how much time are we going to spend looking for him?"

"Oh, wow, Susan." Will stared at her. "You serious?"

"Chill out, Will. No, I'm not serious."

"Wouldn't it be safer if everyone worked in pairs?" Bev asked.

"We don't have time to cover everything in pairs," said Andy. "Besides, nobody should end up lost. That's why I'm setting up this system. We used to do it in the military."

"Senses full alert," said Will. "Sounds like a call for fortifications."

He unzipped the top of his coat and pulled out a fat doobie.

Chapter Seven

Bev sighed, stared at the Douglas fir, blinked her eyes, and searched some more.

Furrowed bark, unmarred by a human's knife.

An hour ago, when she was still buzzing from the pot, the bark had pulsated like the back of some prehistoric creature, massively tall and skinny. Tolkien's *ents* in Middle Earth.

"Have you seen some hidden loot?" she had asked a particularly large fir.

It refused to answer, just like the tree in front of her now, just like the bajillion arboreal beasts she'd already inspected. Looking up just added to the downer. Gray tufts, like stuffing pulled from a cheap pillow, had blotted away the pale blue sky, darkened the woods, magnified her isolation. Cold air slow-danced with the boughs, whispering a tale of abandonment. It smelled like impending snow.

Her stomach grumbled. When she was high, she'd withstood a serious bout of munchies, limiting herself to an apple and half a baggie of the Cheerios-peanut-raisin mix she'd prepared before tiptoeing out of her house.

She shuffle-stepped right and stared at the side of a different tree—nothing. Without her walking stick, she gimped to the next tree, four half steps, leading each with her good leg, though her ankle insisted she should sit her ass down. The ground was a frozen mat of needles, twigs, and little cones. She blinked her eyes and studied the furrows and ridges of yet another fir.

Nothing.

Yeah, she sure had a kick-ass story—a bunch of idiots spent a frigid day-and-a-half tromping around the woods, and they didn't find a damn thing.

A twig snapped upslope to the right, followed by the sound of a boot step. Just as fur-faced Andy came into view, she stepped on a pipsqueak of a cone, enough to bend her bad ankle. It felt like someone had taken a pipe wrench and twisted her foot ninety degrees. Her knee buckled and a little shout squeezed out from her throat. She would have collapsed if she hadn't grabbed a tree and half rammed her shoulder against it.

"You don't have to be in here," he said. "You could've waited out at the clear-cut."

"I've been doing okay."

"I'm going to call it a day. If Cooper had marked a tree on this end of the cut we'd have seen it by now. Even if we missed one, odds are someone would have seen a second one. He must have veered off more to the west."

Fifteen minutes later everyone gathered where the rocked road met the edge of the woods.

"Based on the distance," said Andy, "I don't think we'll have to go too far into those woods tomorrow morning until we find one of his marks."

"Provided this ain't all bullshit," said Ted.

Andy eyed him for a moment. "That song's getting old. At least you're getting a chance to survey some of your future land. Unless that's all bullshit."

Ted took a step toward Andy, then stopped.

"I was wondering when someone would call him out," said Tanya. "We don't get millionaires at the Spar Pole."

"I don't have to prove nothin'," said Ted. "What do you think? I'm going to show up in a three-piece suit with a gold watch dangling from my nose?"

"Don't worry about them." Susan moved a finger down the arm of Ted's jacket. "After we get out of this icebox, we'll be on our way to Acapulco."

"Susan." Will's voice carried a reprimand, and then he rolled his eyes. "Gawwwd."

"Turnabout is fair play, don't you think?" She smooched her lips toward her college mate.

"Cut the crap," said Andy. "Nobody's going to find anything if we're at each other's throats. We didn't find it yet. Deal with it. We'll find it tomorrow."

Will turned and looked downslope over the expanse of clear-cut. "What if he never came this far?" he asked. "What if it's buried out there somewhere?"

Andy gazed the same direction. "They could have shot my buddy out on the tarmac while he waited for the money and the parachutes. He told me he made them turn off all the cabin lights, just in case they had a sniper trying to get a bead on him. So I told him I'd give everything I've got to find his money."

"What's another day?" Jim spat out the shell of a sunflower seed. "We've come this far already. Might as well finish it."

The next shell Jim spat hitched onto a breeze and curved east. "It's fixin' to snow," he said.

Bev looked up. Not one shard of blue tore through the blanket of cloud. The boughs of the firs swayed like boats in a harbor. Cold slithered up the sleeves and down the back of her jacket.

Before this trip was over, she'd probably join her brothers in having camped in the snow. She glanced at her companions staring downslope over the clear-cut.

The only difference was that these weren't Boy Scouts.

Chapter Eight

At the far upper end of the clear-cut, a big bonfire illuminated six tents whose rainbow of colors contrasted the night-muted browns and greens around them. Seated on an unburned stump left over from the timber harvest, Bev accepted the bottle of single-malt Dalmore whiskey and held it at eye level. Flames undulated through the brown glass. Four previous swigs had burned with exquisite purity, and the heat had flowed like a lullaby down her leg to her ankle. A few more pulls would make her amenable to surgery on the spot.

"Don't have whiskey like this at the Spar Pole," slurred Tanya, seated on a log next to Andy, her gloved hand resting on his knee. "Mighty nice of you to bring it, Theodore."

"The hell's a spar pole, anyway?" asked Bev, holding onto the bottle. "Or did someone leave an *e* off the word *spare*?"

"No, it ain't a spare pole," said Jim, "though I s'pose they could call it that. You wanna tell 'em, Ted?"

"Spare pole? Hell, I got a spare pole, any of you ladies want to borrow it. But you go ahead, Slim Jim."

"No, you can tell 'em. You're the loggin' tycoon."

Ted drew from a pipe and blew a ring of tobacco smoke. "Just 'cause I own the land, it don't mean I know the intricacies of it. You're the one that's in there knockin' down the trees."

"I'm just a choker is all."

"Never mind!" Bev took a shot and handed the half-empty bottle to Jim.

"It's a loggin' thing," said Jim, holding the bottle on his thigh. "Cut a tree partway up and it's a spar pole. Run some cables off it and that's how you haul in the logs."

"Sounds complicated," said Bev.

"Well, it is, sort of. You got to limb it and top it and rig it a hundred feet high, maybe a hundred fifty feet. There's all kinds of ways you can fuck it up. You don't choke it right, the log could fall right on top of you. My dad knew someone who biffed it that way."

He took a swig and passed the bottle to Susan.

"Those boys are working rain or snow," said Tanya.

"You don't work, you don't eat," said Jim. "Owner ain't gonna pay if you're not out there."

Ted turned so that his backside faced the fire. "I like your mettle, son. You put your time in, maybe I'll put you up as a supervisor."

"Got a long ways to go before I get to that."

Something moist tickled Bev's nose. She slid a fingertip down the bridge and licked the wetness. Was it starting to rain? She looked up, a booze-fueled pinwheel whirling in her head.

A few fire-lit flakes parachuted from the black night.

If she stood, she'd totter. She might fall flat into the fire, which would be consistent with the rest of her day.

Another tap left a spot of moisture on the back of her hand. "Anyone besides me notice it's snowing?" she asked.

"Guess you could call it that," said Jim.

Andy looked behind them. "It's not even a dusting. Little dots of white on the ground. Might even be a little warmer than when we arrived. Storms will do that."

"We oughta get to bed," said Tanya.

"It's only seven o'clock," said Will. He handed the bottle back to Susan. "I don't need this shit. Look what I've got." He reached inside his coat, then held aloft a doobie and kissed it.

"I didn't get two hours' sleep," Tanya continued. "Thought I might snooze in the van, but not with the crowing and squawking, and all the potholes and curves." She leaned her head onto Andy's arm. "I wanna go to bed."

Ted looked sideways at the waitress. "I got a vacancy in my tent."

"You got a vacancy in your brain," returned Tanya. "Leave me alone, you old fart."

"You ain't exactly a spring chicken." Ted blew another O. "Besides, I was only joking."

"No, you weren't. You don't know how to talk to a girl. You prob'ly gotta pay for it every time."

"You really ought to leave her alone," said Bev. She took the joint from Jim and held the smoke in her lungs as long as she could.

"I know it. Guess the joke's wearing kinda thin. Been a while since I been with a woman."

"I wonder why," said Susan.

"You're not turning on me now, too, are you? We got other places we can go besides Acapulco."

"I'm about to turn on you," said Will.

"Nah. I'll stop." He took a large swig, then tapped the pipe over his knee, emptying the ashes.

"How'd you end up at the Spar Pole?" asked Bev. "Doesn't the Best Western have a lounge?"

"Sure it does, but they ain't my kind of people. Might find me a poker game in a place like the Spar Pole. That ain't going to happen in the goochy-goo lounge."

"Ain't no poker games in the Spar Pole," said Jim.

"Not even a back room?"

"Nope."

"Well, hell, if I end up with Cowlitz Lumber I'll have to set something up somewhere."

Susan moved from a stump to the log next to Bev. "How long since you've had a woman, Ted?" she asked.

"Hell, that's embarrassing. I don't know if I want to admit it."

"You don't seem to mind embarrassing others," said Susan.

He took out a pouch of tobacco. "Well, if I tell you, you're going to feel sorry for me. Maybe that'll work in my favor. Bev hasn't turned me down yet."

"I have now," she said.

"Well, that's three strikes and I'm out, ain't it? Okay, here goes. Almost a year. Nothing since last New Year's Eve."

"Oh, you poor man!" said Susan.

"I was hoping someone would feel sorry for me." He tamped fresh tobacco into the pipe.

Susan turned her eyes toward Will, seated a few feet away. "What do you think, Will?"

Will scowled. "Stop it, Susan. I'm sorry, okay? Do you have to play out this whole fucking thing in front of everyone?"

Susan mimed a kiss toward Ted. "Sorry. Free love isn't as free as it used to be."

"You end up in Longview, you oughta come to my church," said Jim. "They got a singles group. All ages, too. I'll bet you'd find someone."

"Someone looking for a husband," said Ted. "If you're like me, you don't know if they want you for you or for your money."

"Might be one or two like that," said Jim. "But not all of them."

"Well." Ted paused and stared into the fire. "I admit…maybe I ought to do that. When do they meet?"

"Tuesday nights. The thing is, you got to be nice to them."

"I know how to be nice."

"You can't just say, 'Let's go to Acapulco.' And if one of them does go, you can't just expect them to…to…"

"To what?" asked Susan with a mischievous smile.

Jim turned his head and spat. "You know," he mumbled.

"I know how to behave," said Ted. "I admit I ain't been much of a gentleman on this trip. I hereby proclaim my humblest apologies and my pledge to do better."

"That means you're done hitting on my chick." Will's eyes were narrow in the firelight.

Ted bowed toward him. "There are no fish in this pond. I'll behave."

"C'mon, Andy, it's bedtime," pleaded Tanya. She

looked puzzled when Ted, Susan, and Will burst out laughing. Then her eyes showed recognition.

"Oh!" She looked down. "I didn't mean..." She leaned onto Andy's shoulder. "We can read a book. I brought a flashlight. Or you can tell me a story. But not a ghost story. They creep me out."

Andy kissed the top of her head. While she clung to his arm, he rose, and the two of them picked their way over the frozen mud, allowing the light of the bonfire to lead them to a single tent.

Ted drew from his pipe and shook his head. "I'll be damned. He didn't even have to try."

"Maybe you should grow a beard," said Susan.

"I tried it and all I grew was a Brillo pad."

Bev and the other four stared quietly into the flames. One more day and she'd be rid of them.

Or maybe not.

If they found the money and she wrote the story, wouldn't at least one of these people come looking for her? And not exactly in a very good mood?

Jim tossed two chunks of half-rotted wood onto the fire, setting off pops and sparks. After lowering to three feet, the flames absorbed the new fuel and rose to the height of his shoulders.

She'd have to use aliases to protect their identities. But even then, they might be recognizable. She could change the place where they met, put it in another town, give the tavern a different name. She'd have twenty-dollar bills to prove the veracity of the tale.

Then the FBI would come knocking on her door. Would the judge uphold her reporter's privilege to protect the identities of her sources? Or would the judge decide she'd aligned herself with opportunistic criminals and order her to cough up names?

Would she be willing to go to jail to protect these people?

Try explaining that to a four-year-old.

Mommy's not coming home for quite a lot of nights. Some naughty adults took some stolen money. Mommy was with them when they took it, so she knows who they are, but she won't tell on them. Now the police are mad at her, so they put her in jail.

Someday Sandra would understand—maybe by the time the cops let her mommy out of jail.

Chapter Nine

Billy arrived on a magic carpet and parked it outside her tent. Dressed in his Marine blues with brass buttons and a spotless white hat and belt, he glowed brighter than a summer day, exuding joy and confidence. She zeroed in on his cute nose, bent a smidgen sideways where he had taken an elbow playing basketball. He reached out a hand, and she took it. It was a fine carpet, fibers the colors of grape jelly and sunshine woven in paisley patterns, and at the front Billy stood before a turquoise steering wheel and stick shift. It felt like an afternoon in May as Billy steered the carpet out of the woods toward Portland.

"Let's surprise Sandra," he said, despite never having met his daughter. "She'll love this carpet. I bought it for $3.99 at a donut shop."

He put his hand over hers and her whole body tingled. Couldn't she just hold Billy and wrap herself around him before they went to Sandra? No one would see them on this carpet, and it felt so soft and cozy, and why couldn't Billy realize that more than anything in the whole wide world she wanted to be with him the way a woman could be with a man, intimate and close and…

The problem with a magic carpet was there was no toilet, and she needed to use one, and now that they were over the city, there was no place Billy could set it down. He needed to figure out something soon, or she'd...

She woke. Her bladder informed her that she did indeed face an emergency, while a blacksmith pounded an anvil in her head. It was so dark she couldn't see her hand, and it felt like the space inside her tent had shrunk. She wasn't about to go out there in absolute blackness and step on a porcupine. She groped for the flashlight she'd placed near her head, but found nothing. Damn it, she was sure she had put it there. When she'd reeled into her tent about eight o'clock, drunker than she could remember being in years, she was holding it *right in her hand,* for god's sake.

Hadn't Slim Jim bragged his bonfire would still harbor at least a small flame when they awoke in the morning? Where was the light from that? She should be able to see it through the walls of her tent.

At last she touched something metal beneath the wadded-up jacket she used for a pillow. Light. And not a moment too soon. She flipped the switch and she saw right away her tent was half collapsed. Lacking space to sit upright, she slid down to unzip the flap and then the rainfly. A clump of snow fell on her hand.

She pointed her flashlight out into a white world. A breeze hurled a handful of powder into her face. She blinked and wiped the cold stuff out of her eyes.

She pushed her right arm through the snow to the ground, then yanked it out. It was like dunking her arm into the Arctic Sea. The puncture in her palm jolted awake. God, she was probably still drunk. And stoned. What a damned fool she was, to drink like that, surrounded by clowns and out in the wild.

The snow wasn't too deep, not all the way to her

elbow. She didn't want to get her pajamas wet—was it worth the hassle of digging out the rain gear she'd left like an idiot at the bottom of her pack? Her bladder said no, it was time to get moving.

She rolled up the cuffs on her bottoms, shoved her feet into her boots, winced when her ankle objected. Gimpy, she stepped out. Snow fell through the top of her unlaced boot—*whoooo-wee!* But what the hell, she was already outside now. She had one spare pair of socks, plus the smelly pair she wore yesterday. She'd be okay.

She pointed her flashlight toward the woods, identified a white lane between a couple of tents, high-stepped it to the closest sizable tree, and took care of business. Back outside her tent, she stood a moment, shivering like a jackhammer.

Should she wake the others? Should they get out of there now? They could find their way to the van. A foot deep would provide enough challenge for Andy to steer them back to civilization.

Except…

At the moment, no snow was falling. She turned off the flashlight, let her eyes adjust. It wasn't totally dark. She looked up and saw stars, brilliant stars— white pinpoint torches on a backdrop of ink, billions and trillions, the Milky Way chuck full of them, an astral cornucopia.

Well then. She was safe. Somewhere back in those trees, the money called. It never slept, not even at night.

****

Back in her sleeping bag, Bev's stomach burbled like a volcanic mudpot. She hoped to hell she wouldn't have to vomit. If only Billy would return on that magic carpet. If a dream was as close as she could come to touching him, then by God, let her dream a deep dream and wake up in a sweat.

But no, when her sleeping brain brought her back to Portland, she roamed the city at street-level, and eventually all its citizens disappeared. She walked into an empty breakfast diner, where she heard someone calling her full name. *Beverly Wikowski!*

She hated that name, not the Wikowski part, but Beverly. In sixth grade she and her classmates did ancestry reports, and a little punk-ass named Danny Rose found out *Beverly* came from the Old English *befer*, meaning beaver, and *leah*, meaning clearing. Beaver clearing! Clear the way for a lovely beaver!

She'd enjoyed watching the little runt sit on a tack.

Back to the problem at hand—she couldn't determine who was calling or where the voice originated. She was still in downtown Portland, nobody else on the streets, all the buildings empty.

She opened her eyes.

Bev! Bev!—someone was calling her for real, and not her full name. The waitress. It sounded like she was far away. It was more dark than light, the first minutes before dawn. Time to get up.

"I'm up!" she called.

A bulky mass piled against one side of her tent. Had Tanya fallen? But why would she just lie there? Unexpected sounds bored into her groggy brain—wind whooshed, trees thrashed, her tent rattled. She bolted into a sitting position, blinked in confusion—why hadn't her head hit the top of the tent? It was saggy with snow last night. Had Jim cleared it?

Those sounds—a storm. The faraway voice? Right

outside her tent. That bulky shape against her tent? It had to be snow.

What the hell did it look like out there?

Still nauseated from the booze, she twisted around to open the flaps. A white blizzard blew sideways, obscuring her vision.

Shit.

She poked her head out the small opening to examine her tent. Snow had piled half its height. The left third was buried. Pelted by snow, she pulled back into the tent and rezipped the flaps.

How could she have slept through this?

The blacksmith in her head returned to work, hammering a spear point that jabbed her skull with every blow. No way would she ever drink like that again, no matter how fine the liquor, no matter how weird the group.

She scurried out of the bag, pulled jeans over her pajama bottoms and a sweatshirt over her top, donned her parka. From the bottom of her pack she extracted the rain pants. She gritted her teeth and jammed her still-wrapped foot into a boot whose laces she double-tied.

Outside, she sank to her thighs in snow. It felt like a swarm of frozen bees crashed her entire body. Multiple layers of clothing blunted most of the stings, but a few infiltrated gaps around her neck and a full squadron struck her face. The density of blowing snow blotted color and reduced human shapes almost to shadow. Her tent wobbled against the onslaught—would the wind uproot the pegs she'd pounded into the soil and roll it away like tumbleweed?

No—she still had her backpack, sleeping bag, and

air mattress inside. No need to panic.

To her right, with a flashlight in his mouth, Will straddled a flat green tent, struggling to dismantle it while the wind flapped the edges. He handed a shortened tent pole to Susan, who pressed down on an open suitcase to keep the wind from filching its contents. Despite her efforts, the storm grabbed a black sock and skipped it like a rock across an ivory-powdered lake. Beyond them, dim like a specter in the blowing snow, Jim stood watching, a lit headlamp around the wool cap covering his head, his pack on his back, everything stored, ready to go.

On Bev's left, Tanya was yelling Ted's name at a blue tent. On the other side of it, Andy fought a tug-a-war against the wind for possession of Tanya's dislodged tent, pinned against a tree at the edge of the woods. It slipped from his grasp and launched like a miniature blimp, a big blob and then gone, lost behind the screen of racing snow.

Bev pushed her way through the snow until she stood next to Tanya.

"Let's open this tent!" she shouted.

"He's a creep!"

"He won't do anything!"

She bent down, cleared snow from the front to look for the zipper. Damn lecher probably guzzled too much of his own whiskey. She found the zipper, opened the front, leaned inside, and felt for his foot. She grabbed a leg inside the sleeping bag and shook. Stiff as a log, he refused to budge. His sleeping bag felt as cold as the snow.

She stopped, caught her breath, bit down on her lower lip.

A human body.

Cold.

She didn't have her flashlight, but there was enough early-morning light to see that Ted had burrowed most of his head inside the top of the sleeping bag, so she couldn't examine his face. But she didn't have to. She knew.

He was dead.

She backed out fast, bumped into a set of legs, turned and saw Andy, who met her eyes and showed a recognition that something had gone bad. He lowered himself to his hands and knees and crawled into the space.

He remained inside—was he checking for a pulse or performing CPR?

No, it was too late for CPR.

She had touched a dead body. Out in the wild. In a tent right next to hers. For who knew how long? Long enough to freeze like a popsicle. She'd never seen a dead body before, never touched one, except for Billy, and by then the Marines had prettied him up.

Sandra had been an infant the day her daddy came home in a casket.

A shudder snaked up Bev's spine. She pictured where four-year-old Sandra would be later this night— near the front window of her home, waiting for Bev.

Mommy's coming home, little goose. You won't lose both of us.

Andy backed out of the tent, a shiny blue backpacker stove in his right hand, and then he stood, glaring at the dead man's tent.

"Sonuvabitch!" he shouted.

Looking like a lost traveler with his brown

suitcase, Will whirled around in the knee-deep snow. His face was pale and his eyes wide as he gaped at Andy.

Andy turned to face them, and he held the stove upright like a torch. His eyes were narrow and furious.

"Don't you *ever* heat your tent with a propane stove! You won't smell a thing. All you'll do is die."

Like a baseball player aiming for home plate from deep center field, he flung the stove over their heads far into what would be the clear-cut if they could have seen more than ten feet.

The reporter part of Bev conjured a lead sentence for her revised DB Cooper story: *Hunting for treasure can kill you, no matter how much money you have.*

She snuck a quick look at the others, as though they may have read her thought, but they all looked dumbstruck, their minds reeling on unstable ground.

She'd come face to face with death, and all she could do was think of the news angle? What had happened to her?

Wind and snow roared like ocean waves cranked higher than the highest volume. Trees bent like contortionists hiding their heads behind a curtain of blowing white. Cold penetrated all the layers that Bev wore, the cold of winter and the cold of death.

Chapter Ten

Bracing her body against the gale, Bev gazed at the curtain of snow behind which Ted's camp stove had disappeared. His blue dome tent, now a nylon mausoleum, shuddered in the wind.

"His name's not Ted!" shouted Andy against the noise of the storm. Bev and the others turned toward him. "He lied to us. Name was Melvin Ford."

"Holy shit," said Will.

"And he had a gun in his pack. Which will remain in his tent, along with his wallet."

"What do we do now?" shouted Tanya.

"I'll tell you what," said Will. "We leave. Pronto."

His beard turning white from snow, Andy eyed their tall companion. "Would you like to lead the way?"

"No problemo. Follow the tree line."

Jim spat. A brown glob joined the flakes rushing in a white void. "You gonna tell us when we reach the loggin' road?"

Will pressed his lips together, and his eyes widened. "Oh, shit," he said.

In minutes, the foot-holes Bev had made in front of her tent would completely disappear, like prints erased by waves on a beach. To look for the logging road, they'd be struggling into the teeth of the wind, and if they guessed wrong, they'd grope through the shroud of ice until they reached trees on the downhill side, and then they'd wander until the cold had drained their strength.

"How you going to get us out of here, Andy Man?" asked Susan. Her head almost hidden beneath a thick hood and her long coat still pure white, she almost blended into the snow. If she had rain or snow pants, she wasn't wearing them.

"We keep our wits," said Andy. "We get out of this clear-cut."

"So we get nailed by a tree," said Susan.

Jim spat again. "Wind'll knock a few trees down, but odds are none'll hit us. Prob'ly wedge themselves in other trees. It's flying branches you got to look out for."

"What about this Melvin guy?" asked Will.

"He's not going anywhere," said Andy. "He'll be here when we go back after this storm."

While the others withdrew to the trees at the edge of the clearing, Jim stayed to help Bev take down her tent, holding down items against the thieving wind. After she stuffed everything into her pack, he reached out to pick it up.

"I can do it," she shouted.

Snow numbed the pain from her ankle. But she felt its weakness, her body like a post on a wobbly base. She hefted the pack, gritted her teeth, and plowed ten feet upslope to the edge of the woods. In front of everyone, she stepped on something uneven and her ankle bent. It felt like someone whacked it with a pickaxe. She grimaced, her leg buckled, and she went down.

"I'm all right," she insisted, lifting herself up. She brushed off the snow and noticed the others gaping.

She felt her face flush. She was acting like a pitiful

damsel in distress. All her drive and all her pride—hobbled by this? A damned stupid ankle?

She moved past the group, into the woods. Jim hurried by, wheeled, and stopped in front of her.

"Look for a sheltered spot," he yelled. "Clump of brush, thicket, a break against the wind."

Andy joined Jim in leading the slow trek. Each carried a mattock in one hand and a shovel in the other. The blizzard sifted through the obstacle course of trees, obscuring anything farther or higher than fifteen feet. Branches whipped back and forth, launching cones and twigs, the roar like an amplified waterfall—thousands of boughs, millions of needles, captive musicians in a symphonic din. It was pure bedlam, Mother Nature's madhouse.

Snow piled like sand dunes, ranging ankle-deep to as high as the tops of her knees, but because Bev followed Andy and Jim's path, it was easier. On her right the tree trunks were bare, but on her left, wind had plastered snow as high as she could see. Andy had been correct—as hard as the wind blew in these woods, it didn't pummel with the force it wielded out in the clearcut.

No way was she going to make it home by night, not unless conditions improved rapidly. Her family would worry, and they wouldn't have any idea where to look. If she were marooned another day, she'd miss work. She hadn't been on the staff half a year. Would they fire her?

Andy stopped. From a pocket he took out a roll of blue plastic flagging, snapped off a piece, and tied it to a branch.

"Wish I'd marked the road with this," he said. "But

by god, every report said the storm wouldn't hit until tonight."

Bev knew Andy wasn't lying—at least about the weather. She'd checked the forecast when she'd stopped at the *Chronicle.*

"Far fucking out!"

The voice came from behind her—Will. What was he tripping out about in the middle of this shit?

She turned to give him a glare, but he was peering a different direction, and the suitcase lay half buried in the snow. He brought both arms up and pointed at a tree next to Bev. She shielded her eyes from the blowing snow, and in a moment the etching came into focus, light brown against the darker gray, shoulder high. The peace sign without the circle.

"Andy! Jim!" she called. "Stop!"

Both men backtracked to the tree.

"That's it," said Andy. "That's the mark."

Bev felt a shot of euphoria. After all this, she might have a story. Her brain leaped to her desk, fingers clattering on the Underwood typewriter. She pictured Frank, the managing editor, standing behind her shoulder, too excited to sit at his desk and wait for the copy. It wouldn't matter how many days it took to get back—what she'd bring would justify her absence.

Andy held up a gloved hand. "Hold on. There's no clearing here. No triangle of marks. We have to keep looking."

"I can hardly see a thing," said Tanya.

"At least we know the marks aren't on the sides of the trees covered in snow," said Andy. "I'm going to spread us out eight feet apart. We'll keep going the same direction. Keep our eyes open for a shelter, too."

They continued in a horizontal line. Although Bev's nose throbbed with cold, adrenaline made it easier to push through the snow.

With one less person in the group, she'd have even more money.

Wait a minute, she reminded herself. She wasn't going to keep the money.

And what a sick way to think about his death, whoever the hell he was.

To her left, just visible from ten feet, Tanya stared at the trees. Was she also recalculating her share?

Andy paused to flag another tree, and so she waited. Twenty feet forward, he stopped again—it looked like he was listening more than looking, but it was almost impossible to hear anything other than the screaming wind and the turbulent trees. He turned toward her, put hands around his mouth, and shouted.

"Another one—this way!"

A minute later, they gathered where Will stood proudly at the mark on another tree, and then he turned backward and pointed west. At an angle behind them, they could see another mark, also on the lee side of a tree. Bev turned to her right, looking for a mark that would complete the triangle, but snow covered the sides of the trees.

Snow buried the middle of what would be a triangle, if they could see the other corner. The slope was not as steep.

"Looks like we'll be using these tools after all," said Jim.

Andy leaned his pack against a tree and picked up the mattock and shovel. "Well, Jim, you going to help or not? You, too, Will. Get out here and help."

Just like men, Bev thought—grab the glory work, leave the women to watch. They didn't even ask. She could have been a master ditch digger and they would never know.

She walked to the middle of the clearing and grasped the handle of the shovel in Andy's left hand. Andy wiped his beard, but the snow in it had frozen to ice. "All right," he said. "You and Will can start by clearing out the snow. Cooper said it would be in the exact center. We'll have to guess where that is."

The snow weighed light as fluff, but the motion of scraping and throwing it left Bev breathing hard. Andy and Jim attacked the ground with mattocks. After they loosened a quantity of soil, Bev and Will shoveled it away.

"Did he tell you how far down?" Jim asked as they whacked the mattocks hard into the half-frozen earth.

"Couple feet, maybe more," answered Andy.

"Roots and rocks are a bitch."

"Think of your hourly wage."

Forty minutes passed. The shovel work warmed Bev, but each time she waited for her turn against the shelter of a tree, she chilled quickly. Susan and Tanya stood close by, each with her own tree to buffer the wind.

Susan held her arms crossed in front of her chest. Her coat matched the color of the snow. "It'll be more cash than I've ever seen," she shouted.

"Haven't seen it yet," said her boyfriend.

"We will."

"I don't care about the money," said Tanya, her voice shaky. "I just want to get out alive."

"We'll make it," said Bev with more confidence

than she felt.

Feisty reporter helps dig up DB Cooper's loot. The story had to be told. They would get out of this mess.

"You don't know that," said Tanya. "There's too much snow to drive out. We're stuck."

"Andy said he's got chains."

"Won't matter, if there's too much snow. You know what high-centering is?"

"Sounds like a hockey move," said Susan.

Tanya turned her eyes away from the men laboring against the roots and the stones. Beneath the aviator's hat, her face had lost its color. "Your tires dig deep in the snow. You end up like a turtle on a rail, waving your feet with nothing to grip."

"We'll be fine," said Susan. "Going through all this to find the money—it means we're meant to have it. The cosmos is smiling on us."

Tanya moved her hands down over her face and held them to her chin. "You're crazy. We're all crazy. I hate this. I hate it, I hate it, I hate it."

"I'm crazy, all right," shouted Susan. "Crazy for cash. Coo-coo! Coo-coo!" She let loose an exaggerated, maniacal laugh.

"We can clear snow beneath the van," said Bev. "If we have to, we can walk. That river road had houses on it."

Reporter comforts panicking adventurer.

Tanya grabbed her wrist. "Can't you see? It's piling up. This is so stupid. Stupid, stupid, stupid, stupid—"

"Stop it!" Bev yanked her wrist free. "Where are we going to go? We can't see five trees ahead of us. Jim knows the woods and Andy was in Korea. They know how to survive."

"Shovels!" called Andy as he and Jim moved away from the hole. Shoved forward by the wind the moment she left her tree, Bev moved toward the hole. Everything looked farther away than it was. Colors faded—soil appeared more gray than brown. She and Will lowered themselves into the thigh-high hole.

"Thanks for helping Tanya," said Will, throwing soil right while she threw left. "You're a cool chick, you know that?"

"I'm not a chick."

"Well, whatever, man."

"I'm not a man, either."

"Okay. *Female.* Can you dig that?"

"Yeah. Along with all this dirt."

"Pretty weird. Find all this money. Freeze to death."

"You'll be fine. You've got a suitcase."

He chuckled. "I know it looks stupid. Never camped in my life. I wouldn't be here if it weren't for Susan."

From the wall near the bottom of the hole, a rock as big as a toaster jutted out. With her shovel, Bev loosened the stone before hunching down to remove it. Inside the gap that remained, something looked out of place. She took off her glove and wiped away muddy soil.

The object felt like canvas.

She stood. "Andy! Jim! I think I found something!"

Intrepid reporter first to touch buried bag.

God, she hated that stupid headline voice. She wished she could punch it square in the mouth. But then, as Jim and Andy trotted back out, excitement on their faces, elation stirred her blood.

This was starting to look real.

An astonishing story. After a year of nobody finding anything. Not the National Guard, the FBI, all the local badges, every schmuck and his uncle. She, Bev Wikowsky, had stumbled onto the group that located the loot. She had even helped with the unearthing of it.

She could let the headlines percolate now. This was the hour of her triumph, and it was all the sweeter because of the harsh conditions. She'd keep a few twenties to authenticate the story, and she'd make the identities of the people vague, so they wouldn't get caught. She had her reporter's immunity, and no one could ever make her talk.

Then she thought of Melvin. If he were with them now, what would he do with that gun?

Reporter among group found slain.

She shuddered. She wasn't just a reporter. She was Sandra's mom.

But now that Melvin was dead, what would happen if she included him in the story? How could anyone in the group ever acknowledge his presence among them?

She could figure that out later.

Chapter Eleven

Swinging the mattocks double-time, it took Andy and Jim fifteen minutes to extract the muddy green duffel bag. Andy tossed it up next to Bev's feet and boosted himself out. Now she understood why thieves referred to stolen goods as "hot," because it felt as though the bag glowed like lava in the middle of a blizzard.

Andy pulled at the zipper, but it was jammed with mud. He removed a glove and ran his thumbnail across its length and back, and still the zipper would not yield.

"Cut it open," said Susan. "I've got a knife."

Andy shook his head. "I need the bag." He unsnapped a belt pouch, removed a one-quart canteen, and dribbled water across the zipper. After a few tugs both directions, he opened it, revealing a black garbage bag, its top tied in a knot. He looked up and closed his eyes just as a flying twig slapped his forehead. Ducking into the blizzard, he grabbed the duffel bag and a mattock and hurried to the shelter of a tree.

He sat cross-legged with his back against the tree, blew on the fingers of both hands, then rubbed them together between his thighs before he tackled the knot. Like the zipper, it resisted. After a minute, the knot looked the same as when he'd started.

"You can cut the garbage bag, can't you?" said Susan.

He paused to shelter his hands beneath his armpits. Then he stretched out the waistband of his snow pants, dug into the pocket of his jeans, and took out a large single-bladed knife. Bev leaned forward as Andy cut and tore apart the top of the plastic bag. He tossed out a sports jacket, loafers, and a rolled-up white dress shirt, exposing compressed bundles of twenty-dollar bills.

Two hundred thousand dollars. Richard Nixon's salary for a year. At her current wage, she'd have to work more than twenty years to earn that much money.

Tanya wrapped her arms around Andy's neck, almost knocking him backward. "I knew you'd find it, Andy!"

"Wow," said Will. "What's everyone's share?"

"Divided by six," said Jim, standing with both shovels and a mattock, "eight thousand three hundred thirty-three dollars. Seein' how it's all twenties, I'll settle for eighty-three hundred twenty. That'd be four hundred sixteen Andy Jacksons."

Five sets of eyes, including Bev's, spun toward Jim.

"Holy moly," said Will. "You did all that in your head?"

"Couldn't exactly scratch it out on the ground, could I?"

Will pumped a fist in the air. "I get to go to grad school, baby! You can call me Dr. Garfield."

"In two years," said Andy.

"I can wait. Might live on a commune. You want to live on a commune, Susan?"

"No way."

"I don't mean the free love kind. Just you and me."

"I said no."

Tanya let go of Andy and turned toward the couple. "Don't you two have anything in common?" she asked.

Will and Susan glanced at each other, and then they looked away.

"This ain't the time or place," said Jim. "We got the money. Now we better find a place to hunker down."

Tanya turned back to Andy and put a hand on his shoulder.

"Are we ever going to get out of here? Could we...could we..."

He put a bare hand over hers. "We're not going to die," he said. "We just have to wait."

"There's too much snow to drive, isn't there?" she continued.

"I've got chains."

"It won't matter, if it's too high. And there'll be drifts in the road."

"We'll make it."

She pressed her lips together, and her eyes had a desperate look.

Jim held out a shovel. "Who's gonna help me fill that hole?"

****

The same four who dug the hole filled it, leaving DB Cooper's airline passenger attire at the bottom. Before they set out to find a sheltered location, Bev ate a handful of Cheerios and drank the rest of her first one-quart canteen.

God, she could eat a whole pizza. And she still felt thirsty, more than she thought she could be in all the cold. How much snow would she have to melt to refill that canteen?

In the time it took to recover the money and refill the hole, the blizzard had not softened its rage. The exertion had caused her to sweat, and as they resumed the search for a windbreak, she began to shiver. There was no trail, only weaving between trees and gale-driven snow. Jim turned them east, putting the wind at their backs. That made sense to Bev—why keep plodding farther and farther upslope and away from the clear-cut?

But paralleling the clear-cut also meant they were leaving Melvin Ford behind them.

The frigid blast penetrated her clothes and her skin. It was only a matter of time before it froze her bones. Melvin didn't matter now. All she wanted was a spot away from the wind.

Jim stopped, then Andy, who set down the bag and a mattock and retrieved the blue flagging. The woodsman ducked low, crawled across snow beneath a low-hanging fir bough, turned, and called back, "This'll do."

Branches crisscrossed each other in a tight weave. There was no way to join Jim except by crawling. When she reached him, she found herself in a tiny clearing, concave like a little bowl, scarcely large enough to hold the six of them. A dense pack of young firs lined the western edge, blocking much of the wind, while taller trees extended out of sight beyond the blowing snow. Though the break shielded the worst of the wind, it did nothing to quiet the ferocious din. It was dim inside, like late dusk.

At most, only an inch of snow had penetrated the tree-lined bowl. Tanya, Susan, and Will plopped to the ground. Bev remained standing, as did Andy and Jim.

"Can we build a fire here?" Susan still had to raise her voice to be heard.

"How's that even a question?" Jim removed his pack and unfastened the hatchet. "Of course we can. First we've got to find a shitload of twigs, little ones, diameter like a match. Then bigger twigs and branches. Not the crap the wind's been blowin' off the trees. Dry fuel. Little dead sticks pokin' off trees, you can bust 'em off. Or under the snow around the bases of the trees."

He stepped across the clearing and kicked the bottom of his boot against a knee-high mound of snow, shaking loose the icy cloak to reveal a downed branch with smaller branches and twigs jutting at all angles. He broke off a twig and turned back to the group.

"You see the snow rise in kind of a clump, might be a big ol' branch."

"What about cones?" asked Will.

"If they was pine cones, sure. But they're fir. I'd rather have the sticks."

"I don't want to get lost," said Susan, who had taken out her cigarettes but looked unsure if she should try to light one.

"So stay close," said Jim.

"Susan's right," said Tanya. "Ten steps out in the blizzard. That's all it would take."

Andy took the flagging from his pocket. "I'll mark the perimeter. Then I'll go out four trees and mark a larger circle."

"Plus you can backtrack," said Jim.

They found what they could within the little clearing—not much, not enough to start a fire. They ventured farther, out the opposite side of the clearing.

Bev paired with Tanya. Around the bigger trees, they cleared snow with their feet and a shovel before hunching down and probing for twigs. Beneath the third tree she found a branch from which she broke a handful of twigs. Tanya noticed a long clump which turned out to be not just one but numerous branches, longer than their arms, mostly without twigs, shorn of bark, as though they'd been dead a long time.

"I'm sick of this wind!" shouted Tanya.

Bev felt herself shivering again. Her fingers ached. "Let's go back," she urged.

Tanya nodded. "You know what's funny? These branches are more important than all the cash in the world."

They gathered the unwieldy branches and retraced their steps. In the clearing they placed them as well as twigs from their pockets next to a depression Jim had dug. They snapped off more twigs and broke longer pieces.

"I keep freaking out," said Tanya. "Sorry."

"I'm afraid, too," said Bev. "I've got a little girl. She's going to be scared if I don't get home tonight."

Tanya took her foot off a branch she was trying to break.

"You've got a kid?"

"Four years old. I… No one knows where we are."

Emotion swirled in Bev's chest like a sudden eddy. She let her branch fall to the ground.

If Bev didn't return, Sandra might never hear *little goose* again.

Dear Sandra. Little goose.

But they'd found a windbreak. Jim would build a

fire. The snow wouldn't last forever.

"We'll make it," said Tanya. "We have to."

Susan and Will entered the clearing, each holding a skinny branch. Will looked at the pile Bev and Tanya had made. "Cool. You scored!"

A minute later, Andy and Jim arrived with an assortment of small branches. Each emptied a pocket of twigs. Bev, Andy, and Susan lit cigarettes and formed a circle around the oval, watching while Jim, with a pinch of Copenhagen inside his lower lip, sorted the twigs and branches by size. Seated low, where the wind lost even more of its bite, the young woodsman snapped a bigger branch over his knee and placed a piece in the center.

Next, he leaned the littlest twigs like a teepee around a spot in the middle of the branch. From a black film canister, he removed two compressed cotton balls.

"Cotton?" Andy observed.

"Soaked in Vaseline," said Jim. "They'll burn steady for four minutes." He placed the cotton balls within the teepee and used a lighter to set them ablaze. Protected by the thicket, its location in a pit, and the hunched bodies of all six, flame about the size of a fist quickly engulfed the twigs. Jim leaned more twigs onto the branch and then larger and longer ones around them. In a few minutes the fire had grown about a foot high, its heat scarcely registering, and yet they all reached their hands over the pit for the minuscule warmth.

Chapter Twelve

Jim added bigger sticks and the flames rose higher. Bev's shivering intensified, as though thawing somehow released an inner cold.

Andy snuffed his half-smoked cigarette. "I remember pouring gas into 105-millimeter shell casings and lighting them like stoves. Thirty degrees below zero. Half my unit got frostbite. Some lost fingers, toes. We used to light up rice bundles. Had a buddy killed when he lit one that turned out to be booby-trapped with a grenade. Fucked him up bad. Took him a while to die."

"So this is, like, nothing, huh?" said Will.

"No, it's something, if it reminds me of Korea. But I'll bet you it's twenty-eight degrees, maybe thirty. The wind makes it feel colder."

Bev dug into her pack for some gorp, chewed small portions slowly, and let the bits of pulverized oats, raisins, and peanut M&Ms linger on her tongue before swallowing. Resisting the urge to stuff fistfuls into her mouth, she stopped with the bag two-thirds full.

If she saved it, would she have to share it with the others? No one had expected to be stuck in the woods for dinner. Was she the only one who'd brought extra food? The freeze-dried lasagna she still had would not amount to much divided six ways.

It didn't seem fair. She came prepared. She should

be the one to benefit. Holding a hand out to shield the quantity of gorp that still remained, she put it in her pack.

She turned back to the circle and lit another Salem.

"We shouldn't eat everything we brought," she said.

"No, sirree," said Jim, holding a piece of jerky. "That'd be stupid."

Andy and Tanya expressed agreement. Will and Susan eyed the hunk of bread each held.

"We were supposed to be back at the van by dark," said Susan.

Jim glared a moment at the couple, then looked away.

"What if it clears up?" asked Tanya. "We'll go to the van, won't we?"

"Depends more on the wind than the snow," said Andy. "If the wind keeps blowing this hard, we still won't be able to see where we're going. But if it dies down and it's still snowing, we'll go."

Tanya put a hand on Andy's knee. "What about Ted—or Melvin, I guess. We'll go back for him, won't we?"

No one answered. A branchlet dropped from the wind into the fire, but the strong flames scarcely wavered.

"He's buried by now," said Susan. "We won't be able to find him."

"If we did, it would be like dragging a hundred-and-eighty-pound log," said Will.

Andy picked up a broken branch, pushed green needles off the flames, and left the stick in the fire. "Let's talk about the real reasons," he said.

"All right," said Susan. "If we bring his body back, we'll have a lot of explaining to do."

"Oh!" Tanya sounded surprised. "You mean…we should just leave him there?"

Bev watched the flames take hold of the new stick. Everyone stared at the fire.

"Someone's gonna find him," said Jim. "Maybe an elk hunter. A lot of this snow might melt in a week. It ain't even winter yet. For sure the logging crews'll find him in the spring."

"He said he wasn't married," said Will.

"So?" replied Tanya. "That doesn't mean there isn't anybody who cares about him."

"Who gives a shit?" said Susan. "He lied to us. He brought a gun. If he were alive, after we found the money he'd have shot us all. We don't owe him a damn thing."

Jim set two more sticks into the fire. "Said his brother is a sheriff. When you looked at his license did you see where he's from?"

"California," said Andy. "An address somewhere in Sacramento."

"He might've told someone he was with us," said Jim. "What if he was an FBI agent? See anything else in his wallet?"

"A lot of cash." Andy put the half-smoked cigarette back in its pack.

"He sure the hell wasn't very professional," said Susan. "What kind of FBI agent gets plastered and hits on any female around?"

"I just about decked him," said Will. "He was a bad trip. Didn't surprise me he brought a gun."

Susan tugged the hood of her coat over her

forehead and glared at Will. "You put that stove in his tent?"

Will's mouth dropped open. "Jesus Christ! We don't have a stove like that. You think I was hiding one under my shirt the whole time?"

Bev felt her body tense. Sudden wealth and rotten weather—it wasn't a formula for peace and harmony.

On the other hand, peace and harmony never made the front pages. "Hey," she said. "Ease up, Susan. There's no reason to think any of us would do something like that."

Susan looked away.

"We're getting off track," said Andy.

"We're already off track," said Jim. "Let's cut to the chase. We bring that body in, we're givin' up all the cash. No way to separate the two. Now if this Melvin guy was a decent man, that's what we'd do. But to my way of thinking, he ain't worth it."

Bev pressed her lips together. How could she omit the dead man? If she did that, she wouldn't be a reporter. She'd be something else, something she didn't like.

She waited—but no one disagreed with Jim. She glanced around the circle, but none of them raised their eyes.

A gust breached the windbreak of trees and ruffled the flames. A crack sounded in the distance, or at least it seemed far away—the top of a tree snapping, perhaps. On a normal day, it could have been someone stepping on a branch, or a pop from the flames.

"We need more wood," said Jim. "A lot more wood. The way it's lookin' now, we need enough to keep this thing goin' all night."

****

Bev's body begged her to stay at the fire, but she and Tanya departed with Susan and Will in search of bigger pieces, while Andy widened their perimeter with more flagging. She and Tanya moved what she thought was north. The climbing soon gave way to level ground, although it was difficult to determine slope in the middle of a blizzard.

She couldn't see any clumps, and she wasn't strong enough to break a bare branch bending out from one of the trees.

"Let's go a little farther," she said. "We can still see the trail we made."

Tanya put a hand out above her eyes. "I don't know about that."

"Just a little more."

With Tanya's hand clamped around her arm, Bev maneuvered between trees until she spotted several small mounds. She scraped away the snow and found a round of wood with a broken eighteen-inch branch still attached.

It was too heavy to carry, so she and Tanya took turns gripping the broken limb and dragging it like a sled over the snow back to camp, where Jim was hacking at a branch the diameter of a man's arm.

"Hoo-wee! That'll do, if I can split the damn thing. Where'd you get that?"

Bev pointed toward what she thought was the right direction. "Up a little rise and then it flattens out."

"Why don't you two show me?"

Back at the spot where she found it, snow had already whitened the gouge where she'd pulled it from the ground. With a shovel Jim probed the mounds of snow around it.

"I'll be damned." He brushed away snow and exposed a small pile of branches lying parallel to one another. "Would you look at that? They got half their needles. The bark's still on 'em. This was prob'ly cut springtime or maybe last fall."

"You said they thinned it," recalled Bev.

"Yep. Like ten years ago."

"So what's the big deal?"

"I don't know. Prob'ly nothin'. Just…if you was to go to my old house you'd find some rounds in the woods, a pile of branches here and there."

He looked past the two women. "Like that pile over there. Or I'll bet you it's a pile." He moved eight feet to another mound, almost the limit of vision permitted by the blizzard. After scraping off the snow, he stood triumphantly next to his find—three large rounds leaned against each other.

"Someone's been out here cuttin'. Remember what I said about there havin' to be some other access road to the clear-cut? There's got to be something around here."

Bev looked back into the snow the way they came. "I don't want to get lost."

"Me neither." He hesitated. "Look the direction I'm lookin'. I know it's hard to tell, but can you see any trees past that one that's leanin' at a funny angle?"

Bev strained her eyes. All she could see was blowing white, and the cold was penetrating her body again. She could have been gazing into a crater, for all she could tell, or a bunch of trees they just couldn't see because of the blizzard.

"I'm gonna have a look-see," he said.

"No, don't!" called Tanya.

"I won't get lost. It'll only be a minute."

He disappeared into the frozen void. Bev felt her heart pounding. They needed him.

He was gone a minute and then like a ghost assuming corporeal form, he returned.

"We done found ourselves a cabin," he said.

Chapter Thirteen

In the clearing, wind scooped snow from the ground, snatched it as it fell, and blasted it into Bev's face. It pushed against her like a howling bulldozer. She stepped with her hobbled ankle into Andy's foot-holes. The blizzard obscured his figure, as if he were on the other side of a long tunnel.

The cabin appeared like an optical illusion within a blowing white cloud. As she approached, it grew darker and finally clarified itself as a small A-frame, snow piled twelve feet high against the right side and swept bare on the left. Plywood covered a window.

Jim reached for the doorknob. "It's locked!" he shouted.

Will dropped the suitcase. "I'll go down the chimney." He grinned at his joke.

"Like to see you try," yelled Susan.

"Mushrooms, baby! Give me the right kind and I could do it."

Jim held out a shovel to Andy. "Trade you," he said.

Bev and the others stepped aside as the young logger raised a mattock head-high before swinging it at the door. The tool bounced off, leaving only a four-inch scrape. He stepped back and wheeled a three-quarter swing, and this time the blade penetrated with a loud crack. Four more swings produced a hole large enough for him to reach through and unlock the door.

It felt like a miracle to step inside. Susan turned on a flashlight, circled it around the dark interior, reversed, and held it steady on a lantern hanging from a hook on the wall next to a square wooden table.

Andy switched it on. "Looks like the battery's still strong," he said.

They stood near the entry next to a potbelly stove in a single room with white particleboard walls. Next to the boarded window, an open cupboard held unmatched cups, bowls, and plates. A beige Naugahyde sofa backed into the wall opposite the table. Two-thirds back, a ladder leaned up to a loft.

"We just stepped out of hell," Tanya murmured.

Hell refused to surrender. It lowered its shoulder and rammed the cabin. It launched debris at the outside walls. But the little A-frame withstood the charge.

"Hee-hee! I'm going to miss sleeping outside," said Will.

"Don't let me stop you," said Susan.

Bev let her muscles relax and reveled in ordinary sounds—the rustle of clothing while they removed packs, the little whistle in Andy's labored breaths, the knock of a boot on the wooden floor.

Fog puffed out with their breaths. Bev looked back at the woodstove—next to it, a metal rack held a half-dozen pieces of firewood. Little black pellets lay on the floor around it.

Rodent shit. That explained the smell.

She found a broom in a back corner, swept the table, the sofa, the floor upstairs and down, gathered it near the door, and quickly swatted the mess out into the wind and the snow.

Jim had started a fire. She joined the others in a semicircle around the potbelly stove. Despite the icy breeze funneling through the hole in the door, warmth seeped through her jacket and clothing, and finally touched her skin.

Tanya removed her coat, carried it two-thirds up the ladder, and draped it on a rail.

"Dibs on the loft for Andy and me," she said. Andy closed his eyes and looked away.

Soon pairs of gloves lay on the floor near the stove, and the railing could not be seen because of all the coats and hats and rain pants hanging from it. Bev sat in the middle of the sofa with Susan on her left and Tanya on her right, while Jim and Will took the table chairs. A cigarette in his mouth, Andy stood looking through a pile of magazines on a shelf beneath the loft.

Will opened an ice chest the owner had left on the table. He named the items as he withdrew them. "Safe from the rats—half a package of spaghetti noodles, two cans of Campbell's chicken and noodle soup, two tins of Vienna sausages, jar of Cheez Whiz, can of green beans, and what's this? A bag of flour?"

"Some kind of mix," said Bev. "Might be pancakes."

"Where's the potato chips?" asked Will.

"Fritos," said Jim.

"Oreos," said Tanya.

"More donuts," said Bev.

"Last but not least." Will held up a fifth of bourbon whiskey.

Susan leaned forward to read the label. "Old Crow? That'll burn a hole in your gut."

Andy groaned. "That's the last thing we need."

"I'm still hung over," said Tanya.

Andy stepped away from the back wall and tossed a magazine onto the table. "Add this to the mix."

A pouch of Redman in his left hand, Jim picked up the magazine. On the cover, an enormous bear stood gazing at a cowboy and his rearing horse.

"*Field and Stream,* September 1972," he said. "Someone's been here recently. I'll bet you the road he drove in on is the same one the loggers used for that clear-cut."

"How close do you think we are?" asked Susan.

"I don't know. Could be this hunter's got a long driveway. Might not have any neighbors. Might have a lick of 'em. Can't tell in this storm." He stuffed a chaw inside his left cheek and felt for a cup from the cupboard above his head.

"Well, lookee here." He held up a keychain with two keys.

"Awesome," said Will. "Wouldn't it be cool if this dude's got a shed with a snowmobile?"

Jim spat into the cup and pocketed the keys. "Think I'll go have a look-see. How 'bout you loan me some of that flagging?"

"I'll go with you." Andy snuffed his partially smoked cigarette against a saucer and picked up the duffel bag.

"You can leave that here, man," said Will. "Nobody's going to touch it."

"It's simpler this way," said Andy.

"When are we going to split it up?" asked Susan.

"If I do it now, then there are six of us who've got to worry about hanging onto it."

"No worries, man," said Will. "We're cool with

each other."

Andy tugged his coat off the loft rail. "Tonight, then. But I'm hanging onto it for now."

Bev rose from the sofa. "I'm going, too," she said.

"You oughta rest your ankle," said Jim.

"I agree," said Andy.

Bev retrieved her parka. "I'm going. Last I heard from you guys, I was supposed to walk it off."

Her ankle hurt, but so what? Blizzards, riots, crime scenes, Vietnam—she was a reporter, and she followed the action. These people weren't going to shut her out.

At the door, Andy paused.

"You sure you want to go out in this shit?" he asked, without looking back at her.

"Let's go," she said.

Outside, they walked a circle within the cabin's visibility, then probed a second loop beyond it. Wind and snow crashed into her body, draining the heat she had accumulated in the A-frame. On the third circuit, across the clearing from what Bev guessed to be the front of the cabin, the whoosh of trees grew jet-loud. Douglas firs came visible in a white nightmare, and a few steps later, two small structures appeared.

One was a three-sided shed, head-high with firewood, all of it split but plastered with snow.

Jim unlocked the door of the second outbuilding, an enclosed shed that might have been large enough to hold Bev's VW Beetle if nothing else were permitted inside.

It did not contain a snowmobile. A shelf, holding a stack of magazines as well as cans of nails and screws, ran the length of one wall. Above it, wood saws, a hack saw, pruning shears, hammers, levels, and a hand drill hung from nails. Beneath it lay a yellow McCulloch chainsaw, fuel cans, and oil. On the other side in the back, shovels, rakes, a splitting maul, an iron grill, and a set of golf clubs leaned against the wall. Lumber of various sizes and a wheelbarrow occupied the middle.

Jim picked up one of the magazines and held it up to the light of a small window on the right side. A topless woman with her hands over her breasts looked out from the cover.

"June *Penthouse*," he said. "I got that one at home."

Bev shook her head. Of course he would. Her father probably had it, too.

"You see anything in here we can use?" Andy lifted a hammer and examined it.

"Naw," said Jim. "Think I'll bring some of these, though." He picked up a few magazines. "Let's bring some wood back. Can you carry some on that ankle of yours?"

"Yes," said Bev. "Although I'd rather carry it on my arms."

"You got me there." Jim tucked the magazines under his arm. "Hope the weather report's right. We don't need any more snow."

"You drive in snow this deep?" asked Andy.

"Not in a van."

"It's not going to be pretty."

"Well, we can rig a sail on top and let the wind push us home."

Andy hung the hammer back on the wall. "I see us digging out that van pretty damn frequently. Might be quicker just to walk."

He looked across at Bev. "Don't say anything

about this. We don't need to get the other girls riled up."

"The weaker sex, huh?" she said.

"I don't mean any disrespect. It's just… It might not be easy to get out of here. It might be hard."

"And knowing about it is going to make it worse? Shouldn't all of us be mentally prepared?"

"Sure. Of course. What I mean is…"

"No drama—is that it?"

"Sure."

"No wailing."

"That's right."

"No gouging out our eyes."

"Now you're making fun of me."

"Should I question where they are in their menstrual cycle?"

"You ain't gonna win this one, Andy," said Jim.

Chapter Fourteen

Back in the wind-pounded cabin, it was too soon to eat whatever they'd concoct for dinner, although Bev's stomach argued otherwise. After a few tokes from Will's latest joint, she craved the Vienna sausages as though they were cuts of filet mignon.

Seated with Jim at the table, Will held a toke in his lungs, then slowly exhaled. "This is torture. Stoned and we're, like, two hours 'til dinner."

He rose from his chair, opened the suitcase tucked against the wall, and returned with a full length of red rope licorice. He kissed one end. "Six ways, baby. Got to share you this time." He tore and distributed equal-sized pieces.

"You really are the candy man," said Bev.

Awkwardness drifted into the circle. She'd reminded everyone of Melvin, of the decision about his body they hadn't yet made.

Will broke the silence. "Okay, time for the question of the day. Who's going to freak out at home tonight because you're not there?"

Bev felt like spitting out the tiny piece of licorice she'd been gnawing with her front teeth to make it last.

Sandra. Her mom and dad. Alex and Joann and their kids would still be there. Justin, Cathy, and baby Paul would have returned home, but they'd know. Her mom and dad would call them.

They wouldn't have any idea where to search. *Freak out* didn't seem like an overstatement.

"I'll start," said Will, when no one else volunteered. "The grand total for me is…nobody! That's the advantage of being in college. My parents think Susan and me are back in our apartment, rutting like bunnies."

"Do they say that?" Tanya, sitting knees up on the sofa with Bev and Susan, pinched off a tiny piece of licorice.

"No, but you should see the way they look at us. They won't think anything's off if I don't call them Sunday, since we were just there Thanksgiving. A couple of my professors would notice me being gone if we don't make it back by Monday."

"Don't say that," said Tanya.

"I'm not saying we're not getting out of here. But it's not like we can call a taxi."

Susan tapped ash from her cigarette. "Maybe a hearse," she said.

"Oh-ho, that's dark," said Will. "This trip's weirding you out."

"Look at what we're doing," said Susan.

"So? This money's been written off. Nobody's going to miss it. How about you, Tanya? Anyone going to freak out?"

"No." She looked at her knees and rubbed a hand down the back of her dark hair.

"Didn't you say you live with your mom?" asked Will. "She'll worry."

"She won't notice."

Susan laughed. "Welcome to the club. I don't even know where my dad and stepmom are. Somewhere in

Europe."

"What about your real mom?" asked Will.

"She won't notice, either. She's six feet under."

"Oh. You never mentioned that. You just said you live with your dad."

"That sounds sad," said Tanya.

Susan stared at the white plywood wall next to the table. "Mysterious circumstances. She didn't wake up. Medical people never determined the cause."

"Oh, jeez, Susan. I'm sorry." Will stepped across the small space between the table and sofa, and hugged her at the shoulders. She stood up, pulled loose, walked to the stove, and drew from her cigarette.

"It's like Hamlet in reverse," she said. "My mom dies. Dad cashes in a big fat life insurance policy. Two months later he remarries. Doesn't have much time for his old family."

"Susan," said Will, his eyes showing concern.

She turned back to the group. "I'm fine. Hamlet should have gone to college. I've learned to be independent. And I like it."

For a few moments, the gale provided the only sound, whooshing between loud and louder, flinging an occasional cone or branchlet against the outside wall.

Will retook his chair at the table. "Wow. Guess I asked a dumb question. We'll get back, and when we do, let's give some love to the people who care about us. Sorry, everyone. Sorry, Susan."

"Love has its limits," said Susan. She looked at Andy. "Now that you've agreed to divvy up the dough, any reason for waiting until tonight to do it? And how about we plug the damn hole in the door? It's like having an air conditioner right next to the stove."

"I got it." Jim popped up and went to his backpack.

Bev kept her eyes on Andy. Why was he hesitating? Did he really think distributing everyone's share would lead to problems?

Susan stepped aside to let Jim go by with a wadded-up T-shirt. "You are planning to share it, aren't you?" she said.

Andy sighed, then slid the ice chest against the wall. He set the duffel bag on the table. "You had it figured out, Jim. What's everyone get?"

"Four hundred sixteen bills apiece. You said you get the same cut as the rest of us."

"That's right." Andy took the rubber band off a bundle and began dealing twenties into six different stacks.

Will mocked the voice of a game-show host. "Sixteen bills apiece—three hundred twenty dollars. Care to trade it in for what's behind Door Number One?"

Jim played along, adapting the voice of an overwrought housewife. "The one with the hole in it?" he asked.

"That's right, but you can't peek," said Will.

"It's Sasquatch, isn't it?" Jim maintained the female voice.

"Ma'am?"

"Fuckin' Sasquatch. You heard me, Mr. Hall. White fur. Frigid breath. Groans like the wind and stinks to high heaven."

"Ma'am, we wouldn't put your mother on the show."

"Shut up, you terrible man. I'll keep the money."

"Then I suggest you invest in toothpaste."

Andy paused from the divvying. "You two clowns are going to make me lose count."

"My goodness." Jim stayed in character. "We wouldn't want that, Monty, would we?"

"No, ma'am."

"You like your mothers hairy, don't you?"

"Those are trade secrets."

After distributing the loose bills, Andy handed each person four bundles of a hundred twenties each.

Bev ran her thumb down the ends of one bundle—not a blank among them. More than enough to have paid all her fees and tuition for her undergraduate years. She picked up a second bundle. Four thousand smackeroos. More than enough for a brand-new Chevy Camero.

What if she didn't write the story?

Now *that* was a stupid idea. She set the money back on her lap.

What if she got caught? Sandra's mother—a jailbird. She wouldn't do that to Sandra.

The world was going to hear the truth, and she'd surrender her share to prove it.

And maybe Melvin Ford, if that's who he really was, would get a decent burial.

Chapter Fifteen

Bev put the money in her backpack and returned to the sofa, while Andy loaded the remaining bundles into the duffel bag.

"Hot damn," said Will, eyeing a bundle in his hand. "Can't spend it. Still going to have to take out loans to get through grad school."

"William Garfield, doctor of psychology," said Susan. "And thief."

"I never stole anything. This dude with a big black beard just gave it me. Happened to find it in the middle of the woods."

Susan took a seat next to Bev. "Try explaining that to a judge."

"You know where I was when Cooper skyjacked that plane?" said Will. "Grandma's house on the Oregon coast. Drove straight there after my last class at PSU. My cousin Rob and I had to sneak out in the rain just to smoke a joint."

"Your granny doesn't smoke pot?" asked Bev.

"The point is, I've got an alibi. I can prove I wasn't on that plane."

"Yeah, like you look a lot like DB Cooper," said Bev. "He was in his forties. That's what the stewardesses thought. Polite. Offered to pay for his drink and tip the stewardess."

Andy strained to zip his pack after squeezing the

duffel bag inside it. "You found all that out on Thanksgiving?" he asked.

She looked him in the eye. "Like I told you, I went to the library."

"What's the name of that heating and air conditioning place you work at?"

Panic almost froze her brain. What the hell was it?

"Rose City," she said. Straight face. Eyes neutral. Nothing to hide.

"How'd you end up in Kelso?"

She felt the eyes of the others.

"What the hell?" She tried for aggrievement. "I grew up in Longview. My grandma still lives there. We had Thanksgiving at her house."

With a fresh dip of Copenhagen under his lip, Jim spat into a mug. "I never seen you before."

Great. A group inquiry.

"That's because you're from Kelso," she said.

"No, I'm from Longview. Which high school'd you go to?"

"R.A. Long." She felt damn lucky she'd just interviewed that hotshot basketball player. Otherwise, she'd have had no idea what name to pull out of her hat.

"What year'd you graduate?" asked Jim.

"Jesus Christ. 1968. What else do you want to know?"

"I was a freshman. I don't remember you."

"It's a big school. Probably all you noticed was the cheerleaders."

"Ha-ha!" Will chortled. "I saw the smut you brought from the shed. You going to share?"

"I'll sell you one. Twenty dollars."

Will held up a bundle. "I might happen to have one

right here."

"Fuck you, Will," said Susan. "You think I'm going to let you bring that magazine to bed?"

"Oh, yeah, that's right." Will raised his eyebrows exaggeratedly at Jim. "You keep the magazines. I'll keep the girl." He brought his twenties to his suitcase, zipped them in, and removed a half roll of toilet paper. "Where's the nearest tree out there?" he asked Jim.

"Hell if I know. One direction's as good as another. I wouldn't stay out long, though. Wind'll swallow your tracks."

"Why would I want to stay out there? I don't even think I'll make it to the trees. Don't worry, folks. I'll take a shovel."

Susan rose from the sofa. "I'm going, too. But I'll find my own tree, or whatever."

"That makes three of us," said Tanya.

****

Bev waited for them to leave before she lit a cigarette. Eight thousand bucks. She could keep that stash secret for a long time, more than two years. There'd be plenty of hijackings and bank robberies and armored car heists by then. The serial numbers on her twenties would be far down the list of illicit cash.

Her twenties. She'd gone through a lot of hardship to get them. She'd endure more before she escaped these woods. In a way, she'd earned them. Hell, she'd even helped dig them up.

But no.

That little voice in her head trying to tempt her needed to shut the fuck up. It was probably the weed. Get stoned, put eight thousand dollars on your lap, and see where the buzz took you?

She'd made her decision.

"So, we've got two Lumberjacks on this here crew."

"Huh?" She realized she'd been staring into space.

"I said, we've got two Lumberjacks." Jim rubbed a forefinger across his chin. "Didn't mean to hassle you when I was askin' those questions. Guess we're all kinda paranoid."

High school, that's what he meant. The R.A. Long Lumberjacks.

"That's all right." She was in a fog, an easy, lounging-in-the-head buzz. At the table next to Jim, Andy turned the page of a magazine, but she couldn't see if it was a *Field and Stream* or *Playboy* or *Penthouse* or whatever.

Something bopped the side of the cabin where the table was. God, it was a fucking gale out there. Like a movie. Like a Hollywood set where they had all those huge wind machines. No, more than that.

"Did you ever have Swanson for a teacher?"

"Huh?"

"Swanson. You know, for history?"

His eyes were squinty and red, but he looked earnest. He just wanted to talk about old times.

"Sorry to disappoint you, but I hated that school."

He spat into the mug, then stared inside it as he swirled the spittle. "Oh. Well, I kinda liked it. I mean, I graduated. Half my friends dropped out, soon as they turned sixteen. If it wasn't for football, I'd have prob'ly joined them. We don't have to talk about it. So your mom runs a library?"

"Um, yes. In Gresham."

He had probably never set foot in it. Neither had

she.

He glanced at his cup of spittle, then looked toward the boarded-up window, his eyes neutral, perhaps downcast, like she was still the senior and he was the freshman, beneath her interest. But they never would have found this cabin without him. They'd never have been able to start a fire back in the woods. He was the most valuable member in the group.

"Hey, tell me about your girlfriend," she said, donning her reporter's curiosity look.

"Awww." He pushed back a grin, and he looked down at the table. "She's nice. Funny you said something about the cheerleaders, because that's just what she was. I couldn't even talk to her 'til I was a junior, and then I could barely say a word. But I guess she kinda liked me, too, and she could talk a lot more. She always found a way to hang around with me until I finally got the nerve to ask her out."

"Sounds like she had her eyes on you for a while."

"You know how some girls, they know they're pretty, and they think they're above it all? She's not that way. She's nice to everyone. She's smart, too. She's gettin' her A.A. degree."

"Sounds like you're in love."

"I guess so."

Bev took a puff from her Salem.

Young. In love. In lust, for that matter.

Bev remembered that feeling. She still had time to find love. People would understand. They'd say she'd grieved long enough.

But Billy…despite the passage of time, she could still picture him as clear as if he were right next to her. She could feel his presence.

How could she let go, and not let go? How could she move on and yet hold what was dear?

"Jim," she said. "Where are you in the draft lottery?"

He looked up—apparently, this was a safer topic for him than love. "Right now? I'm a long ways from the top. They're gonna do another one in the spring. I'll be watchin' on TV, just like I did the last one."

"Would you go?"

Andy looked up from his magazine.

"What do you mean, would I go? Of course I would. I wouldn't let my country down."

Andy opened his mouth as though to speak, but he said nothing and returned his attention to the magazine.

"Not everyone sees it the same way," she said. She pictured the Park Block Riots, a long-haired man ten feet from her heaving a Pepsi bottle toward the riot-geared cops, the cops swarming him, swinging three-foot batons. The screams, the anger.

"I won't be a fuckin' draft dodger. I don't want to go, but I'll go."

Billy had been the same way. "Well, I hope you won't have to go."

Covered with snow, Tanya hurried inside and shut the door, stifling the wind. She examined the cabin.

"They're not in the loft?" Her face was pink, and snow crusted her brows.

"No," said Bev and Andy.

"How long was I out there?"

"Ten minutes, maybe," said Jim.

She stepped past the wood stove. "I've been looking for them. I circled the cabin."

"Did you see their tracks?" asked Jim.

"I saw lots of tracks. I didn't follow them. I kept the cabin in sight the whole time."

"Well, they can retrace their tracks," said Andy, looking back at the magazine article. "Let's give them a little more time. Maybe they went out to the trees."

"Might be bringin' back some firewood," said Jim.

"What if they need help?" asked Bev. "Like a tree fell on them or something?"

"Tree falls on 'em, another five minutes won't matter," said Jim.

"It might," said Bev, eyeing Tanya. The waitress's eyes were agitated and her jaw looked tense.

"It might," agreed Andy without looking up. "But I don't want us to get panicky every time someone has to take a dump. They've got their tracks. They'll find their way back."

Tanya shook out her coat near the stove and carried it up the ladder into the cloud of cigarette smoke. She came back down to retrieve the broom and a flashlight from her pack. Soon afterward, the sound of sweeping in the loft accompanied the outside howl of wind, along with the occasional turning of pages and spits into a cup.

Several minutes passed. The sweeping stopped, and Tanya came down with the broom and a loosely wadded cover she'd torn off a magazine to use as a dustpan. She dropped the glossy cover and sweepings into the woodstove, walked to the table, and stood next to Andy.

"It's been at least fifteen minutes," she said.

"Maybe they're checkin' out the shed," said Jim. "I left it unlocked."

Bev snuffed her half-smoked cigarette and rose.

Her ankle had stiffened. She dreaded the idea of dragging her body back out in those conditions, but if no one else would do it, she would. Andy closed the magazine and put his hand on Tanya's arm. "You're right," he said. "I'll go look for them."

"Same here," said Jim.

The door swung open again. Wind had worn Susan's face raw, and snow clung to her blonde hair. Her eyes were wild. She hugged herself tightly and scanned the cabin.

"I can't find Will!" she said.

Chapter Sixteen

Bev jumped up, grabbed her rain pants, and pulled them from the railing.

Andy was standing next to her when she turned around. "Not this time. It's too dangerous. You women stay here. Keep the fire going. See what you can cook for dinner. Will's going to be hungry when we bring him back."

She looked him in the eye. "I'm going." She moved to step past him, but he grabbed her arm below the shoulder and spun her back.

"No, you're not. If I have to stand here and force you to stay, that's what I'll do. That means Jim will be out there on his own. Is that what you want?"

"You have no idea what I want."

Susan stepped next to Andy. Desperation filled her eyes. "Stop it, Bev. Every second you fight this, it's a second against Will. Save it for another time."

Bev let her arms go limp, and when Andy released her, she remained standing at the wall.

The men bundled up and left, and the women stared at the door. A gust threw itself against the side of the cabin and moaned, long and loud. In half an hour, it would be dark—not that the day had offered much light.

The damned fool. Probably stoned out of his gourd. She didn't need another death for her story. It was already dramatic enough.

She held back a sob.

Susan lay face down on the sofa and gave in to her sobs. While Bev stroked the back of her head and Tanya rubbed her back, Susan shivered, despite the A-frame's warmth.

"So cold, so cold, so cold," she murmured.

Without warning, she spun into a seated position and pointed a finger at Tanya.

"You!" Her eyes flung hatred. Her mouth twisted with fury. "What did you do to him?"

Tanya staggered back a step. "Nothing. Why would I?"

"It had to be you! Who else was out there?"

Tanya knelt down and met Susan at eye level. "Oh, Susan, I never even saw him. I looked for you both."

"You want his money. One less person means a bigger share."

"No! I'd give up my share to get Will back."

Bev moved between the women. "Stop it, Susan," she said, the same words Susan had spoken to her moments before. "Blaming someone won't bring him back."

Susan took a breath and closed her eyes. When she opened them again, the anger was gone and confusion had taken its place.

"I looked and looked. I thought I found his tracks, and I followed them into the woods, and then I couldn't see them anymore and I couldn't see the cabin. I kept looking anyway, and I couldn't find him. I was yelling. Then I thought maybe he was back in the cabin already, or maybe he was looking for me, so I went back on my steps and I found the clearing. But I couldn't see my path after that. I thought I went forward, but the cabin wasn't there. And…and I thought I was going to die."

"Andy will find him," said Tanya. "He's a good man. He won't come back until he's found Will."

Susan peered at the waitress. "I don't know if I can trust you anymore."

Bev leaned forward. "Susan. That's not helping."

The college student took another long breath, her jaw clenched, her lower teeth scraping her upper lip. Still shivering, she extracted a cigarette from the inside pocket of her coat and lit it.

Tanya took a medium-sized pan from the open cupboard. "I'm going to make dinner. "Spaghetti with green beans and sausage. Those three men will be starving when they get back."

"There's a pasta dish you won't find in restaurants." Bev reached a hand to Susan's shoulder. "C'mon, let's get that coat off you and get your stuff drying."

Susan allowed Bev to remove the jacket, and then she unlaced her boots and peeled off the rain pants. She sat down on the arm of the sofa. "What if it's my fault?" Like a child hoping for acceptance, she looked at Bev.

"You can't say that," said Tanya, opening the ice chest. "That's a crazy storm out there."

"Maybe he wouldn't have gone so far if I hadn't gone out there with him."

"Don't you say that," said Tanya. "He made his own decisions. Besides, Andy and Jim are going to find him."

Bev took a plastic pitcher from the shelf and poured snow water from the stockpot into it. She guessed all the snow from the pot had melted to less than a quart. If they were going to have enough water, they'd have to keep filling that stockpot. She stepped out into the blizzard and scooped up more snow. Darkness had nearly vanquished the day. Wind had transformed the path of the men from boot holes to mild depressions.

"It's up to my thighs," she said when she returned.

"What if we never get out of here?" Susan asked from the sofa.

"We'll get out," said Tanya. "Andy said the storm is supposed to stop tomorrow."

"He was already wrong about the storm. What if he knew it was coming sooner, but he wanted to get the money? What if it keeps snowing and snowing?"

"It'll stop sooner or later," said Tanya. She sounded more confident than Bev felt—or maybe she was better at hiding fear from her voice. "And I'll bet you Jim could go get help. He knows the woods. We could wait for him. As long as he walks south, he'll hit some kind of road."

"Can we trust him?" Susan asked.

"He's true blue," said Tanya. "They're looking for Will right now, and they don't have to do that. They'll bring him back."

"Suppose he does find a road and he gets away. He knows people are going to ask questions. It would be a lot simpler if he didn't say a damn thing. He could wait a couple of months until we're all dead, and he could come back on a snowmobile and take the rest of the money."

She looked across the cabin as though she could see through the walls. "Two hundred thousand dollars," she said. "That can change a person."

Tanya went to the stove and put the stockpot on the floor. "Oh, Susan, you're just feeling bad because of Will." She placed a smaller pan, half full of water, on the stove. "They'll come back. We'll be fine."

The water heated faster in the smaller pan. It boiled softly, and in eight minutes the noodles were al dente. Tanya stirred sliced Vienna sausages and the green beans into the pasta, and Bev added freeze-dried peas from her pack.

Dinner was ready, but the men had not returned. Twigs and branchlets continued knocking against the outside wall, and the little cabin shook.

Chapter Seventeen

Bev lit another cigarette, put a chunk of wood in the stove, and peeked out the door. It was dark, but the sound of wind described the scene—sideways, blinding snow. Even with their headlamps, how far could Andy and Jim see with the beams reflecting off a torrent of snow?

Could the blowing snow have concealed a narrow ravine? Did a cougar lurk at the edge of the trees? Had a tree fallen and pinned Will by the leg—or worse?

It felt as though Will's fate connected with her own. If Andy and Jim brought him back alive, it would portend her own survival. If they didn't...

What would it be like to die out there? How long would it take?

She set the pasta on a hot pad on the table and placed the stockpot on the stove.

"How much food do we have?" asked Tanya.

"I have some gorp and two rolls," said Bev. "I did bring one extra backpacker meal—lasagna and meat sauce."

"I have half a pound of trail mix," said Tanya. "I thought we'd be back by now, or at least on our way."

"I have two frosted cherry Pop-Tarts," said Susan.

"We've got the rest of the food in the ice chest," said Tanya. "Can I have a puff of your cigarette?"

"Sure." Bev handed her the Salem. "I've got a

whole other pack left. It hasn't exactly been good conditions for smoking."

Tanya barely took a drag before handing it back to Bev and exhaling. "I quit three years ago. Not that it matters when you work in a bar. It's like breathing in a forest fire."

Bev handed Tanya the cigarette. "Keep it. I'll light another. How long have you been a waitress?"

"Nine years. But I still paint. I never quit. It's not exactly a painting type of town, unless you're talking about house painting. When I was younger I brought some paintings to Portland. I thought I was good enough. Guess I was wrong."

"Why don't you try again?" asked Bev. "Things are different now. Women have a better chance."

"Like hell," said Susan.

"It wasn't because I'm a woman," said Tanya. "I don't think about things that way."

"Don't kid yourself," said Susan. "Maybe you aren't good enough, but if you were a guy that wouldn't matter. You could swallow the paint and barf all over the canvas and they'd say you're a genius. If a woman did that, they'd say she needs a Valium."

"I don't know," said Tanya, taking a seat on one of the chairs. "Anyway, you probably think I'm a slut."

"What, because of Andy?" Bev lit another cigarette.

"Yeah, that and the whole barmaid deal."

"Are you?" Susan's eyes were hard.

"No, I'm not. Not that I don't have opportunities. I have to see something in a man, something special. I want it to last. Sometimes it does." She took another puff. "I haven't had much luck with men. Andy's kind of special, don't you think?"

"He's a little old for me," said Susan.

"Well, I'm a little old, too, I guess," said Tanya.

"If you're a slut, then so am I," said Susan. "I got it on with Will the first day I met him. I thought he was cute."

"That's the only criterion men use, and nobody calls them sluts," said Bev. "They don't have a term like that for men."

"Yeah, they do," said Susan. "Men."

They laughed.

Tanya blew a smoke cloud toward the loft. "The other night, there was a group of them sitting on the barstools yakking back and forth, and I was right in front of them, and one of them said 'find 'em, fuck 'em, fill 'em, and forget 'em,' and they all laughed."

"That's disgusting," said Susan, "but I'm not surprised."

Bev wanted to tell them she was going to be different. She was going to make it on her own smarts and guile and persistence. She was going to get off the Women's Page, and she was going to write some serious shit. She'd talk to important people, actual leaders. She'd ask tough questions, get both sides of every story, and her work would make an impact.

But she couldn't tell them.

If this group knew who she really was and what she meant to do, would they let her live? People did crazy things for money.

"What are you going to do with your major?" she asked Susan.

"I wish to hell I knew. I suppose I could be a teacher, but I don't want to put up with all the little shits. I could maybe do public relations, but I don't want to be someone's shill. I used to think I'd write books, but I don't know."

"Do you think you and Will might get married?" asked Tanya.

"He's not anything long-term. Look at him. Fucking lost." She closed her eyes. "Jesus. What a mess."

"I'll bet they're on their way back right now," said Tanya. "I'll bet they walk through that door any minute."

"Will you cut the Pollyannaish crap?" Ash tumbled off the tip of Susan's cigarette. "It's a shit storm out there, just like everyday life."

The women were quiet for a moment.

"How long have they been gone?" Susan asked.

Bev looked at her watch. "Thirty-two minutes."

When the door finally opened, the two men who entered barely resembled the ones who had left. Jim flicked off his headlamp and revealed a face without color. His eyes were snow-encrusted slits. Andy leaned onto the young logger's shoulder. His nose, the only portion of his face not covered by either beard or cap, looked rubbery, with a bluish hue.

Both men went no farther than the stove.

Susan dropped her burning cigarette on a saucer, sprang off the sofa, and retreated to the loft.

"Andy!" Tanya recovered from open-mouthed shock, left her chair, stopped halfway when Jim held up a hand and shook his head.

"We tried," he said, his voice scarcely audible.

For several minutes no one moved or spoke. Firewood popped inside the stove. Water dripped from the stockpot lid and sizzled on the hot black metal. Breathing hard, both men held their pink hands in front of the stove, occasionally squeezing them into fists or shaking them.

Bev smoked, and her fingers twitched.

No more Will.

Unless he'd wandered into another cabin none of them knew about. Unless he'd found a hidden hot spring or a Jeep with the engine running or an angel with warm arms.

Two of them now. Gone.

She leaned her head on the sofa and considered what the woman in the loft was feeling, because even if Susan hadn't loved Will, his loss would squeeze her heart.

Four years and eleven months ago Bev had lived in a second-floor apartment when the doorbell rang just after two p.m. She lugged her pregnant belly to the door. When she opened it, two men in dress uniform stood grim-faced before a backdrop of drenching rain, and she knew.

As they departed, she thanked them, a strange thing to be thankful for. She went to her bedroom and cried. She and Billy had planned a lifetime together, and all they received was ten months. Sandra had kicked in a particularly hard and painful manner, as though from inside her nest of amniotic fluid she understood and did not approve.

And now, stuck in this cabin, Bev felt those jabs in the gut and the bigger punch of loss.

The voice of the wind held no remorse. If anything, it seemed to gloat.

Jim rubbed his thighs and slowly turned his head

left, then right. Like an old man, he tottered a step and offered an arm to his companion.

"C'mon, Andy," he said. "Let's get you to the couch."

Chapter Eighteen

Shivering, Andy sat on the sofa near the stove, leaning forearms across his thighs.

His mouth was partly open, and his small eyes, set back in their sockets, seemed lost in a different kind of storm.

"You ladies think you can get his coat and boots off, and maybe rub him down a bit?" Jim's voice shook, just like the rest of his body, although not as much as Andy's. "Almost didn't make it back. Had his whole weight on me, and he still didn't want to come in."

"Oh, Andy!" Tanya pulled off his wool cap, pressed her head to his bearded cheek, then kissed his forehead. Lifting his arms one at a time, she removed his coat, sat beside him, and squeezed the warmth of her body against his. Bev pulled off his boots and the snow pants he wore over his trousers.

"You lie down, honey, and I'll lie right next to you," said Tanya. He didn't roll his eyes or shrug his shoulders. He obeyed, his face against the backrest, while Tanya squeezed onto the narrow space behind him.

Bev retreated to a chair at the table. She took the lid off the pasta mixture and verified it was no longer warm. Jim returned to a spot on the floor across from the stove.

"You tried, honey. I know you tried," said Tanya,

her lips an inch from the back of Andy's neck.

"I'm sorry," he murmured into the back of the sofa. "Tell Susan. Sorry."

"She knows, honey. She knows you tried."

For a while, all was still, except the ceaseless wind and the objects it propelled. Then Susan backed down the ladder. She took a chair next to Bev and stared with hardened eyes at the resting couple. After a few moments she stood, reached over Tanya, and tugged a wallet out of Andy's back pocket.

In an instant Andy revived, pushing up his body and knocking Tanya to the floor, but Susan had already stepped back from his reach. She opened the wallet and examined something intently. He rose to his feet, tottered a moment, flopped back down, his eyes glazy, his nose bluish in the light of the electric lantern. Next to the stove, Jim stood up and watched, while Tanya looked up from the floor.

Susan extracted a card from the wallet, flicked her gaze in turns from it to Andy, and then she set it down with a snap on the table next to Bev.

She glared at the bearded man. "You son of a bitch. Tell the others who you are."

Bev glanced at the card. It was a driver's license— no beard, hair short, eyes dark, a long face. No white dress shirt, no tie, but she knew who he was.

He rubbed a fist inside the palm of his other hand, glanced from Jim to Bev to Susan and finally to Tanya, who sat on the floor in front of him.

"Jordan Balfour, at your service," he said, mustering what strength he could to his voice. "Some people know me as"—he paused to scan the group again—"DB Cooper."

He reached under his coat. When his hand appeared again, he was holding a gun.

Chapter Nineteen

Facing a gun only a foot from her nose, Tanya scrambled back until she bumped into the chair next to Bev.

Bev stared at the gun. Pointed in her general direction, it seemed to triple in size.

Any second could be her last—ever. How could she have been so stupid? It was clear to her now—shave away ninety percent of the hair and it was him, just like the drawing on the FBI poster.

"Oh, god. Andy—don't," moaned Tanya.

"I've got a child"—that's what Bev wanted to say, but her throat was locked tight. She could barely breathe.

Cooper's—or Balfour's—arm still shook. How much control would he have if he pulled the trigger? How much time did she have until he tried?

"Susan," he said. "Give Bev the wallet."

Bev felt the wallet press against the back of her shoulder. She took it from Susan's hand.

"Bev. Put the license back in the wallet and gently toss it next to me on the sofa. And Jim—don't try to sneak up on me."

Bev glanced at the young logger. He stood in Cooper's peripheral vision, and it did seem he was half a step closer than he had been before the pistol came out.

She did what Cooper—she figured that's what she'd call him—told her to do. He returned the wallet to his pocket.

"Sit down, all of you," he said. "Right where you're at. Tanya, take the chair next to Bev."

After they complied, he set the revolver on his lap, his hand still on the grip, the barrel pointed toward Jim.

"If none of you does anything stupid, nobody will get hurt. We'll all walk out of here alive, at least those of us who remain. You can keep your money, and I will keep mine. Do you understand that if I wanted to kill you, I'd have already done it? Do you see how easy it would be? I've killed enough people in my life—what's a few more?"

"What did you do to Will?" asked Susan.

Cooper regarded her with what seemed like a mocking puzzlement. "What did I do to Will? Why don't you tell her, Jim?"

"He was with me the whole time," said Jim. "We never found Will. Sorry, Susan."

Cooper nodded toward Susan. "I'm sorry, too. I don't want to sound callous, but there are worse ways to die. When you die of cold you suffer for a bit. Your extremities ache. After a while you stop feeling them. You get tired. You don't know what's happening. You lie down to rest and you never get up again. But at least there's an explanation for your demise."

He took a cigarette from the pack of Pall Malls in his shirt pocket, put it in his mouth, and withdrew a set of matches from the same pocket.

"No disrespect, sir," said Jim. "But what are you talking about?"

"I can sense you calculating, Jim," he said, without

looking toward the logger. *"He's about to strike a match. His hand will be off the gun."*

Cooper turned and eyed his potential adversary. "I'm a warrior. Attack me, and you'll die." He lit the Pall Mall. His body shuddered as he drew from the cigarette. Exhaling slowly, he cast his gaze from person to person before setting his focus on the table. His eyes seemed to look somewhere else, perhaps into his own mind. His shaking diminished greatly.

"Explanations. Now that Susan has given me a proper introduction, I suppose I should reveal what this is all about."

He smoked again.

"In Korea, men were drafted to fight. They agreed to fight. Cold killed some of them, but they knew why they were there. There was an explanation. They might not have agreed with the explanation, but at least they had it. Same in Vietnam. One of my men was trying to avoid the enemy. He died of hypothermia in seventy-five-degree water. He stayed in too long, but he understood why he was there.

"But to die without an explanation—that's a different animal. You're boiling rice and a bomb falls. You hear the whistle, just a second to pray—please let it fall somewhere else. But it doesn't. Boom. No explanation. You happened to be there, that's all. You have nothing to do with the war."

He looked up from the table and eyed the others in the cabin. "Multiply that times thousands. Tens of thousands. Two of them, the parents of my wife. She goes to them, in Hanoi, to pray at their grave. Another bomb falls."

"You're talking about them gooks, aren't you?"

said Jim.

Cooper shook his head. "Gooks. Let me ask you something, Jim. Suppose the Soviets came to your town and said they were in charge now. Would you allow it?"

"That ain't the same."

"Why? Because you're not a gook?"

"We're trying to save them from the Communists. We're dyin', too. I lost a buddy. Another come home missing half his leg."

Cooper looked back at the table. "I have also lost friends. Such as that man hiding in the delta. If I hadn't married one of those…gooks, I might still feel the same way you do."

"You're goin' to give that money to them gooks, aren't you? That's why you don't want us to know. That's like—"

"Shut up, Jim!" Bev glared at him.

Cooper looked at Bev. "You're worried I'll get angry and start shooting. I won't do that." He turned to Jim. "And I have no intention to give so much as a dollar to the Communists. I have no illusions about who they are."

Tanya wiped a tear from her cheek. "You were married?" she asked.

"Yes."

"And she was killed and now you're crazy."

"Perhaps."

"I really liked you."

"I'm sorry. I should have kept more distance between us."

"How can we trust you now?" continued Tanya. "How do we know you won't…" She stopped herself.

"Won't…?" Cooper asked.

Tanya wiped both cheeks and kept quiet.

"Won't kill you? Is that what you mean? I already told you. I could have done the deed as soon as we found the money. By then, I'd already concluded it would be easier to get out by myself than with all of you. But that's not who I am."

He picked up a saucer from the end table and set his cigarette on it. "I'd like to think you'll buy that home on the coast, Tanya. And Jim, it would make me happy for you to buy that land you want. But if you think things have changed, that it's your patriotic duty to give up your share and capture what you believe is a Communist-loving traitor, you'd be mistaken."

"I don't know who you are," said Jim. "All right if I get me a cup? Might as well have a chew."

"Go ahead. We should eat, too. It smells as though you ladies did some cooking."

Jim took a step forward, hands up in submission. He slowly turned to the cupboard, grasped a teacup.

Then he spun around, flung the mug in a bullet line at Cooper's face. He let the momentum of the throw spring him forward to a pounce. Cooper raised his free hand to deflect the mug and ducked beneath Jim's arms. In a crouch, he whirled on the young logger, whose grasp captured only air, and he slammed the revolver down on the attacker's head.

The gun discharged. Bev dropped like a rock to the floor, then glanced up. Had anyone been hit?

"Oh, god!" shrieked Tanya, while Susan darted to the door, hand on the knob, ready to flee without a coat into the freezing night.

Bev's ears rang from the explosive bang, and her

eyes squinted in terror. The smell of gunpowder hung in the little room. Was she next? Would he kill them all now?

"I'm sorry! I'm sorry! I'm sorry!" Jim shouted. He had landed on the sofa, face down, as Cooper stood looming over him, pointing the gun at the back of his head.

"Don't!" cried Tanya.

Cooper panted softly. "Jesus, kid, you don't listen very well."

"I'm sorry, I'm sorry, I'm sorry," Jim whimpered.

Tanya rose to a knee. "Don't, Andy! He's just a kid!"

"I thought you had a fiancée," said Cooper, "or was that a lie?"

"No, sir. I mean, yes, sir, I do. I'm sorry."

"She'll think you ditched her. Is that how you want her to remember you?"

"No, sir."

"Are we done pulling stunts like this?"

"Yes, sir."

Cooper took a step back, picked up the mug, and dropped it on the sofa next to Jim. He stepped back again. "Get your ass up that ladder."

Jim slowly rose. Holding the mug loosely by the handle, he ascended to the loft.

"I don't want to see your face looking over the side." Cooper raised his coat and shirt and holstered the handgun. "I don't even want to know you're here."

He sat on the edge of the sofa, elbows on his knees, forehead resting on his hands.

Bev unlocked her frozen limbs, rose on quivering knees, and felt her way back onto the chair. This wasn't a story anymore. This was about getting out alive. About getting home to Sandra.

She looked up at the loft.

"Jim!" she called.

"Yeah."

"Don't be a fucking hero!"

"I won't. I'm sorry."

She looked at the man in front of her.

"Cooper," she said, "or Balfour or Jordan or whatever you want to call yourself…"

He raised his head off his hands. "What?"

"You did the right thing. Thanks for letting him go."

His lip twitched. "What about before? The wars? My dead wife? Did I do the right thing then?"

This guy was fucking crazy. "Does my life depend on my answer?"

"Of course not."

"I won't judge you. I just want to live. I've got a little daughter. Maybe that matters, if you care like you say you do."

"So no judgment," he said. "Just survival. You'd do all right in 'Nam."

Chapter Twenty

Cooper rose from the sofa. "Let's divvy up dinner. Four ways. Jim can stay upstairs and think about his actions."

Bev glanced toward the loft. Cooper meant for Jim to hear—bad boy, no supper. Her heart raced. She said a silent prayer that no one would anger the man with the gun.

"We could heat it up again," said Tanya. Nobody answered, so she scraped out four portions of sausage-green-bean spaghetti on black ceramic plates. Bev divided one of her two remaining rolls into four pieces.

Cooper ate three forkfuls, chewing slowly. After the women finished, he picked up his plate and climbed the ladder.

"I want this plate emptied," he said. "And that doesn't mean feeding rats or chinks in the wall."

"Yes, sir," came the reply.

Back on the ground floor, he picked up Bev's dish. She put a hand on his wrist.

"That's okay," she said. "I'll take care of my plate."

"You ladies did the cooking. I'll do the cleaning." He set dishes and silverware on the floor by the woodstove, dipped a portion of a dish towel in the stockpot, picked up the first plate and washed it.

Maybe he wouldn't kill them.

After he put the plates away, he touched Bev's shoulder. "We need more wood. This time you're going with me."

Her legs felt weak. If she went out there with him, would she ever come back? She sensed the gazes of Susan and Tanya, probably wondering the same thing.

He lifted his hand from her shoulder. "I'm not going to do anything to you. As hard as it might be to believe, I don't want anything to happen to any of you. We just need to get wood. Two people will bring back more than one. Is your ankle up to it?"

She managed to nod her head.

"Good. I've got an extra headlamp you can use." He looked up at the loft. "Jim. I'm going out for wood. That gives you enough time to plan an ambush. Would you like me to bring you your hatchet?"

"No, sir. What I did… It was stupid."

"That might be the smartest thing you ever said. Some day we might have a nice chat about Vietnam, but for now getting the hell out of here with our skins intact takes priority. You sure about that hatchet?"

"Yes, sir. Thanks for the food, sir."

"Oh, that's right. Tanya, I missed a plate. Would you mind?"

"No. I'll do it, Andy," she said.

Outside, Bev ducked her head as the arctic blow iced her cheeks, grabbed her by the shoulders, and shoved. The light from her headlamp reflected off a stampede of snowflakes and bounced back into her eyes. Beyond Cooper and his tan-colored coat, the world was a black hole.

How long would it take the wind to erase the pathway they carved? She dared not look behind her. In

that short pause she could lose sight of Cooper's coat—
she would be in outer space, the tether between her and
the ship snapped in half.

After a couple of minutes, Cooper stopped at the
edge of the clearing, facing a wall of firs bending and
waving, flinging silhouettes of cones and twigs.

He turned to Bev, tilting his headlamp down so it
wouldn't shine in her eyes. "Missed it!" he shouted.
"Has to be that way!" He pointed left, turned, and
resumed the slog, this time head-on into the screaming
wind.

They reached the first shed, trudged past it, and
stopped in front of the open shed with snow-pasted
wood stacked head high. She grabbed a piece,
somewhat fat—would it fit through the door of the
wood stove? She put it back and selected a different
piece, and her headlamp caught an edge of bright blue
against the windward side of the shed, strange to see
color in this dark and white world.

It was a blue plastic tarp. Perhaps it sheltered
kindling—they could use some, in case the fire went
out and they had to start over. She stepped past the
stacked wood, found the edge of the tarp, and tugged it
away from the wall.

Will's white face and open eyes stared back at her.
Out of his partially open mouth, a seepage of blood had
frozen in flakes over his scruffy beard.

Her stomach roiled, and she stumbled backward to
fall into the snow at Cooper's feet. For an instant she
felt like a beetle on its back, trapped in a tomb of icy
fluff. She scrambled up and backed into Cooper. His
hands grasped her by the shoulders, held her in place.

"Stay put!" he shouted.

Of course. She couldn't flee into the night. She would die if she did.

"I'm okay." She willed her legs to quit backpedaling.

Steeling herself, she spotlighted Will's face. His eyes were frozen in shock, as though facing an oncoming locomotive in the last microsecond of life. It looked like he had managed to sit down, lean back against the wall of the shed, and cover himself with the tarp against the cold before he died. On the ground, his legs protruded into a narrow space behind the stack of wood.

"I didn't see a tarp the first time," Cooper said.

"Neither did I."

She remembered a photograph that had appeared on page four in the *Chronicle* a week ago. It was a Ford Pinto—its front end smashed like an accordion, its roof three-quarters shorn. Charlie, one of the police-beat reporters, had taken the photo. He told Bev it hadn't been easy, but somehow he'd held off vomiting and kept his wits, despite the decapitated young woman belted into the driver's seat, an image that didn't make it into the newspaper.

This was her car-crash moment. To be the reporter she wanted to be, she had to face death. While Cooper peered down at Will, she bent low and placed two fingers over his carotid artery. His neck was as cold as the snow.

Cooper pulled away the rest of the tarp. Will still wore all his clothes, his army surplus coat, his snow pants. Grasping the corpse by its shoulders, Cooper pulled it away from the wall. He tried to peel off Will's green wool cap, but it was frozen to his head.

"Blood," said Cooper, nodding toward a dark spot on the back of the cap.

Bev forced herself to look.

Cooper eased the body back against the shed and covered it with the tarp.

"Let's go to the other shed," he said.

Inside the other shed, Bev took out a cigarette and lit a match. The stillness of her hands belied the shaking she felt inside.

"You all right?" he asked in the midst of lighting his own cigarette.

"I'm not under a tarp."

They smoked for a couple of minutes. It was a relief not to have the wind yelling in their ears while trying to yank them off their feet.

"They'll be worrying about us," he said.

"They'll be worrying about me. You're the one with the gun."

"Are you worried?"

She blew out smoke. She'd been trying to quit cigarettes ever since she became pregnant with Sandra, but now she was glad she hadn't.

"Would you be?" she said.

"Yeah. Except I know my mind. You're not in any danger from me. Neither is anyone else."

"What happened to Will?"

"I'd like to know." A mixture of fog and smoke streamed out his mouth and nostrils.

She glanced around the shed—everything looked the way it had in the afternoon. "I can tell you what I want to believe. Whatever whacked him in the head wasn't held by human hands. A big branch. A glancing blow from a falling tree. He stumbled around. Found the woodshed. Didn't see the one we're in now. Wrapped himself in the tarp to stay warm. Prayed about living."

He nodded. "But then there's Susan, and there's Tanya."

"You're thinking maybe with a shovel?"

"Something blunt. There were no cuts in his hat."

They smoked some more.

"What should we say?" she asked.

"Right now? What good would come from telling them what we found?"

"Susan has a right to know."

"Maybe she already does."

"Then how'd he get here?"

"Maybe she didn't finish the job. Thought she did, but she didn't. At least, not right away."

"Did you see her when she came in? She looked for him. She was out of her mind."

He let his arm down at his side, his cigarette pointed at the ground. "So did Tanya."

"Susan's going to freak out. I can see her running out, trying to find the shed, trying to find Will. While you and Jim were out looking, she starting accusing Tanya. She said one less person meant more money for everyone else. Tanya swore she didn't have anything to do with it."

"So if we tell them what we've seen, she'll go after Tanya."

"Probably."

"Back to my question—what good will come from telling them now?"

"I can't see either of them doing this to Will," said Bev. "But if one of them did, what's stopping her from doing it again?"

A gust blew louder, shaking the small enclosure. A crack resounded above the squall. Bev braced, ready to hit the floor, but if a tree were to smash through the roof, there was nowhere to dive for cover.

A muffled thump followed, sending vibrations beneath their feet.

Cooper, who'd squatted low to the ground, rose.

"That had to be close," said Bev.

Another gust slammed the shed. It was as though the big bad wolf had come to blow their house down. Bev held herself still, her senses alert for the sound of another crack. But none came.

"I don't like it here," said Cooper. "At least in the cabin there's no tree that can hit it."

Bev caught Cooper's eye. "You get the idea that maybe, after you buried the money, Mama Earth didn't want to give it up?"

"I'm starting to wonder now."

"I think you're right—we shouldn't say anything."

"And I think you're right. If one of them did the deed, she might try to kill someone else. Maybe tonight."

"I don't feel so sleepy anymore."

"One of them's going to want to sleep right next to me."

"You don't have to go along with that."

"Might be for the best. I can keep an eye on her. You really think you can stay awake?"

"The way I'm feeling now? A bottle of sleeping pills wouldn't knock me out."

"All right." He threw his cigarette to the ground and stamped it out. "You hear Susan getting up, put your headlamp on her. I want you to yell your lungs out if you see anything remotely like a threat."

Bev extinguished her cigarette on the ground. "Let's get some wood before the wind swallows our path."

Cooper opened the door, then shut it before stepping out. "Bev—thanks. I think I can trust you."

"I've got a kid. Remember?"

He nodded. "You mind if I ask—where's her father?"

She closed her eyes. Almost five years later, the question hurt as much now as it did then.

"Sorry," he said.

"No. It's okay. What you said about no explanation? He was in 'Nam too, and he came back in a box."

Chapter Twenty-One

Wind continued to rattle the cabin walls. Bev turned the page of the book she'd brought in her pack, *I'm Okay You're Okay,* although she wasn't sure what she'd just read—something about staying in an adult ego state? Across from her at the table, Susan turned up a card. Freed from banishment, Jim sat on the floor against the back wall, occasionally turning a page from a *Field and Stream,* the same as Cooper, who had a different issue on the sofa next to Tanya. The waitress stared at an open word-search magazine she held on her lap.

It was hard to imagine either Susan or Tanya whacking Will on the back of his head with a shovel. Would it have required multiple swings? Or would one hard smack have been enough to let the cold take care of the rest?

She liked the tree theory better. A chunk of treetop could have knocked Will face first into the snow, unconscious and bleeding from the skull. He could have bitten his tongue, which would explain the blood in his mouth and on his beard. Regaining consciousness, he could have staggered to the woodshed, covered himself with a tarp to stay warm, and died.

Tanya closed the puzzle book. While Bev and Cooper had been discovering a corpse, she had obviously spent time brushing her hair. It had an ebony luster, softened by the light of the lantern. She looked at Bev a moment, then Susan, who ignored her or didn't notice, and then Cooper.

"It was hell while you were out there," she said in a quiet voice.

"We were never in any danger." Cooper didn't look up from the magazine.

"You took so long."

"It's hard moving around out there. It's hard to know where you're going."

"Well, I'm not talking about that anyway." She glanced toward the table again. "I'm talking about Susan."

Susan picked up a card and held it, looking across the table at Bev.

"Why am I imagining a nine-year-old ratting out big sister when Daddy comes home?" She placed a three on the diamonds pile.

"I'm older than you," said Tanya.

"Then start acting like it," said Susan.

"You don't want me to bring up the things you were saying."

Cooper closed the magazine and put it on the end table. He looked at Bev. "We might learn something," he said.

"That's right," said Tanya. "She's still saying I did it. That I did something to her boyfriend. That's just—"

"Who else was out there?" Susan slapped a partial deck onto the table. "Just me and you. He might be stupid, but he can find his own tracks back to the cabin. Something happened, and you know it."

"See what I mean?" The waitress wiped a tear. "Why is she doing that?"

Jim looked up from his spot in the back corner. "I told her to stop. She wouldn't listen to me, neither."

Susan pushed all the cards together, face up and face down. She turned toward Tanya, and they glared at each other. "He's my boyfriend," she said. "Maybe not enough to get married, but I care about him."

"That doesn't give you the right to…to accuse me of something horrible."

"What other explanation is there? All of a sudden he's gone. Tracks all over the place, and he's gone. I looked everywhere. Gone. Fucking gone."

Tanya leaned her head back. She squeezed the puzzle book, then leaned forward again. "I'm sorry for you," she said. "Terribly sorry. I wish I'd never come here." She looked at Cooper. "I mean, I like you, Andy, but this is just too horrible."

Cooper, who'd been ping-ponging his eyes between the two women, looked over at Bev. "You learning anything?"

"No," said Bev.

He put a hand on Tanya's knee and eyed Susan. "There is another explanation," he said. "Neither of you harmed him."

Susan flinched, and her eyes grew wide.

"That's right—you, too," he continued. "You could have done something just as easily as Tanya. But given the conditions out there, it's more likely that whatever happened didn't involve either of you."

Bev put a hand on Susan's hand, over the stack of cards. "I told you before. None of this helps. None of it will bring back Will."

Susan pulled her hand back. "She's just going to walk away. When we get out of here, nothing's going to happen. She'll have more money, just like she wants."

"Jeez!" Tanya brushed her hands across the side of her head. "Tell you what, Susan. If we don't find Will…if something bad happened, you can have whatever my extra share would have been. How about that? Why would I hurt him and then give you the money?"

"Oh, that really helps. I can get that much money with one phone call. I'd rather have Will. Can you give me that?"

Cooper slapped his hands together. "No more accusations. You want to accuse someone, go outside and shout it to the wind. That's about as much as it's worth. I don't want to hear it anymore. So, Susan, what's it going to be? Are you finished with this crap?"

Susan sifted through the cards, stopping each time she found one facing opposite the others.

"He asked you a question," said Jim, still on the floor.

She set down the cards, rose from the table, and walked to the stove, facing away from them.

"Okay," she said.

Something pounded three times on the outside door. Susan sprang back, whirled toward the others, her eyes astonished and fearful.

Jim bolted up from the floor. "What the…"

Bev rose from her chair, kept a hand on the table, stared toward the door.

They waited a moment, and then the knocks came again.

Someone was out there.

Chapter Twenty-Two

Bev exchanged a glance with Cooper and knew in an instant that he also understood the implications.

It was not Little Red Riding Hood on the other side of that door.

"Just a minute!" Cooper yelled, unholstering the revolver. He motioned for Susan to step against the wall and whispered the words, "Open it fast."

But Susan couldn't move. Her eyes glassed over.

Bev hurried past the paralyzed woman and pressed her back against the wall by the door. After Cooper positioned himself so that Susan would not be in the way of a bullet, Bev grabbed the knob and yanked open the door.

Frigid air barged in, scattering cards and flapping the pages of magazines. Against a backdrop of blowing snow, faintly lit by the inside lantern, an ice man stood breathing heavily. Snow covered his outerwear and wool cap, and his beardless face was white and rubbery. Beneath the bulk of clothing, he appeared short and scrawny. Although his eyes looked drained of color, they flickered in recognition of Cooper's gun.

The man turned off a silver metal flashlight and moved his arms away from his sides.

"That's right—keep your hands where I can see them," said Cooper. "Step in slowly."

The man complied. Once inside, he held his gloved

hands closer to the stove, close enough to grab Bev if he had a mind to do it. He whimpered like a puppy, and his body shook. Snow granules clung to the sandpaper nubs of whiskers, and ice encased his dark gray brows. He looked older, perhaps in his sixties.

Bev fought an urge to cower like a mouse. She made her eyes hard, examining him as she shut the door.

"Okay, mister," said Cooper. "What the hell are you doing here?"

The man took his eyes off the stove and scanned the room before settling on Cooper.

"Oh, my god!" cried Tanya. "What are you doing here, Clint?"

He opened his mouth, struggled to find his voice, then answered through chattering teeth. "Freezing…my ass off."

"The woman next to you," said Cooper. "She's going to remove your pack and your coat. Let her do it."

Although Bev didn't mind Cooper volunteering her for the task, she paused. How was she going to do it without getting between Cooper's gun and the ice man? Also, if Tanya knew this ice man, what did that mean?

Then Bev recognized the one-inch cleft on his chin, and fear tightened its grip on her spine.

"You're the man who walked away while"—she looked at Cooper—"*Andy* was talking at the Spar Pole."

Clint said nothing. His legs quivered. His whole body shook. Bev took a breath and moved behind him to take off the pack.

Cooper kept his eyes on Clint. "Tanya, did you tell this man when and where we'd meet?"

Tanya clutched the edge of the table. "You only told us not to bring somebody else. I never thought he'd...Clint, what are you doing here?"

"S...same as you."

Bev pivoted to Clint's side and reached for the zipper to his green canvas jacket. She removed both of his gloves—his reddened hands were cold and damp.

"You did it," said Susan.

"Wait, Susan," said Cooper.

"You can't tell me to wait. Not when *this man* killed my boyfriend."

Bev removed the coat, dropped it next to the pack, and retreated to a spot between the stove and sofa.

Fear reanimated Clint's eyes. "I ain't killed nobody."

"Hold on, mister," said Cooper. "First things first. Unbutton your shirt. Slowly. You make a sudden move, it's your last one."

"I got a pistol, if that's what you're after," said Clint.

"Where is it?" said Cooper.

"Above my right hip."

"You put him up to this." Susan pointed a finger at Tanya's face. "You're the reason he's here."

Tanya backed into the sofa, lost her balance, and let herself fall on the middle of it. "I did not," she said.

"Shut up!" Cooper's eyes narrowed, and his face grew hard. His finger was poised at the edge of the trigger, his grip on the revolver tight.

"Susan, you've got to stop this," said Bev.

"Okay, Clint," said Cooper, his voice low and edgy. "Bev's going to take your pistol. You got a problem with that?"

"No."

Christ—she'd never touched a gun before. What if she couldn't get it out of the holster?

It turned out to be easy. She had to unfasten a pair of snaps. Holding it by the tips of her fingers, she brought it to Cooper.

Cooper took Clint's gun and handed his revolver to her. "Hold onto this. Keep it pointed at Clint. Keep your finger on the trigger."

Holy Christ—could she shoot it?

If Clint dove for it, she'd have to shoot. And if she missed? If that ice-man creep pulled it out of her hands, then what?

She'd do whatever she had to do. She held out her hand for the revolver. It was heavy. Her finger on the trigger, she propped a hand beneath her wrist to hold the gun steady and pointed it at Clint.

His eyes grew more fearful.

Cooper released the magazine from Clint's pistol and pulled back the slide. A bullet popped out and clattered onto the floor.

"Ready for action, aren't you, Clint?" said Cooper.

"I always pack in the woods," said Clint.

Cooper pocketed the magazine, set the pistol on the table, and retook possession of his revolver.

"I know what you're thinking," said Clint. "But if I wanted to shoot ya'll, you think I'd have knocked on the door first? I been at that fire you started. Fuckin' tree fell right across it. Branch knocked me on the side of the head. Fucked up my tent."

"Shut up." Cooper backed a step past the table, opening a pathway for Clint. "Sit down on the sofa. Bev, clean out his pack, check his coat, inside and out.

Leave everything on the floor."

Tanya sprang off the sofa, and Clint took her place, rubbing his hands together while his body continued to shake. Cooper spun a chair away from the table and sat directly across from the newcomer.

Clint's pack had only two compartments. Bev took out a half-full package of beef jerky.

"How is it you know this man, Tanya?" asked Cooper.

Bev glanced over to the waitress, whose eyes shot poison at the man on the sofa.

"He's a regular. He was there that night. He was listening. And then he went over to the bar. He called me over and asked if I was going, and I said I didn't know. Later on, after everyone left..." Her eyes darted from Susan to Cooper. "I told him I was going, and I told him when we were leaving. And that's all. I swear. I had no idea he'd follow us."

Cooper slapped his free hand hard on the table. "Son of bitch! Who else did you tell?"

"No one, Andy, I swear. Not even my mom, not that she'd care."

Cooper swept a glare from Bev to Susan and Jim. "How about the rest of you? Who knows what you're doing right now?"

"My girlfriend thinks I'm huntin' turkey," said Jim.

"My daughter and my parents think I'm looking for mushrooms," said Bev.

"No one," said Susan. "Except Will, if he's...if he's..." She didn't finish.

Tanya leaned down with her hands on her knees and stared at Clint. "You'd better not have done anything," she said.

"I don't know what you're talking about." He looked from face to face, shuddered beneath the heat of everyone's eyes. "I know about the cowboy man. Don't know how he died, but I was watching you folks this morning."

"In the middle of a blizzard?" asked Cooper.

"Hard to see, but ya'll didn't see me, neither."

"Why'd you hide?"

Clint blew warm air onto his thumbs, lowered the hands, and kept rubbing.

"Didn't want to deal with you if you didn't find anything."

Cooper leaned forward. "What do you mean—deal with us?"

"If ya'll found the money, I thought I'd ask for some, too. Small amount, just to keep me quiet. I figured it would be a bargain."

Bev scanned the items she'd placed on the floor. The jerky and a can of pork and beans. Smashed package of white-powdered mini-donuts. Blue spray paint. Binoculars. Rope. Two cans of Sterno. Matches in a waterproof container. The flashlight he held when he showed up. She'd emptied underwear from a plastic bag.

She picked up the jacket, felt something heavy, reached into an inside pocket, and pulled out a box of bullets.

Cooper glanced at the box, then returned his gaze to Clint. He took a pack of Pall Malls from his shirt pocket, considered them for a moment, and put them back.

"That's a lot of bullets," he said.

"It's what I always carry."

"Where have you been these last few hours?"

"I told you—over by the fire. Figured when the wind died down I'd beat you back to your van, and we could negotiate a settlement when you arrived."

"What makes you think we'd settle?"

Clint's lips twitched, as though fighting back a smirk. "Oh, I got me a little insurance policy."

"What do you mean by that?"

"Let's just say, without my help, transportation's going to be an issue."

"I'm the one with the gun, Clint. Don't play riddles with me. You think I won't kill you?"

Clint stopped rubbing his hands together. He looked Cooper in the eye. "That'd be a mistake," he said. "You need me to get out of here. That's all I'm going to tell you."

"I don't believe you," said Susan. "If that tree hadn't fallen…" She crossed her arms below her chest. "You were planning to sneak in here tonight. You'd have killed every one of us."

"I told you I wouldn't do a thing like that."

"Then where's my boyfriend?"

Clint scanned the room. "I don't know. Up that ladder, maybe?"

Susan stepped away from the table and spat on Clint's face. "You bastard!"

Clint wiped a shirt sleeve across his face. "He's the tall guy, ain't he? I swear to you, whatever happened to him, I didn't do it."

"Sounds like you know something, Clint," said Cooper.

"I don't know a damn thing. But I can see he ain't here and you don't know where he is."

"Stand up," said Cooper.

Alarm seized Clint's face. "What for?"

"Just do it."

He stood. "I swear I ain't hurt nobody."

Cooper lifted the revolver from his thigh. "No sudden moves. Empty your pockets. Place everything on the sofa."

Clint pulled out a comb, a set of keys, coins, a wallet, a pocket knife, a handkerchief. A droplet fell from his forehead. Whether it was melted ice from his brows or nervous sweat, Bev couldn't determine.

"Now take off your boots."

"I need them boots."

"We'll take 'em off for you," said Jim, standing next to Susan, "after we put a bullet in your brain."

"C'mon, Jimmy," said Clint. "You know me. You know I'm okay."

"Okay for what?"

"That I wouldn't hurt nobody."

"I can't tell people what I don't know."

"Shit, Jimmy, you ever see me pick a fight?"

"That's enough," said Cooper. "Jim's right, though. You don't take those boots off, we'll take them off for you."

"Okay, okay." Clint sat on the sofa and unlaced a boot. "Jesus Christ. People find a little money, they get mighty paranoid. What you think I got, anyway? A little derringer?"

Cooper said nothing. Clint pulled off the boot, held it upside down, and shook it. He smiled a look of *Who, me?*

"Next one, Clint," said Jim.

A look of worry passed through the newcomer's

eyes, replaced by his thin smile, a borderline smirk. "Only going to ask for a thousand dollars," he muttered while unlacing the second boot. "Thirty years I been mixing chemicals at the paper mill. A little bonus, is all. I know how to keep my mouth shut."

Upside down, the second boot yielded nothing.

"Socks," said Cooper.

"Jesus. You want me to strip naked?"

"Maybe."

"I ain't taking off my socks. There ain't enough nose plugs in here for that."

"Bev," said Cooper. "See what he's got in his socks." He cocked the revolver's trigger.

Clint raised both hands chest-high. Bev knelt in front of the sofa and lifted up one of his pant legs.

"He was already dead," said Clint. "I swear, I swear. Oh Lord Almighty, you're going to think I done it."

"What are you talking about?" Susan shrieked the question, silencing Clint. His breathing quickened and the quiver increased.

He'd been right about the odor, but Bev assumed her own feet didn't smell any better.

She caught her breath at the sight of a rectangular lump in his sock. She reached inside and took out a wallet, stood, and backed a step. It was damp and held the odor of the old sock.

She opened it, and the thing she dreaded, that they all dreaded, was there.

Chapter Twenty-Three

William Thomas Garfield looked pensive on his Oregon State driver's license, expiration date March 17, 1973, a twenty-second birthday he would never have. On the day he went to the license office, he'd been wearing a light blue dress shirt and a black tie. He didn't look like a goofy guy with a taste for marijuana and cocaine.

Susan darted around Cooper and threw a punch. Clint raised both arms, but her fist blasted through the defense and smacked his cheek. Then she swung an uppercut between his arms, this time connecting with his chin.

Cooper rose from his chair and took a step back, holding the revolver at his side. "Get her off of him."

Bev had already backed away to the woodstove, but Jim sprang forward, wrapped both arms around Susan's waist, and yanked her away while she continued swinging her fists.

"You son of a bitch!" she shouted.

"Stop it, Susan," said Cooper, watching Clint, who kept his arms raised and his eyes wary.

Jim pulled her back another step. "C'mon, girl. Hold your horses. Let someone else take a shot at him."

At the back of the cabin, Tanya stood with her hands covering her face. "Oh god, oh god, oh god, Clint, you…oh god."

"Shut up, Tanya," said Cooper.

Susan twisted left and right to get loose, but Jim kept her in a squeeze. "You fucking bitch," she yelled at Tanya. "You're part of this."

"I'm not, I'm not, I swear I'm not."

Cooper slapped his free hand onto the table. "Both of you, shut up!"

Bev kept her eyes locked on Clint. He rubbed his cheek and rotated his jaw. Perhaps the show of pain was a ruse. In a second he'd be a dart and Bev would be the bull's eye. He'd grab her, thrust her in front of him like a shield, drag her outside, twist her neck, bite her, vicious like the animal he obviously was.

In the pause after Cooper's command, a wind gust whooshed in the darkness outside.

Clint massaged small circles on the back of his jaw. "It ain't like it looks," he pled.

"Shoot him, just shoot him," said Susan, no longer flailing but still inside Jim's grasp.

"Lord almighty." Clint closed his eyes and whimpered. "These people ain't going to believe me. Why'd I have to take that wallet? Why couldn't I have just left it there?"

"Look at me, Clint," said Cooper.

Clint opened his eyes. There was a tremble in his shallow breaths.

"You've been lying to us." Cooper kept his voice even. "You told us you didn't know what happened to Will or where he was. But you do know. You took his wallet. Why should we believe anything you say?"

"I thought..." He sighed. "I thought if I told you, you'd be thinking what you're thinking right now, that I done it. But I didn't. Tanya, you know me. Am I the kind of man who'd kill someone?"

"I don't know you. You're a customer in the bar."

Susan scowled at the waitress. "I don't trust a thing you say. You told him we were going and when we'd leave. You spread your legs for Cooper. If Cooper didn't have a gun, we'd all be dead, and then you two would split the money."

"I told you I'm sorry I told Clint."

"You didn't seem sorry when you told me," said Clint.

"You're the one who asked," said Tanya. "Stop trying to get me on your side, you murderer."

"I didn't do it."

"Explain how you got the wallet," said Cooper.

"Can I have one of them Pall Malls? How come she's calling you Cooper? Wait a minute—are you him?"

"No cigarettes. You can call me Andy."

Clint looked around the group as though searching for a sympathetic face.

"Like I said, I been following you. Just… All I wanted was a little cut of the proceeds. Last night when the storm got bad, I figured I'd better stay close. Saw you leave that cowboy behind, find the money, start a fire, find the cabin, all of it. I didn't want to stay outside the cabin freezing to death. Figured you'd leave when the wind died down. Went back and forth a couple of times between the fire and the cabin just to make sure you weren't leaving some other way. Poked around a little, not too much, didn't want to get lost. Found those sheds. Went back in the woods behind the sheds, and I damn near tripped over him."

He looked at Cooper. "If you're going to kill me, at

least let me have a cigarette."

"Nothing's decided yet," said Cooper.

"I'll give you a cigarette," said Susan. "After you're dead I'll stick one in your ass and light it."

Clint took a long, trembling breath.

"You're not finished yet," said Cooper.

Clint gave a questioning look.

"You took his wallet," said Cooper. "You say you didn't tell us because you thought we'd think you killed him—or maybe because we'd know you did. What did you do then? Did you leave the body there?"

"I didn't do it. You'll never get me to say I did, because that would be a lie. I didn't want to leave him lying there, if that's what you're getting at. If you found him under the tarp in the woodshed, I'm the one that dragged him there."

Bev looked at Cooper, who shook his head once.

"I got a little heart," continued Clint. "I didn't want him to get buried in the snow. If I killed him, wouldn't I want to leave him out in the woods? Let the bears and the beetles find him in the spring?"

"Stop it!" Susan wiped tears from her cheek. Jim let go of her but stayed close. "That's not just a body. That's my boyfriend. I can't take this anymore. Bring him outside and shoot him."

"Are you married, Clint?" asked Cooper.

"Sure. Good woman, too. Worried about me, I'd guess."

"Well, I'm hurting right now for that young lady behind me. I know what it's like to lose a loved one. I know what it's like to want revenge."

"I'm telling you, I'm the wrong somebody. He was already…deceased."

"Then what caused him to be deceased?"

"He was froze solid. Maybe he got lost and run out of energy. Or he could've had, I don't know, a heart attack or something."

Cooper shook his head. With his free hand, he pulled at a tuft of beard, deliberating, holding the cocked revolver. Wind battered the cabin, rattling the lantern on its hook.

Half a minute passed. Then Cooper nodded toward the floor. "Put your boots on."

"No!" It wasn't a refusal that fell from Clint's lips. It was a plea.

"Now."

Clint bent down and pushed his left foot into its boot. "This ain't right. You're making a mistake. I know how it looks. Tanya, help me out here. I thought me and you was friends."

Tanya sniffled and closed her eyes. "I hate this, Clint. I wish I'd never come."

"I've got a question, too," said Susan. Her eyes bored in on Clint. "Did you and Tanya plan this together?"

Clint paused with his right boot in his hands. He looked up at Tanya, saying nothing.

The waitress turned her eyes away from his glare. "Stop it, Clint."

He turned his head to Susan. "No," he said, before putting his right foot into its boot.

"It's not enough to kill people, you son of a bitch," said Tanya. "You want them to think I'm with you."

He tightened the laces of his left boot and tied them in a double knot, lamenting aloud, "Lord almighty, don't let it end this way. They know not what they're doing. Ain't that what Jesus said?"

He tied the right boot, jabbering all the while. "I knew I should've left that body out there. Lord, this is what I get for that? I know—I should've never took that wallet. That one's on me. But that don't mean they should shoot me."

"You believe in God," said Cooper, "or are you just now getting religion?"

"God's my only hope."

"You might be right about that, because here's what I'm going to do. I'm going to throw you out into the storm with what you're wearing right now. No flashlight, no coat, no hat, no pistol or knife. Nothing. If I find you anywhere near this cabin, I'll put a bullet in your chest. If you pray a lot, you might end up better off than Will. Now get up and walk out that door, and don't stop walking until you get to town or drop dead, whichever end God wants for you."

Clint rose from the sofa. "You…you might as well shoot me."

"I'm not going to be the one who kills you," said Cooper, "unless I find you anywhere around this clearing."

"You're killing me by sending me out there." He scanned the room, and when his pleading eyes met Bev's, all she felt was revulsion.

"Why can't you shoot him?" asked Susan. "Can't you see he's dangerous?"

"Susan's right," said Jim.

Cooper looked at Bev.

She didn't know what to say. Her freshman year in college, she'd decided she didn't believe in capital punishment. But now she was on the jury, and the crime was close at hand.

She averted her eyes.

She wasn't supposed to be a player in this game. She was an observer. An objective reporter refrained from impacting the story.

"Get out, Clint," said Cooper.

Clint did not move.

Cooper stepped forward and thrust the gun against the flesh below Clint's chin. He wrapped his hand behind the little man's neck, turned him, and shoved him toward the door. Clint stumbled but kept his feet.

"Get out," said Cooper, his tone unchanged.

Clint backed a step, and Cooper matched it with a step forward. "Turn around and leave," he said.

"Lord almighty." He turned and opened the door.

"Three minutes. Then I'm coming after you. You'd better be well into the woods by then."

"I can't see a thing!"

"Ask God to guide you."

"You're killing an innocent man."

"You're not innocent, Clint. None of us are. Now go."

Clint pushed out into the night and disappeared in the blowing snow.

Chapter Twenty-Four

Cooper closed the door, lowered the revolver, and uncocked it. For an instant he wavered on his feet, caught himself and stiffened. He glanced at Bev, then the logger.

"Jim," he said, "can I trust you?"

Jim nodded.

"Then get your boots on."

"You're going to leave us here?" said Tanya. "What if he sneaks back while you're out there?"

Susan scowled at her. "Isn't that what you want?"

"No! I hate him."

"Tanya didn't know," said Cooper.

"Like you know what you're talking about," scoffed Susan. "Just like the weather. Are you certain your confidence has nothing to do with her cunt?"

"Fuck you, bitch." Tanya took a half step toward Susan and stopped, arms at her side, hands pressed into fists.

"I don't have time for this," said Cooper. He grabbed his boots and went to the sofa, setting the gun next to him.

Tanya followed him with her eyes. "But Andy, what if he sneaks back in?"

"Any of you ladies ever shot a handgun?" he asked.

Bev shook her head. He might as well have asked

if she'd piloted a ship to China.

"I have," said Tanya. "My brothers taught me. I used to have a gun, but I sold it."

Cooper retrieved the pistol from the table. He put the magazine back in.

"Keep your finger off the trigger unless you mean to use it." He offered the pistol to Tanya.

"No," said Susan. "Don't give it to her. She'll shoot us."

"No, I won't."

Bev's heart quickened. Maybe, she thought, she should have pretended to know how to use a gun.

Susan put both hands behind her head, pulled on strands of her blonde hair. "This is crazy. Her boyfriend killed my boyfriend, and now she's going to kill me."

"You're the one who's crazy. Stop trying to blame me."

"You told Clint."

"I hate that bastard."

Cooper put the pistol on the table in front of Tanya and leaned down in front of Susan. "If you're worried about Tanya, you can come out with us."

Susan shook her head. "You heard what that bastard said. Will's out there. Right where you were. Didn't you see the tarp?"

Bev and Cooper exchanged a glance. "I saw it," said Bev, "but there was no reason to look. All we wanted was firewood."

Susan strode halfway to the ladder, then turned back to the others. "You're all liars. You knew he was there. I can see it in your eyes."

"Think about what you're saying," said Bev. "If we saw Will's body under the tarp, why wouldn't we say anything?"

"I don't know. You're all in on it together. Everyone except me. Just…just don't bring him in here. I couldn't stand it. It's bad enough that he's…"

She couldn't finish the thought. She climbed the ladder and disappeared from view.

Tanya picked up the gun. "If Clint walks through that door, I'll kill him. Don't stay out there so long, Andy. You darn near killed yourself the last time. Jim, don't let him stay out there long."

Bundled and waiting near the door, Jim didn't reply. Cooper joined him, then turned to address the women.

"We need to get out there before the wind covers his tracks. When we get back we'll have someone guarding this door the rest of the night."

****

While the wind moaned and hurled cones against the wall, Bev sat next to Tanya, facing the door and sharing a cigarette. Perhaps the men would find Clint and kill him out of sight and sound. Maybe that was Cooper's plan. Get Clint outside so he could kill him away from the women.

Perhaps they would never return.

The keys to Clint's vehicle remained on the floor near the stove. She pictured herself leading Susan and Tanya to his vehicle when the wind died down—but could she or anyone else drive it in all this snow?

Susan came down from the loft and stood in front of Tanya. "Here I am." She lifted her arms. "If you're going to shoot me, now's the time."

"Don't tempt us," said Bev, her jaw tight with anger.

"I don't want any of this." Tanya turned her eyes away from Susan. She held the gun at her side. If she raised it suddenly, Bev planned to grab her hand and push it away.

"Use your brains," said Bev. "Tanya could have shot Cooper as soon as she picked up the gun. Then she could've killed the rest of us."

"And then how would she get home?" asked Susan.

Bev tapped ashes onto a saucer. "She follows the tracks, catches up to Clint, tells him she's taken care of everyone else."

"That's a horrible thought," Tanya whimpered. "I could never kill you guys. Please stop talking about it."

Susan walked to the sofa and sat cross-legged. "Tell you what, Tanya. I'll stop. That doesn't mean I trust you. But I'll stop."

The lantern light flickered before dimming to half brightness.

"Shit," said Susan.

Bev went to her pack and took out the headlamp Cooper had loaned. "I'm not using it unless we have to. I don't know if he brought extra batteries."

"How long are we going to be stuck in this fucking cabin?" asked Susan.

Bev and Susan smoked quietly for a minute and then the lantern went out. The only visible objects were the orange-red tips of their cigarettes. Bev was next to Tanya, yet she could not see her.

"Turn on the headlamp," said Tanya.

"I'd better not," said Bev. She felt for Tanya's arm and handed her the cigarette. The burning tip quivered in the dark as the waitress took a puff and handed it back.

"Clint's out there," whispered Tanya.

Bev's body tensed. It felt like a centipede walked up and down the back of her neck.

How long were the men going to be gone? What if Clint ambushed them and wrestled away the gun from Cooper? If she heard a gunshot crack within the wind, which man would be pulling the trigger?

"Turn on the headlamp," said Susan.

"Am I outvoted?" asked Bev.

"Yes," said Tanya.

Bev flipped on the headlamp, took down the lantern, and hung the smaller light in its place. It illuminated the table, dimly capturing Susan a few feet away on the sofa and outlining a silhouette of the potbelly stove. If Clint came in, they'd see his diminutive shape before they recognized his face.

Minutes crawled by.

"What's your daughter's name?" asked Tanya.

"Sandra," said Bev.

"Where's she at now?"

"With my mom and dad. That's where I live. Her daddy…he was killed in Vietnam."

Tanya touched Bev's hand. "I'm so sorry."

"Fuckin' politicians," said Susan.

"You don't know how I feel about the war," said Bev. "I might be all for it. Saying what you said would just make it worse."

"All right," said Susan. "How do you feel about the war?"

"Fuckin' politicians." Bev tapped ash onto the saucer.

"I'd laugh," said Susan, "but I can't laugh."

"Do you get my point?" asked Bev.

"Can't say I do."

"Be careful what you say when you're around people you don't know."

"People need to know the truth."

"People need to have their hearts protected."

Susan drew from her cigarette. "At what cost?" she asked.

"Let's not fight." Tanya leaned her head on her hands, then looked toward the door. "What are they going to do tonight—your parents? Do they have any idea where we are?"

"Any idea?" Susan cut in before Bev could answer. "Were you listening back in the van when Cooper told Jim the circle on the map isn't where we are?"

Tanya shook her head. "I guess…I guess I was hoping someone might know." She looked at Bev. "What are they going to do?"

Bev felt dread and guilt in her stomach. What information would her parents have for the cops?

Their daughter had gone mushrooming somewhere in the Cascade Mountains. That narrowed it down—to thousands of square miles.

The cops would assume she was just another nitwitted hippie-type looking for magic 'shrooms and getting herself into trouble. It wouldn't be worth mobilizing a search crew, especially when a blizzard was laying siege.

Bev rubbed the back of her neck. "They're going to worry their heads off. They'll try not to show it to Sandra. They'll think either I'm in trouble or I've gone off the deep end."

Bev took a drag from her Salem. "I'm supposed to be at work tomorrow, too."

"Sunday?" said Susan. "At a heating and air conditioning store?"

Damn. Damn, damn, damn. Blabbing again. Now she had to think up a reason.

"It's paperwork. Stuff we can't get to during the week."

More minutes ticked by. Although she couldn't write the Multnomah Gardening Club feature she had planned, a lead sentence popped into Bev's mind.

The hazards of gardening apply mostly to the plants, rarely to the gardener.

If she didn't get to work tomorrow, whenever she did get back they'd have her clean out her desk and leave. Adios. Fired from her first job for pursuing a story she couldn't tell them about.

But that wouldn't matter if she could feel the tight hug of Sandra's arms. Sandra wouldn't condemn her. She'd be overjoyed, and her mommy would feel the same.

Chapter Twenty-Five

The door opened, and wind barreled inside. Tanya grabbed the pistol and aimed.

"Tanya!" cried Bev.

A headlamp beam followed the wind, and then a figure, tall and bearded.

Tanya had a finger on the trigger, and she did not lower the gun. The headlamp beam swept across the table, blinding Bev.

"Jesus, Tanya, put that thing down!" yelled Cooper.

"Andy!" Tanya set the pistol on the table, bounced from her chair, and dashed to the door. She hugged him just the way Bev imagined Sandra would greet her when she came home.

"Hey!" said Jim. "I need in, too."

After the coats and hats were draped, boots left by the fire, cigarettes lit, and chewing tobacco inserted, they sat in a circle, Cooper and Jim on the sofa and the women on chairs. By then, Cooper had described following Clint's tracks into the woods. He confirmed, as though he'd never seen it before, Will's body beneath the tarp.

"It's after nine o'clock," said Cooper. "I could use some rest. We can't keep these headlamps lit all night."

"Clint's still out there," said Tanya. "Probably where we built the fire. It wouldn't take him long to get here."

"Chances are it's out," said Jim. "He said the tree fell on the whole works."

"So he claimed," said Susan.

Bev took a long draw from her Salem and scanned the circle. Tanya had a link to a killer. Susan had anger. Jim could buy a hell of a lot more land with two hundred thousand dollars than with whatever his share was now. And however much he might gussy up his reasons, Cooper had already demonstrated his thirst for cash.

They were a scruffy, smelly, frightened group. She couldn't trust any of them.

Each individual had a plausible motive.

One thing they didn't have—allegiance to each other.

A loaded pistol lay on the table.

Clint was outside.

She couldn't figure out what was safer—drunk and stoned in her tent the way she was last night in the midst of a howling blizzard, or levelheaded and sheltered in a cabin with two hundred thousand smackeroos that everyone wanted.

No way was she going to sleep.

Jim spat in a teacup. "You said something about keepin' a watch."

"That's right." Cooper held his cigarette up to his face, as though to study it. The bags under his eyes had puffed out even more. He looked welded to the sofa.

"So what's the setup?" asked Jim.

Cooper blinked his eyes, rotated his neck in a circle, then looked at the young man sitting next to him. "Think you can split the night with me?"

"You trust me with a gun?" asked Jim. "I won't do it unarmed."

"Put my life in your hands, after what you did?"

"Pretty much."

"Wait a minute," said Bev. "You two sound like my bosses. Planning things out as though I'm not even here. I can take a watch, too. It doesn't take much to pull a trigger."

"We should all take turns," said Susan.

Cooper studied his cigarette. "Every one of us, at some point, holding onto the pistol."

"Would've been easier to shoot Clint," said Susan.

"You think?" said Cooper.

No one spoke. Bev sensed they were all eyeing each other, appraising, calculating.

Defense or offense. Or both.

"Even if we don't sleep, we can at least rest," said Jim.

****

Lying on a bed in the loft, Bev heard every noise in the night. Rodents scraping behind the walls. Rustles of people turning inside sleeping bags. Cooper clearing his throat. The click of a flashlight and whispers during the transition between watches.

Five hours into the night, she heard a click, watched a flashlight beam fidget across the ceiling, heard whispers, the swish of a coat pulled from the railing, the tapping of boots on the wooden floor. The door opened. Wind burst inside, and the door tapped closed.

The sounds assured her that the opening door signified someone leaving, not someone entering. Without those noises, it would have meant Clint. It was the first time the door had opened all night.

That is, if she hadn't dozed without realizing it.

Someone had to pee real bad. Her own bladder had started a conversation, but she could wait until daylight. There was nothing suitable in the cabin to pee in. They had teacups, coffee mugs, the empty green-bean can, and an even smaller one that had held Vienna sausages.

Nothing like a coffee can.

They had discussed this scenario and made a decision. If a person absolutely couldn't wait until daylight when everyone was up, then stay against the cabin, take care of business on the leeward side, bring a flashlight or a headlamp, and make it quick. And if a certain side of the A-frame became an open sewer?

At least they'd be alive.

The door opened and closed again. No click, no rustle of coat.

Jim might do that. Walk out there in the dark, sandals or barefoot instead of boots, warm the toes when he got back to the sleeping bag. Or maybe Cooper—did he have flip-flops? Sneakers?

Bev jacked up the sensory dial in her ears.

No tiptoes. No squeaks on the floorboards. Even the mice had gone to sleep.

Whoever had gone out had not come back. A second person had left. Or maybe just opened and closed the door for some reason. It was Susan's watch. Maybe she threw out a cigarette or took a peek outside.

Bev waited for the next sound. And waited. It was blacker than night—she could not see her hand in front of her face. Her ankle throbbed a small reminder of its injury.

Wouldn't it be terrible to get diarrhea? Because

that would explain why the someone out there hadn't returned.

Nothing like Vienna sausage, green beans, and terror to produce a bad case of the runs.

A corner of her stomach contracted, just a little squeeze. But she was okay. A sympathy pain, maybe. Her mouth was dry like cigarette ash, but no way was she taking a sip of water, not when some of the liquid would find its way to her bladder.

Still no sound, nothing but the ceaseless wind. How long could it keep blowing so hard? Three years ago, a Christmas blizzard had shut down the main east-west highways through the gorge on both sides of the Columbia for three days. *Please,* she prayed, *don't let it be like that.*

How long had it been since the door opened and closed? Ten minutes? Twenty?

Too long. If that door didn't open within two minutes… She felt for the flashlight next to the rolled-up jeans she used for a pillow, and she began to count.

When she reached seventy-four, something sharp and human cut into the howl of the wind, the way a rodent might shriek at the sudden squeeze of an owl's talons.

She stopped counting and rose up sitting.

No, God, no.

The door opened and even before the wind's entrance, Susan screamed a name…

"Clint!"

Chapter Twenty-Six

Bev pushed herself out of the sleeping bag and hurried into her jeans.

"He's out there!" shrieked Susan on the ground floor below Bev.

"Close the door!" yelled Cooper. "Where's Jim?"

Bev jammed her foot into a boot, barely noticing her ankle's painful rebuke.

The door closed, cutting off a blast of cold air.

"He's...he's..."

Bev double-tied both boots, straining to hear Susan's reply.

"Where is he?" repeated Cooper.

"Clint... He flew out of the snow... He grabbed Jim's hatchet, and he...and he...he hit him in the neck. It was awful. And he turned around and saw me and I thought I was next and I screamed. He ran back into the blizzard. I don't know where he is."

Bev grabbed her flashlight, snatched her coat off the rail, and set a leg down the first rung of the ladder. If she could burst out the door and like a hare bound across the snow all the way to Portland, she'd do it. But Clint was out there, waiting, holding a bloody hatchet.

Jim. He was the one they could least afford to lose. Maybe he was only wounded. Maybe he needed their help.

"Where's Jim? You've got to tell us where he is,"

said Cooper.

"I tried to help him. There was blood everywhere. It was horrible. I think…I think he's dead."

"Where is he?"

"The right side of the house."

Halfway down the ladder, Bev jumped to the floor. It felt like someone whacked her ankle with a pipe wrench, but she kept her feet.

Next to the door, Susan pressed her back against the wall, her flashlight pointed at the floor. Cooper thrust his right arm into the sleeve of his coat while stepping toward Susan. Tanya leaned with her back against the table, both hands behind her, clutching the edge.

"Which way did Clint go?" asked Cooper, now directly in front of Susan.

"That way." She pointed toward the door, toward the woods, where Jim had built the warming fire.

Unless, obscured by the blizzard, he'd circled them. Could he be outside their door at that very moment?

Cooper put on a knit cap and headlamp that he pulled from his coat pocket.

"Don't go, Andy!" Garbed in only a sweatshirt, white panties, and socks, Tanya dashed to Cooper and grabbed his arm.

Susan snatched Tanya's arm away from Cooper. "Get away from here, you bitch. Go out there to your boyfriend."

Cooper grabbed Susan by her coat and yanked her close. "Shut up! Leave her the fuck alone. If you touch her while I'm gone…" He stopped, deposited her back against the wall, and stared at his hand. Even from across the room, Bev saw that his hand was darker than it was before he touched Susan. Susan slid along the wall, then broke away and didn't stop until she reached the ladder next to Bev. Blood smeared half her face and much of her jacket.

"Cooper!" Bev felt stunned by the force of her own voice.

He hesitated at the door, showing only his back.

"I'm going." She tucked the flashlight beneath her armpit and put on a glove. "You can't stop me."

He turned around to face her, his headlamp already on.

"You can't do it alone," said Bev. "You need someone else."

She couldn't see his eyes, but his hesitation communicated for them.

You? Bev Wikowski?

She put on the other glove.

Tanya took a step backward. "Don't leave me with Susan."

"You're going to have to take care of yourself." Bev went to the table, pulled the headlamp off the hook, and put her flashlight on the table. "Where's the pistol?"

"I have it." Cooper took it from his coat pocket and held it out, barrel down. He aimed his headlamp into Bev's face. "You've got a kid."

"That's why we need to kill the bastard. And you can get your headlamp out of my face."

He lowered the beam. "Take it. I can't shoot two guns."

She met him at the door and took the pistol.

"Safety's off," he said. "Keep it pointed down. Can

you get your finger on the trigger with that glove on? Don't press it. You'll shoot it if you do." He wore black liners instead of the gloves he'd worn during the morning.

Her gloved finger had just enough room to poke between the trigger and the trigger guard.

"You ready?"

Hell no, she wasn't ready. But she nodded. He reached beneath his coat and removed his revolver.

"I'm moving across the front of the house to the side," he said. "You stay behind me near the door and sweep your headlamp out the front and behind us. If you see him, shoot him. Brace your wrist with your other hand. Don't hesitate."

He opened the door and scanned left to right. Wind and snow swept into the cabin.

"Be careful, Andy!" called Tanya.

He stepped out and left the door for Bev to close. A torrent of snow blasted her from the left. Her knees shook, though not from the cold. She could not hear her breathing or their steps, only the invisible trees thrashing in the gale. Cooper moved to the right front corner, while she edged away from the door.

The wind behind her heaved its icy breath down her back. Her mind played an image of a hatchet swinging at the back of her head. She fought the instinct to whirl a hundred eighty degrees before it struck, and instead she swept her head slowly across the front, staring for a face, a figure to spring out of the sprinting thick flakes blindingly white in the reflection of her headlamp. She pivoted to bring the beam of light behind her, into the mouth of the blizzard.

Snow pelted her face.

There was no one.

No one that she could see.

She reversed the arc and caught Cooper's back as he turned the corner and disappeared. She moved forward through the mini-trench in the snow and stopped at the corner, so that she could cover both the front—what little she could see against the snow peppering her face—and the side.

Again, she scanned a semicircle. Light ricocheted off the flurry, the space beyond it black and empty. When she reversed the sweep, she found Cooper hunched to the ground, leaning his head on his left hand, while his right hand and the revolver drooped onto the snow. Jim lay slumped against the cabin. His neck hung open like the gill of a big fish. In the bright beam of the headlamp, blood gleamed red on the white snow. The sheltered air cradled the smell of excrement.

Jim's mouth had contorted into an open-mouthed grimace. His eyes stared at her, fearful and wide, as though she were the one who'd stolen his life.

Her legs begged to bolt away, to zig and zag into the dark frozen night until exhaustion brought her down on a bed of snow, and so what if she never woke from the sleep, as long as her death didn't spring from violence and blood? But she held her place. This was like the scene of the Pinto crash, its front end smashed, its top sheared away like the head from the driver's body. A competent reporter observed details and took photographs. She had to do more than that. The shots she might have to take would come from a gun, not a camera.

She forced herself to look again and noticed that although Jim still had on his coat, his headlamp was missing. She raised her head, swept her headlamp around the side and the corner and the front of the A-frame, because this moment of shock was the perfect time for a half-frozen Clint to burst out from the darkness, hatchet upraised, face wild and desperate. The pistol weighed like an iron bar. Her arm shook, and her legs wobbled. It would be difficult to make an accurate shot.

When she completed the reversal of her arc, Cooper was standing next to her, and beneath the beam of light cast from his forehead, his eyes blinked from fury to exhaustion to fury again.

"He's cold." Cooper held his gun down at his side and wiped his free hand down the back of his head. "So cold so fast."

Bev touched his arm and looked him in the eyes. "We have to find Clint," she said. "We have to kill him."

Chapter Twenty-Seven

From the door of the A-frame, footprints formed a path of compressed snow leading toward the clamor of trees. Wind kicked up powder and blew it east. Bev and Cooper knelt to study the prints, noted toes pointing away from and toward the cabin.

Clint's movements were clear. In retreat he'd paused outside the door, bloody hatchet in hand, murder churning in his veins, and yet he had not chased Susan inside. He'd withdrawn to the trees.

But how far?

Surely he'd know that Cooper would come after him. Clint could lurk behind the first line of trees, or he could parallel the edge, obscuring his tracks. If they rushed by him, following the trail to the old fire, he could dash back to the cabin. Susan and Tanya would be the next victims. From the backpacks he'd gather two hundred thousand dollars in cash while Bev and Cooper probed deeper into the woods, to the old fire, where they would find nothing.

Bev rose and opened the door a crack. She called out her identity before opening it the rest of the way. Tanya sat with a flashlight at the table, her face taut and pale. Susan peered out from the loft above the ladder.

"We're going after him!" she yelled. "He went into the woods. One of you needs to grab the poker. Hide behind the door and smash his head if he sneaks in."

Neither woman responded. They looked like human automatons with the power shut off.

"Who's going to do it?" asked Bev.

After a moment, Tanya said she would. Bev shut the door.

"You have to watch my back!" Cooper shouted. "If he's hiding, he'll attack from behind. Shoot him before he gets me. Keep your headlamp off. He won't know you're here."

He moved quickly through the thigh-high trench that traffic to the sheds and the woods had carved in spite of the wind. The din of flailing trees grew louder with each step. They paused at the edge of the forest, the firs like dark pillars behind gusts of gleaming white in Cooper's headlamp.

He turned toward her. "Ready?"

"Ready."

He demonstrated—hand under the wrist of the hand wielding the gun, pointing the weapon down, just like the cop shows. She followed the example.

"Ten feet behind me," he said.

He turned toward the woods, taking a moment to study the tracks ahead of them. Bev's mind flashed onto Billy, pictured him the way she'd imagined him in 'Nam on patrol, peering into a sauna-hot jungle, dark even in daylight. In the riot of greenery, hidden perils waited—men with rifles and grenades, pits bearing bamboo stakes, trip wires set to spring spiked bamboo whips—a dozen ways to die, some immediate, some excruciating.

How many times had her Billy fought back fear to patrol those jungles? In the end, what killed him? How much pain did he feel?

Cooper moved forward into their own jungle. She waited for the ten-foot gap, then followed him, her chest so tight she could hardly breathe. The volume of noise overwhelmed her senses, except for a thin zone of concentration between her and Cooper's back. Something airborne flicked against her cheek, prickling her skin—a cone? A twig? She passed one tree, and another, her heart skipping a beat each time. If Clint were there, he could let two people pass as easily as one, and then attack. What would it feel like to have a razor-sharp hatchet swing into the soft skin of her neck?

She shivered, but she didn't hesitate. She moved forward.

Another tree. Another. Wind whiplashed the boughs. She smelled the evergreen and the snow and the metallic taste of fear.

Cooper stopped. His headlamp revealed a fallen tree, devoid of needles, its finger-width branches poking out like spokes. He stepped between branches and over the trunk, moved past it, then paused. Though she tried to remember the way he'd gone, she walked directly into a branch, jabbing her thigh. She winced but dared not stop. Pivoting sideways, she moved to the trunk. Her foot hit something solid, like a loose rock, but it didn't feel like an object from nature.

She bent down, freed one hand from the gun and felt for the object. There was a handle, smooth, and when she slid her hand up she touched the thing that had felt like a rock beneath her boot.

A hatchet.

She leaned across the trunk and grabbed Cooper's arm. Amid howling wind and snow, he turned, his headlamp swiveling past her face before aiming down where she pointed. Next to the blade end of the hatchet, two dark droplets speckled the powdery white ground. Bev's stomach lurched, but she picked up the hatchet and brought it closer beneath the headlamp beam. She looked up to meet Cooper's eyes at the same time he looked toward hers.

In his haste to escape, had Clint jabbed himself on a branch from the tree like Bev? He might have been going much faster. Was that how the hatchet ended up on the ground? Or did he drop it on purpose, hoping they wouldn't find it, so he could convince them of his innocence when they found him at the fire?

Because he had to know they would come for him.

The hairs on her head prickled in even greater terror.

What better distraction could a murderer leave than the murder weapon itself? She lifted the hatchet and whirled around, expecting to see a wild-eyed man pouncing at her. But there was no one.

She pulled Cooper close.

"Look around us," she whispered.

She stared into the darkness while invisible snow pelted her cheek.

She felt a tap on her back and turned.

"Give me the hatchet," said Cooper.

She climbed over the trunk and handed it to him, let him move ten feet ahead, and followed.

If the hatchet hadn't been part of an ambush, then what was it?

When it came to hiding his crimes, Clint didn't have much competence. He showed up at the cabin carrying Will's wallet. And now he had abandoned a murder weapon on a path between the fire and the site of the crime. He could have stormed into the cabin with that hatchet. Maybe Susan's screaming caused him to panic.

Following Cooper, Bev looked left and right, expecting Clint to jump out of the night. She passed three trees, four, five. They had to be getting close.

He paused, motioned for her, and turned off his headlamp.

"No more light," he whispered when she reached him. Iced frizzes in his beard brushed her earlobe. "We move by touch. Feel for the trail. Look for the glow of the fire."

Her eyes adjusted enough to detect the dark shades of trees, the outline of Cooper's figure, the black mop of beard contrasting the faint paleness of face. Daylight was coming.

"I thought he said the fire went out," said Bev.

"Remember—he's a liar. Keep five feet behind me."

He dropped to his hands and knees. She waited the length of five feet, then followed. Snow dampened her gloves. The puncture wound in her palm prickled as though the thorn had entered anew. Cooper's cotton gloves had to be like ice water—how could he stand the aching of icicle fingers?

She marveled that her own pain wasn't worse. Somehow adrenalin blunted it, freed her mind to focus on the bigger threat.

And then, toward her left, an orange fingertip pulsated beyond the trees. She hurried forward, grasped Cooper by the boot. When he stopped, she scrambled to his side and pointed his head toward the glow.

On a normal night, a glimmer that faint would

suggest a distance of a hundred yards, but in the blowing curtain of snow, it was difficult to guess how close they were. She recalled they hadn't gone far away from their woodland shelter before they found the clearing with the cabin. On a normal day, they could probably have walked the distance in a few minutes, maybe less.

So they were close.

He leaned his mouth to her ear. "You can stay here," he said, and then he drew back, as though he could read her face in the dark for hesitation and fear.

"Let's go," she said.

Chapter Twenty-Eight

In the gloom of the dark forest, the orange glow grew larger as Bev crawled forward. Snow iced her body, while wind swept across her back. Ahead of her, Cooper passed between a pair of trees. Her muscles tensed—would Clint leap out from the one on the left or the right? Could she roll to her side, slip a gloved finger on the trigger, point up and shoot in time to save Cooper, to save herself? She reached the two trees, glanced left and right, saw no one, and allowed herself to breathe.

She passed another tree. And another.

Like an unleashed devil, the gale moaned through waving branches and boughs.

She passed three trees on the left, two on the right. A hint of evergreen smoke slithered into her nose.

Orange transformed from glow to actual fire, twitching through the mesh of vegetation that sheltered the tiny clearing. Faint, like the tap of a finger on a tabletop, wood popped in the firepit. Bev crawled alongside Cooper, and they crept to the bramble that bordered what had become Clint's lair. Wind and snow lashed at them, while on the other side of the thicket, less than ten yards away, flames tilted with the sheltered breeze. Sitting next to it on a chunk of wood, a sleeping bag over his body and around the top of his head, Clint stared at the fire.

Beyond him, a tree had indeed fallen, its trunk perhaps two feet in diameter. If they had stayed at this site overnight, it would have killed more than one of them.

But two had died anyway.

Cooper leaned over and spoke into her ear.

"I'm going around. I'll sneak up on him the way we first came in. Wait here. Cover me."

She pictured Cooper on one side, she on the other. "We'll shoot each other."

"No, we won't. Different angles. But you won't need to shoot. I'll do it."

He drew back as he had earlier, as though he could read her face. Maybe, this time, he could.

He crawled off to the left and disappeared from sight and sound.

Bev rose to a sitting position. She found a triangle between the weave of branches, threaded her finger through the trigger guard, and aimed at Clint's chest. Seconds ticked by, and then a minute. What was Cooper waiting for?

Bev watched a wisp of her consciousness rise above the scene. From the branches above her, she observed herself sitting with her butt on the snow and a gun in her hand, nervous but determined, focused as she had never been before.

And to do what? To kill a man, perhaps.

Sandra's mommy, finger on the trigger. How did she get here? What had happened in two days since Thanksgiving dinner?

A terrible grief, heavy as iron, sprouted in her chest and radiated into the fullness of her body.

I'm sorry, she whispered, uncertain if she was

directing the apology to Sandra, or herself, or God, or the universe. She had let them all down.

There could never be a story. Sandra must never find out. She would have to keep these grim events confined to her own memory and no one else's, forever and ever, amen.

Cooper rose straight up from the other side of the downed tree. With a gun in one hand and a hatchet in the other, he stepped over the trunk. In the firelight, visible behind the screen of falling snow, Clint pulled his head back and gaped, as though the Grim Reaper had stepped in front of him.

"Goddammit, what are you doing here?" Clint demanded in a shaky voice.

"I'm here to send your sorry ass to hell."

"Why? Lord almighty, why?"

"Don't give me that shit." Cooper tossed the hatchet to the ground on the opposite side of the fire from Clint. "You drop this on the way back here? Let me guess. You don't know what I'm talking about."

"You're goddamn right I don't know what you're talking about. I don't have a fucking hatchet. You took every goddamn thing I have. I ain't left this spot since you kicked me out. Now you're going to kill me anyway?"

Cooper cocked the hammer. "You didn't know a fucking thing about Will, either, did you? Just happened to find him dead. Just happened to take his wallet."

Clint slid back half a foot. "I told you the truth. God in heaven knows I ain't lying."

"You lied, Clint. You're lying right now."

"I don't know what you're talking about. I swear I never seen that hatchet in my whole life."

"You think you can kill people and lie your way out of it? I gave you a chance, Clint, and now another man's dead. I should have killed you the first time."

"No, Jesus, no. This ain't right."

His pistol aimed at Clint's chest, Cooper glared at the wide-eyed man. From behind the jumble of little trees, Bev watched Clint tighten the sleeping bag around his neck and tremble.

The wind howled, and the snow blew, and the fire cast its light on the surrounding trees. Both men stared at each other, one with fury, the other with pleading and terror. They froze in that posture, and another minute went by, and Cooper started shivering like the man who cowered on the ground.

Damn it. Shoot. They couldn't stay that way while the sun rose and the day ticked by and the other women waited back at the cabin. That man was evil. A lying, killing, deceitful monster. Bev was sure that as long as he breathed, all their lives were imperiled.

"I'll go right now, if that's what you want me to do," said Clint. "Leave and take my chances. Wander around this hell-shit and probably die anyway."

"No," said Cooper. But he didn't do anything.

Bev rose to her feet. Her legs were stiff from cold, and her whole body quivered, but she stepped around the brush and showed herself in the opening where their trail entered the clearing. Cooper and Clint both gave her a glance before locking their eyes back onto each other.

"Cooper," she said, her voice vying with the wind. "We have to do this."

"I'm leaving now." Clint pressed the palm of his hand to the ground and pushed himself up. But in a flash he launched the bag loose, spun a half-turn like a wrestler on the mat. He reached an arm for Cooper's leg.

Just as quickly, she raised the gun and squeezed the trigger. The blast screamed in her ears, and the pistol yanked back her arm, and when her eyes refocused Clint was squirming and groaning. She stepped forward and shot a second time, and it seemed as though the world slowed down. The ringing in her ears muted the wind and trees, and the snow fell silently, tapping her face.

She staggered a moment. Instinct urged her to drop the gun, to turn and leave, but she forced herself forward, in quivering half steps, until she stood next to Clint. Blood spurted from a hole in the side of his neck. His eyes rolled back in their sockets. He panted shallow breaths. Blood dribbled out his mouth. For half a minute his arms and his legs and his head twitched. His breath slowed, and then it ceased.

She hated Cooper for getting them into this mess, for his inability to finish it, for forcing upon her the role of executioner. She wanted to spit in his face, batter him with her fists, kick him in the groin. Instead, she collapsed into him, sobbing. His arms embraced her like it was their last moment on earth.

Chapter Twenty-Nine

Holding the gun, Bev trudged behind Cooper away from the firepit and Clint. She and Cooper had agreed they could dispose of the body later. She didn't have the strength to dig a grave.

At the edge of the clearing, Cooper stopped. Blowing snow blunted the early morning light.

"We need to talk," he shouted. "Let's get to the shed."

All she wanted to do was sleep, if her body and her mind would allow it. The sleeping bag, the bed, the loft beckoned her. She saw herself burrowing deep and closing her eyes and collapsing in slumber.

She followed as he skirted the edge of the woods until the enclosed shed came into view. He fought the door open, and they stepped out of the assault of wind. She leaned back against the left wall while he stood across from her against the long shelf, backlit by the dim light of the window behind him. With the jet-noise now outside, she heard herself panting and felt her heart pounding. Cooper set the revolver on the shelf, struggled to remove the frozen gloves, and placed reddened hands beneath his armpits. Miniature icicles coated his beard and brows.

They stood that way for a minute. Bev gazed toward Cooper, but her mind played the film of Clint, blood pumping from his neck, eyes rolled back, the spasms, the stillness.

"I'm sorry," he said.

She knew what he meant, or at least she thought so—leaving it to her to do the killing. She didn't reply. It was not okay. He was supposed to be the soldier.

"I don't know why. I just froze. I've seen other men do that. Just…freeze." He pulled a piece of ice from his moustache. "But never me."

Bev understood this was the moment when the woman consoled the brave warrior who wasn't so brave as he thought.

She'd be damned before she gave him that.

"I don't want either of us to say what happened back there in the woods," she said.

"I saw too much. Did too much. All for a lie." He blinked his eyes, confused, like a dog wandering in the rain. "I choked. I never choked before. I was the one who showed the men what to do, how to act under fire."

Bev broke the eye contact. If Cooper wanted a pity party, he could stage it somewhere else.

"We'll tell them he's dead now," she said. "That's all they need to know."

He nodded. "If you'd seen me on the plane, you wouldn't have known what I was going to do. What I did. Just a regular passenger. Nerves of steel. Truth is, I'd never have hurt a soul. I'd have let them arrest me before I hurt someone."

She rubbed both hands down her mouth, then clasped them to a fist beneath her chin. "That would have been a better outcome," she said.

They took out cigarettes and smoked. They looked past each other, he at the wall and she out the window. Waiting this long in the A-frame had probably made

Susan and Tanya frantic, but Bev felt no urgency to make an appearance for their sake.

"What about you?" he asked after several minutes. "I talked about myself. You must be...well, I know what it's like to do what you did."

"I don't want to talk about it."

"I get that. Neither did I. What's to talk about, eh?" He exhaled smoke and held the cigarette down next to his leg. "The thing is, it will come back to you. When you least expect it. In a store. Walking down the sidewalk. When you hear a song on the radio."

She snuffed her Salem, half-smoked, and put it back in the pack. "We need to move Jim."

He considered the idea. "I'll put him with Will. Tarp was big enough."

"We'll do it together. You drag him through the snow, his head might come off."

"I don't think it was..." His eyes darted from the wall to her and back. "All right."

She stepped across the small space and put the pistol next to Cooper's revolver. "I don't want this."

Cooper picked up the pistol. "The safety's still off."

"So switch it. It's not mine."

He snuffed his cigarette against the bottom of his boot and put the quarter-length stub on the shelf. "No, it's not yours. But I need you to carry it. Or would you rather have it in Susan's or Tanya's hands?"

"What? You can't carry it?"

"One's enough for me. Given my performance back in the woods, the nature of what we're doing, and what's happened so far, someone else should have a gun."

She felt like snatching the pistol and heaving it out into the blizzard. It was outrageous to ask her to keep it, to hold this evil, killing thing.

"I don't ever want to shoot a gun again."

"That's how I felt, and look what happened. I let everyone down, especially you."

"Especially Jim."

He looked away, toward the back of the shed. "Especially Jim," he mumbled.

She stepped over, took the gun from Cooper, and retreated to her side of the shed. She flipped the safety on. "Fuck you, Cooper. Fuck this whole trip, your fucking money, your bold and daring hijacking, your fucking beard, and all your deceptions."

He closed his eyes a moment and then opened them. "I deserve that. The thing is, I meant to do something good with that money. Stick it to the man. The whole lying apparatus. I never meant for any of this other shit."

"Next time get a real job."

He blinked his eyes and pressed his lips together. It looked like he might cry. He turned around to the shelf and made a show of inspecting the revolver. In a minute he pulled back his coat and his shirt and holstered the gun. Then he turned around.

"You can put the pistol in your coat pocket. Just make sure Susan or Tanya don't get hold of it. Don't let it out of your sight."

He stepped toward the door but stopped with his hand on the knob. "You did the right thing. Probably saved all our asses."

"Let's remember Jim."

"You couldn't have saved him. That's my fault."

"No. I mean, let's put him in the shed."

****

Jim's body was frozen in its posture, knees bent nearly to his chest. For a little guy, he was heavy. But Bev didn't typically hoist 140-pound weights, even with a partner. She held him by his boots while Cooper grasped the coat at the shoulders, cradling Jim's head between his arms. Crossways in the buffeting wind and snow, they retraced the steps they'd taken from the shed to the cabin. By the time they reached the stacked wood, Bev's arms felt as though they'd been pulled from their sockets.

After they uncovered Will, she pulled his head back from the wall. She did not allow herself to acknowledge he had been a human being with whom she'd spoken, who'd shared a joint with her. It was just a body, an unliving thing. Wherever the person had gone, it was far from here. The head was not round in the back. The curve of it had been flattened. If it were not frozen, it would be mushy, the skull beneath the hair and skin crushed into fragments.

He had to have been struck more than once. More than twice. A dozen times, or twenty, with great force. Clint must have bashed him until he no longer breathed.

"There was another tarp in that shed," said Cooper. "I'm going to go get it. We'll keep them separate."

She laid the head back gently against the wall.

Will had gone on the wrong trip.

So had Jim.

So had she.

Chapter Thirty

In the lead on the way back from the woodshed, Bev had almost reached the door by the time the cabin revealed itself. She couldn't count how many times a thought had popped into her head—*I killed a man. I killed a man. I killed a man.*

She planned to walk through the doorway straight to the ladder and up the loft to the bed and a warm sleeping bag. She'd get in, let the bag defrost her body, and she'd sleep a delicious sleep. Clint was dead, and it was safe to sleep.

Dim outside light rushed in with the wind when she opened the door to the dark interior. Susan was absent. On the sofa, Tanya rose from her back. Her face showed joy but switched to fear.

"Don't!" she shouted.

Bev stopped, then reversed her forward momentum just as Susan jumped from behind the door, an iron poker raised above her head. Bev thrust up an arm and ducked, but Susan lowered the poker, closed her eyes, and staggered.

"Thanks," said Bev. "It smells better when you lower your arms."

She delayed her dash for the loft as soon as she felt the woodstove's heat. It stung the cold on her face, and when she removed her gloves and dropped them to the floor, it burned the cold in her fingers, too. She shuffled sideways half a step for Cooper. He didn't look quite as bad as he had when he returned with Jim after searching for Will, but it was nearly dark in the cabin, with only a silver flashlight hanging from the hook over the wooden table.

Tanya and Susan stood gaping at Bev. She wondered what kind of sight she presented. Her nose throbbed the most—if she had frostbite, would it be blue? An ugly purplish blue? She'd seen pictures of severe cases. It would blot her nose, like a scarlet letter, to remind her every time she looked into a mirror: *I killed a man. I killed a man.*

"Well?" asked Susan.

"He's dead," said Cooper.

"Thank god," said Tanya.

Susan gave the waitress a sideways glance. "Yeah, right," she mumbled.

Bev lifted the lid of the stockpot. All the snow had melted. Water filled the bottom fifth, lightly simmering. At least Susan, whatever she'd done to clean herself, hadn't contaminated it with blood. But neither she nor Tanya had done a damn thing for their water supply—how much of it had boiled away?

"Why can't anyone fill this damn thing besides me?" Bev dislodged herself from the stove, grabbed a dishtowel to keep her hands from getting burned, and poured the water into a smaller kettle. She stepped out into the blizzard and collected more snow.

Afterward, she rubbed her hands together next to Cooper in front of the stove. Her fingers were red, but at least they weren't purple. Tanya had withdrawn to a chair at the table, while Susan took a spot on the sofa. Cooper looked back at the table and grunted.

"Got to get the damn board off that window so we can get some light in here." He picked up his ski gloves, pushed the hood of his coat back over his head, and stepped back into the storm. Bev couldn't imagine how he'd get the plywood off, unless he found a crowbar in the tool shed.

Minutes later, a thumping on the outside wall competed with the noise of the wind, followed by the squeak of a nail pulled from wood. The process repeated itself three times, allowing teaspoons of light to sift inside. After two more screeches, Cooper's bearded face replaced the plywood cover, like a peeping Tom getting a look at the women inside.

Although dimmed by the blizzard, the light that spilled into the cabin illuminated the interior like a sudden spotlight. From the stove, Bev glanced at the faces of the two other women inside and the man outside. None bore the horrible emaciation that she recalled in photographs of Holocaust survivors, but their eyes showed the same exhaustion, the same haunted intimacy with death. They had found two hundred thousand dollars, but joy had blown away with the wind.

She smoked the second half of the cigarette she'd begun in the shed, announced her intention to sleep a few hours, and climbed into the loft.

The sleep she hoped would bury her thoughts failed to occur. *I killed a man, I killed a man* wouldn't stop. She remembered when she was seventeen and she'd tried to rush through a left turn on a yellow light. She miscalculated, and the driver of a Pontiac on the intersecting street moved forward when her light turned green and Bev's turned red. Bev slammed the brakes too late, skidding into a T-bone on the Pontiac's passenger side. Metal crunched. Glass shattered. Smoke tinged the air.

Her Chevy Nova was on fire. She scrambled out. A man with a fire extinguisher opened the hood and put out the fire. The woman in the Pontiac, who turned out to be the mother of one of her classmates, ended up with a bruised arm and little bits of glass that a doctor in the hospital removed from around her eye, but that was all. Since that incident, every time she sat behind the wheel of a car she reminded herself that it was a killing machine, and she never took chances on the road.

Later that same year, at a different intersection, a nineteen-year-old guy from Corbett did the same thing, except his mistake killed the driver of the other vehicle. They arrested the kid for manslaughter. He did time in prison.

It shocked her, how thin the line was that separated an ugly mistake from a life-altering tragedy. Only random chance kept her on the good side of that line.

Now she had crossed that line. Her life would never be the same. She had not been careful. She'd made an impetuous choice.

Maybe it had been necessary to kill the man to protect her own life and the lives of others, but the fact remained she had killed him. She would have to inform the police. Who knew if she could talk her way out of it, if the evidence supported her rationale?

They had a bunch of money that didn't belong to them.

She could claim she intended to write a story about it. But she hadn't bothered to tell anyone. In fact, she'd lied to her family about it.

Couldn't a reporter lust for a windfall of cash as much as any other worker?

She was in deep trouble.

Unless…

She opened her eyes and blew a breath through taut lips. Her shoulders tensed. Prickles spread across her scalp.

Unless nobody found out.

The idea grated against her being, all that she was raised to be, all that she believed about right and wrong. A good person and a good citizen took responsibility for her actions. She didn't lie—well, most of the time— and she didn't sneak.

Would Cooper and Susan and Tanya go along with her to cover up Clint's death?

Clint had told Cooper he was married. Did he tell his wife where he was going?

And what about the others? If they hid one death, wouldn't they have to hide all the deaths? Could they get away with it?

She rolled to her side, overwhelmed and scarcely able to think. Oh, she had crossed a line, all right. And now she was about to cross some more. It was bad enough to kill someone, but it sure looked worse if the killer tried to cover it up.

The watch on her wrist showed 8:22 a.m. She had been lying in bed for half an hour. On a normal Sunday, she'd be up along with everyone else in the house. She and her mother and father would be trading sections of *The Oregonian.* Sandra would be "reading" a book to her stuffed Winnie the Pooh. Would that scene ever occur again?

Hours ago she had worried that Sandra might be left an orphan if she didn't make it back alive from the storm. Now she foresaw her daughter being raised by grandparents because Mommy was in prison.

Clinging to the sleeping bag, she rolled to her other side. If only she could sleep. It might clear her mind, help her sort through the dilemma. But there wasn't going to be an easy answer. She had messed up, big-time.

Dumb-fuck reporter kills man, goes to prison.

That was the new headline.

Chapter Thirty-One

"Bev...Bev..."
Someone jostled her arm.
"Bev."
It was Tanya, hunched over and shaking Bev. A clump of Tanya's dark hair stuck out in a snarl, and the skin sagged below her reddened eyes.

Bev blinked, surprised she had slept, a black sleep, dark and absolute, so that she woke without remembering a single snippet of dream. But with her eyes open and Tanya's worn face a foot from hers, the image of Clint's body quivering while blood spurted from his neck thrust itself into her mind's vision, and the words echoed in her head: *I killed a man, I killed a man.*

"What? What time is it?" she asked.
"A quarter after one. The storm's slowing down. Andy says let's all talk."
"Yeah. I'll be there. Give me a minute."
"Don't fall asleep again."
"I won't."

As Tanya lowered herself down the ladder, Bev pulled herself out of her sleeping bag. The tobacco cloud that gathered below the ceiling of the loft stirred a craving. She lit a Salem. Her body resisted awakening, and the air seemed to hum a silent buzz.

I killed a man, I killed a man.

Had Billy spasmed like that when he died? The lieutenant who wrote her a letter—Johnson Smith, a weird name—never mentioned it, but why would he? The platoon had been ambushed by mortar fire. Billy died instantly. But had it been that way actually? What kind of officer would tell a soldier's widow that her husband had suffered horribly before death relieved the pain?

She exhaled smoke through her nose and felt the warm tingle in the sinuses.

For the millionth time she told herself she needed to let Billy go, that he would want it that way. But if he were here, he'd understand why she did what she did. Choosing life sometimes meant taking it from someone else.

Help me through this, she whispered, sitting on the side of the bed, directing her prayer to the Billy in the photograph on the fireplace mantel at home. He had other faces besides that one, had worn other clothing besides the dress uniform in the photo, but as the months and the years dribbled by, those other images faded. In memory, ninety percent of the time he appeared with that same confident smile, the buzz-cut hair, the khaki dress uniform.

Downstairs, the other survivors stood looking out the window, Cooper between Susan and Tanya as though to keep them apart. They all had cigarettes, even Tanya. Bev took a spot on the end next to the waitress, who pressed her body to Cooper and wrapped an arm around his waist.

"We think it stopped," said Tanya.

Bev looked out into a bright white blur of snow. Wind continued to shake the cabin, to rattle the dishware, to moan and howl.

"What are you talking about?" she asked. "It's still fifty miles an hour out there."

"Yes," said Tanya, "but do you see any snow falling?"

"How can you tell?"

"Just look."

Bev took the cigarette from her mouth and stared. It was hard to determine what was falling and what was flying up. A fathomless mob of white flakes blitzed left to right across the front of the cabin, blotting out the sheds and the trees that couldn't have been more than thirty yards away. But a kind of sameness characterized the sprinting snow, all of it powdery, as though a giant beast with endless breath were blowing talcum powder off the palm of its hand.

Possibly it was all lifted from the ground and off the unseen trees. Perhaps it snowed in tiny granules, mixing with what had already fallen.

"What's it matter?" asked Susan. "We can't see anything in that shit."

"I think Tanya's right," said Cooper, who had shown no reaction to Tanya placing an arm around his waist. "This storm was supposed to pass through, and then there was supposed to be clearing."

"Like everything's gone according to prediction," said Susan.

"Either way," said Cooper. "We need to talk, especially you three. We've got decisions to make. They won't impact me, because I'll be long gone before certain things are discovered, if they're ever discovered."

Tanya took her arm from his waist. "Things?

You're talking about people, aren't you?"

None of them looked at each other. They gazed into the white-out. Bev felt the spot between her shoulder blades tighten.

"Possibility one," said Cooper. "The three of you tell the authorities. Except I can't let you do that, not right away. I need a day after we get back. How are you going to go an entire day before you tell the authorities? Answer: you can't. Not without causing considerable grief to yourselves."

"What do you mean?" said Tanya. "We have to tell. We can give you time to get away, but how do we avoid...I mean, we can't just leave...leave the...you know..."

"The bodies," said Susan. "Stiffs. Corpses. Whatever."

"Yes," said Tanya.

Susan blew smoke hard. "Shit, Tanya, why can't you just shut the fuck up? You're not a goody two-shoes. You're with us. You went after the money. You blabbed to Clint. You slept with DB Cooper or Jordan Balfour or whoever the fuck he is. I'll bet the license is phony, too. So this son-of-a-bitch Clint kills at least two people, maybe three if we count the corpse at our first camp. And then we kill him. And Cooper here, if you can't take a hint, he's not so keen on our being blabbermouths. I'll tell you what, Cooper. I'm not saying a fucking thing. If Tanya can't keep her mouth shut, you go ahead and make sure she does. I hear what you're saying. I've got a clue. And I'll bet Bev over there, whoever the hell she is, she's going to keep her mouth shut, too. So in my mind there's only one question to answer, and that's how do we keep our asses from being busted?"

Bev glanced sideways at Tanya. She looked tense, fearful.

"The game has changed," said Cooper. He stepped away from the group, and instantly adrenalin raced through Bev's body. If he suddenly took out his gun, could she jump him? Could she get out the door before he did anything? Her own gun—or Clint's—was still in the pocket of her coat draped over the upstairs railing.

They watched as Cooper took another step, opened the woodstove door, and threw the stub of his cigarette inside. He stood up and turned his back to the stove.

"You ladies still think I'm going to kill you." Surprise tinged his voice. "I can see it in your eyes. That's not going to happen. If you decide to go to the authorities, I'll need to put you someplace where you can't talk to anyone for a day or so. Then I'll be the one to contact the authorities to tell them where they can find you. At that point, you can blab all you want."

He took out another cigarette and lit it. "Prison has no appeal to me. But no one was ever supposed to be hurt. Killing would be inconsistent with the plan. I'd go to prison first. The whole point was to do something good and at the same time thumb my nose at a few people."

"That's worked out real well, hasn't it?" said Susan.

"Shut up," said Bev.

"Don't worry," said Cooper. "She can't provoke me. But she sure knows how to try."

"I can be quiet," said Tanya. She slid her free hand down the side of her hair and looked at Cooper. "Do you think...could you, wherever you're going...take me?"

"Are those your terms for keeping quiet?"

"No, I don't mean it that way."

"It doesn't matter. No, I'm not taking you. You're a nice person. But no. I can't take you or anyone else."

Although it appeared she might cry, she nodded. "Okay."

"So," said Cooper. "Possibility two: everyone keeps quiet. There are complications."

"No shit," said Susan.

"Bev, you've been quiet," said Cooper. "What are your thoughts?"

Bev examined the wall with the sofa and looked up the ladder at the back, toward the loft. Dry and faded, the walls and the roof of the cabin had absorbed smoke from the stove and cigarettes as well as a whiff of rodent excrement. The dishware and cups were chipped and mismatched. Only the magazines seemed relatively new.

"Burn, baby, burn," she said.

Chapter Thirty-Two

"What the hell are you talking about?" Susan flicked ash to the floor. Outside, snow blew like a storm of ivory dust.

"Bodies increase the chance the cops will connect us to them," said Bev. "There's plenty of gas in that shed out there. This cabin will burn hot."

She stepped to the table and tapped ash onto a saucer. "Suppose we do keep quiet. Springtime comes. Snow melts. The hunter shows up. Maybe he's got kids. Maybe he's got a dog. Guess what they find in the wood shed? Over in the trees? The loggers show up. Guess what they find? How long will it take for the cops to come knocking on our doors?"

"This is fucking crazy," said Susan.

"I know," said Bev. "I can't believe I'm saying this. I can't believe any of this."

Still at the stove, Cooper adjusted the fire with a poker. "You're taking this conversation to a place I think it needs to go."

Tanya pressed her lips together.

"Problem is," said Cooper, "Skeletons have teeth. Won't be my problem, but it will be yours."

"What do you mean?" asked Tanya.

Bev squeezed the filtered end of her cigarette.

She knew what it meant.

"When there's a fire, they use dental records to ID

the bodies," she said. "So if all the skeletons are in the cabin, it's the same as leaving them out in the open. It'll take more time to figure out who they are, but that's what will happen."

"Do we want to dig four graves or two?" asked Susan. "Because we can do either."

Susan picked up the small pot from the table and drank water from it. Bev wanted to knock it out of her hands, but they couldn't afford to waste any water.

"Two bodies in the cabin that no one will connect," continued Susan. "Who are they?"

"I beg your pardon, Susan, but Will is one," said Bev. "He and Melvin. They're not regulars at the Spar Pole. Wednesday was the only time either of them had been there. And who knows if Melvin gave his real name to anyone? There's a chance the cops won't identify Will. The missing person report will come from his parents, and they're on the Oregon Coast."

"I'm like Bev," said Tanya. "I can't believe we're having this conversation, but what about Jim with Ted...or Melvin, if that's his name? I don't think anyone knows Jim went to the Spar Pole. Wednesday was only the third time I saw him there. He wasn't hanging out with any friends. He told me not to tell anyone, because he didn't want his old man to find out. He's not twenty-one years old, and he never drank too much."

She paused a moment before continuing, "I razzed him about his Copenhagen and how he was going to lose all his teeth, and he told me his whole family had strong teeth. None of them had ever been to the dentist and none of them ever had a cavity. I don't want to say this, but they won't be able to identify him."

"You're in it now," said Susan. "You're helping us plan."

Her hand still shaky, Tanya took a puff from her cigarette.

Cooper stepped to the table and helped himself to the water in the pot. "So sometime in the spring, the authorities might identify one man, if anyone files a missing person report on Melvin, plus another skeleton whose identity they'll never know. If they do ID Melvin, they may find out he was at the Best Western Hotel, and that might lead them to interview everyone who was at the Spar Pole, including you, Tanya."

"And I'll say I didn't know who he was. If they show me a picture, I'll say he was there, but I don't even remember what it was he drank. And anyway, I'm going to quit that job. They pay me crap, and the customers don't tip, and I don't ever want to be in that place again, not after all this."

"Something else," said Susan. "Melvin and Jim would be the only skeletons without any damage. If Clint...well, how bad did he hit Jim in the neck? Did it go through far enough?"

"No," said Cooper. "Not to the bone."

"Then it would look like they died in the fire," said Susan.

They were quiet for a moment. Bev turned around to look back out the window. Behind a mist of blowing flakes, the ghost-dim silhouettes of trees appeared, and then a gust erased them in a wash of white. "I just saw the trees," she said.

The others joined her, but renewed wind blocked the vision. Had she seen the forest, or was her mind playing tricks? She turned to the table and took a drink from the pot. If that's what everyone else was doing, she wasn't going to drain her own canteen.

Tanya took another puff. "I feel so bad. Jim's girlfriend will never know. Maybe she'll think he ran off so he wouldn't have to marry her. Will's parents will never know. Neither will Clint's wife. How will she collect insurance, and what about his retirement, if he's got one?"

"We have to turn those feelings off," said Susan. "They won't be any more or less dead."

"There might be a way we can let families know," said Bev. "Not right away. Maybe with a typed note. No details, though."

"The authorities will put that together, too," said Cooper. "They'll connect everyone to the Spar Pole. Like I said, I'll be long gone. For your sakes, it'll be better if the others just disappeared. No explanations. Nothing. Just gone. My recommendation is that we bury them all, separate graves, in the clear-cut, where the land has already been disturbed. The one thing we can't do is put them all in the same place."

"Through all that snow?" said Susan. "And the frozen ground? Jesus."

More ash dropped from Cooper's cigarette. "Do you want to save time, or do you want to save your freedom?"

"Time and freedom go together," said Bev. "The longer we're out here, the greater the odds we'll never get out. I say we burn Tanya's two choices and we use the hole where the money was for the other two."

"All right," said Cooper. "It's your choice. No more graves than what's necessary."

Within the stream of snow, a sprig of fir blew by

the window, and Bev recalled her dream of Billy on a magic carpet. Her family had to be frantic, trying to hide their worries from Sandra, devising excuses for her mommy's absence.

I'm still alive—if only they could hear her thoughts.

But on the other hand, if she survived, no one could ever know her thoughts. She had memories that could never be revealed.

She decided she didn't care about the newspaper. If they fired her, they fired her. All she wanted was to return home alive.

Mommy comes home, holds her child.

That was the only headline that mattered.

The wind eased again. The roaring white train slowed and the cabin walls seemed to sigh.

"I see trees," said Tanya.

Chapter Thirty-Three

They stepped out of the cabin and paused before beginning a scouting expedition to make sure no one else resided nearby. Bev was astonished at how small the clearing was. In front of the cabin, the forest and the sheds were no more than twenty-five yards away. On all sides, at most thirty yards distant, Douglas firs surrounded the cabin. They had been vulnerable to falling trees after all.

Within sight, no slopes ascended. The hunter had situated his cabin on a small flat. To the right, a truck-wide gap extended into the snow-heaped woods. It had to be the access road.

She looked at her watch. Darkness would fall in two hours. At night, flames would be visible for miles. It was too late in the day to burn down the cabin.

She should have been at her desk by now, working on the Monday morning paper. Her pages had one of the earlier deadlines, seven p.m. She usually stayed to help copy-read, lay out pages, assist in the darkroom—whatever they needed. But now they were going to fire her. No more Bev hanging around the police beat reporter, hoping to snag a surplus crime story. They'd replace her with a bubbly old lady who *absolutely adored* rose gardens and debutante balls.

Cooper plowed a furrow mid-thigh deep in the snow down the open lane, followed in a line by Tanya,

Susan, and Bev. Although the snow was light and fluffy, Bev wondered how many collective pounds Cooper displaced to push through ten yards, fifteen, twenty—progress was slow. At least her ankle didn't bother her much.

Branches, cones, and twigs littered the smooth bed of snow. Whenever the breeze stilled, the sound of their breathing and the crunch of their footsteps seemed to magnify in volume.

I killed a man, I killed a man.

The weight of the pistol in her pocket pushed down the right side of her coat. It accused her, convicted her. She pictured herself flinging it full-force into the woods as though to purge her conscience.

She sought a different mantra than the one that plagued her. *I saved our asses. I saved our asses.* But her brain didn't cooperate.

After a hundred yards, the gap widened and forked, one road to the left and the other straight ahead until it curved out of sight. Another narrow path on a slight incline opened to their right. Leafless alders and black cottonwoods clustered where a creek gurgled on the other side of the path.

"Wish we had Jim," said Tanya as they considered which direction to explore.

"Might as well flip a coin," said Cooper. "We go right, it might loop around to the clear-cut or it might go to another cabin. We go left, it might go to a road that goes to the clear-cut. Straight ahead, we might eventually hit pavement."

They chose the right turn. Sixty yards up the gentle rise, they found a single-wide mobile home beneath a steel-roof canopy. Snow piled to the top step in front of a metal door with a small window. On the right end snow piled like a ramp to the roof, while on the left end only a dusting of snow partially covered the cement pad. Mildew spotted the bottom third of the weathered white siding.

"No vehicles," said Tanya.

"Hello! Hello!" shouted Susan.

"Not so loud," said Cooper.

Susan looked skyward. "Nobody's going to be out in this fucking weather. We could torch the whole damn forest and nobody would be around to see it."

"Andy's right," said Tanya. "We should be sure. Besides, there might be some food inside."

Susan walked past Tanya and Cooper to the steps, then turned back. "Andy, Andy, Andy. Tell me something, Cooper. Do you like being called Andy?"

"Don't give a shit one way or the other." He approached the trailer and walked its length. Bev followed. They circled around to the back, where the woods almost touched the trailer and an outhouse stood half buried in a drift. The single-wide smelled ancient, mossy like the woods. It had probably cost more money to get a cement truck out this far to pour the pad than to buy and haul and park the trailer on top of it.

"It's locked," said Susan after Bev and Cooper reversed their path and returned to the front.

Cooper climbed the steps and peered at the bottom edge of the window. With a pocketknife he slit the bottom and one side of the screen before sliding up a shutter, reaching inside, and opening the door.

"They're not too worried about burglars," he said.

"Probably nothing worth taking," said Bev.

The door opened into a living room that smelled

like a football team's laundry. Foam stuffing poked through slits on a blue couch patterned with pink flowers. A green recliner looked like it had been towed on its side down a dirt road. Along the wall between the sofa and chair, a wooden plank and white-painted cinder blocks served as a shelf that held paperbacks and hardbound Readers Digest Condensed Books. Beneath it, a dried-out mouse carcass lay squeezed in a trap. Cigarette burns pocked the linoleum floor.

Past a kitchen without appliances and a bathroom without running water, Bev found a plastic sled with a pull rope leaned against a bedroom wall. She carried it to the kitchen, where Susan and Tanya had gathered a can of green beans, a can of creamed corn, two cans of fruit cocktail, and three tins of Spam, plus a package of votive candles. From the other end of the trailer, Cooper brought a half carton of Chesterfield cigarettes, a book, and a transistor radio. He turned it on to a station airing a football game between the Oakland Raiders and the Kansas City Chiefs. He moved the dial past country-western, rock-and-roll, two preachers, and, finally, a news station out of Portland.

"Maybe they'll tell us the weather," said Tanya.

The reception was remarkably good. Someone had set off a bomb in a Dublin theater. President Nixon was at Camp David reorganizing his administration. An anonymous source reported that Lieutenant William Calley planned to ask for clemency for his role in the My Lai Massacre.

Then the local news began.

Law enforcement officials remain baffled by the identity and fate of the hijacker known as DB Cooper. Exactly one year from yesterday, this modest, well-

dressed man hijacked a Northwest Orient 727 jetliner between Portland and Seattle. After collecting two hundred thousand dollars ransom in Seattle, he forced the pilot to fly to Reno, and in the dark of night he parachuted out over the Cascade Mountains.

Federal Aviation Security Chief Max Shaffer believes the man known as DB Cooper is probably dead.

Cooper gazed out the small window above a two-person table. His expression gave no indication of pride or anger or shame. He seemed distant, as if the broadcast chronicled the deeds of someone else.

On the radio, Shaffer's voice came next.

"One of these days some hunter in Oregon or Washington is going to find the skeleton of this man."

The newscaster continued on the story.

Cooper's heist is the only unsolved skyjacking out of more than seventy such incidents in the past four years. Numerous con men claiming to be DB Cooper have stepped forward. One of them, Donald Sylvester Murphy of Bremerton, Washington, was arrested with an accomplice earlier this month on charges of extortion. Mr. Murphy allegedly bilked $30,000 from a Los Angeles weekly tabloid which published what turned out to be a phony confession entitled "The DB Cooper Story—the man who got away with it." In order to convince the tabloid that his story was genuine, Mr. Murphy allegedly doctored two twenty-dollar bills so that they matched the serial numbers of the ransom money.

Meanwhile, DB Cooper's legend grows in popular culture. Underground radio stations have been playing a ballad, 'The Story of DB Cooper,' portraying the

219

hijacker as a man with an incurable disease who has already given the loot to the poor and to his mother. DB Cooper T-shirts are sold in a variety of stores.

The question remains, who is DB Cooper, and where is he now?

The broadcast switched to a report about a murder in the Pearl District. Cooper sank onto one of the wooden chairs, and he pulled at the bottom of his beard.

"Dan Cooper," he said. "Not DB. It wasn't a real bomb. If there had been a cop on the plane, it would have been over just like that. I'd have gone to prison. I made a promise to myself—no one gets hurt. Now look what's happened. Shit."

He turned toward Bev and the other two women, his eyes focused mostly on Susan.

"I'm sorry, ladies. You don't know how sorry. None of this was supposed to happen."

Tanya wiped a tear off her face. "You've done all you could. You tried to do right. I never dreamed Clint'd come after us. I'm the one's that's…"

"Shhhh!" said Susan. "It's the weather."

Variable westerly winds as a low-pressure system creeps in from the coast on the heels of the big blow. Light rain is already falling in Beaverton. Metro temperatures are twenty degrees warmer than yesterday, returning to seasonal norms. Snow level will rise to 7,000 feet overnight. The Oregon Department of Transportation expects to have eastbound lanes of Interstate 80 North open by nine p.m. Expect more rain throughout the week.

In sports, University of Oregon head coach Dick Enright said he expects senior quarterback Dan Fouts to…

Cooper turned off the radio. "You ladies see any nine-volt batteries in here?"

They hadn't.

"What's this weather mean for us?" asked Susan. She put canned goods into the bottom of a grocery bag Bev found beneath a sink with no pipes.

"It'll be darn near impossible to drive in," said Tanya. "The snow's going to be like wet cement."

Susan threw the package of candles down so that they banged against the cans at the bottom of the bag. "Shit! Shit, shit, shit. We need to get out now, but we can't because of all these dead bodies. We waste a fucking hour in case there's some other wacko out here in this shit. We don't have time for this. We could've had half of Clint's grave dug by now. Let's get the fuck out of here and take our chances. Let the fucking wolves find the bodies and drag them off to their dens."

"There aren't any wolves out here," said Tanya.

"Coyotes, bears, hyenas, elephants. Who gives a shit? It'll be five months before anyone comes back here."

Bev took the bag from Susan and set it on the counter.

"We can't afford to take that chance," she said. "We've talked it through already. You know it. There aren't any good options, but we'd better stay with the best one we've got. We need to keep our heads on straight, and that includes you. And Tanya, you cannot—cannot—go to the cops."

"I said I wouldn't. I don't want to go to jail."

Bev grabbed the waitress by the arm. How could she make Tanya understand, or even care, how thin was the string on which the rest of her life hung?

"It's more than that," she said. "You want to know who killed Clint? I did. I killed him. Do you want to send me to prison and separate me from my daughter? They could say we decided to kill him because we didn't want to share the money with him. We can't prove he did anything."

Susan's face broke into an odd, creepy smile. Bev let go of Tanya and turned her attention to the California girl. She could feel the lack of sleep, the lack of food, her bum ankle and her bum future, the killings, all of it, boiling up like a geyser.

"What's so funny?" she demanded.

"You?" Susan's smile was contorted. "You killed Clint? That's so cool."

At the table, Cooper opened his book.

"I could use your help, Cooper," said Bev. "We need to stick with the plan. Right?"

Keeping a hand over the title, he closed the book and looked toward the women. "Funny. Having this book here. If you were a god watching all of us and you wanted some entertainment, you'd plant this book here just to watch our reactions."

He took his hand off the cover and held it up for them to see.

Ordeal by Hunger: The Story of the Donner Party.

"What's the Donner Party?" asked Tanya.

"Every California kid learns that in school," said Susan. "A wagon train that got snowed in. Whoever died, the others ate."

"Oh, my god!" Tanya closed her eyes.

"No one's going to eat anyone," said Bev. "C'mon, Cooper. The plan."

He set the book down. "You're right, as long as we

don't panic. Let's stick with the plan."

On their way out, Cooper stopped at the doorway and held an arm up to halt the others behind him. Whatever he was looking at prompted him to slowly reach beneath his coat for the revolver.

Another person after the loot? A deputy or an FBI agent?

He brought the pistol in front of him.

How many more years on the prison term? How many more nightmares?

Gunfire blasted in her ears, and she staggered back.

"Looks like turkey's on the menu," said Cooper. He moved aside so Bev and the other women could look. A dozen turkeys were flying up into the trees, while on the bare snow a single fat bird lay.

Chapter Thirty-Four

Bev's ears rang.

"Smart move," said Susan. "Like we've really got time to do whatever the fuck you've got to do before we can cook that bird."

"Oh, I think we do," said Cooper, stepping off the stairs. He hurried to the turkey, near the tracks they'd made on their way to the single-wide. Bev and the others waited while he determined the gobbler was full-fledged dead and picked it up by the neck.

Bev dragged the empty sled down the steps and pulled it behind her as she started the return trip to the cabin. The others fell in behind her.

"I've been thinking," said Cooper. "I like Bev's idea about using the hole where I buried the money. The soil will still be loose."

"It's going to have to be deeper and longer," said Tanya. "Otherwise, the coyotes will dig it up."

"Fine sense of smell, coyotes," said Cooper. "That'll still be a lot easier than digging two separate ones from scratch. Let's go to work right away, two on the grave and two of us to go get Melvin. We've still got some daylight."

Bev craved a warm bed or, short of that, any flat surface. She could lie down on the boot-compressed snow and fall asleep—if her brain could somehow snap the Clint film and turn off the projector.

But Cooper was right. They had to keep going. How much strength did she have left in her arms? Could she swing a mattock without whacking her foot?

"I'll do the digging," she said.

"I'll help," said Tanya.

"All right," said Cooper. "We'll pick up Will on the way to the gravesite. We can use this sled, along with some rope I've got in my pack. Susan can help me get Melvin. We'll bring him to the shed, and then we'll pick up Clint and bring him there. We'll help you finish digging the grave if you're not done yet."

"I won't touch that grave." Susan's voice wavered.

The grief engulfing Bev magnified on behalf of Susan—Will would be one of the occupants.

"Of course." Cooper hurried to correct his mistake. "Sorry."

Bev backtracked the way they'd come. The breeze blew a long breath, dusting her cheeks with snow lifted from the ground. Her brain bubbled up an image of a sweltering jungle and placed her there. At her feet lay Billy's mangled body, and the fates had placed in her hands a shovel. In her imagination, she snapped the handle across her knee, flung both pieces out of the atmosphere, and she howled.

At the intersection where the creek gurgled, she turned them left, toward the cabin. Her mind blinked to her last real view of Billy, his paste-colored face peaceful inside the flagged coffin before the last ceremony. In the green manicured ground, a neat rectangular hole waited. Although surrounded by mourners on that day, she had felt alone, except for the fetus inside her swollen womb.

One foot in front of the other, and again, and again.

The back of the A-frame came into view, and above it an uneven tear in the clouds revealed a ragged patch of pale blue. The breeze felt heavier, on the brink of warmth. They stopped at the cabin only to put the food inside and obtain tools and rope, a small length of which Cooper used to tie the bird to a nail outside near the door.

At the woodshed, Bev motioned for Susan to look away, and then she pulled loose the tarp. Cold had preserved the confusion of fear stamped into Will's stiff eyes, his body L-shaped like a frozen hinge. She and Cooper lifted the oblong weight, wrapped it in the tarp, centered it on the sled, and with the rope secured it at the calves and across the shoulders. From that point, Cooper dragged it behind them, while Bev led the other women into the woods. It took less than a minute to reach the thicket that bordered the shelter where Clint lay, and she took them around it, the way Cooper had gone the night before. It took only a few minutes to go downslope from there, following the blue flagging, to the triangle where they'd unearthed the ransom money. In the clarity of sight, freed from the bullying storm, Bev marveled how much distances shrank. She helped Cooper unfasten the tarped body from the sled.

"Susan and I will be back as soon as we can," said Cooper.

If she paused for a moment, Bev worried she'd never get started, and though she moved in a stupor, she leaned down and used the mattock as a rake to pull away snow. Tanya joined her, scraping with a shovel. Behind them the sound of the sled sliding across snow faded away. Despite the blizzard's freezing cold, the soil they'd displaced—was it only yesterday?—still lay loose and clumped. It was easier to remove than when she'd first attacked it, but she lacked enthusiasm and strength for this second occasion. She moved like a woman triple her years, and felt like one, too.

They'd excavated half the soil by the time Cooper and Susan returned red-faced and panting, each with a rope, pulling the sled upslope. Bev guessed the distance was closer than what she remembered, but for those two, dragging Melvin's hulk in the snow, it probably seemed farther.

Susan unzipped her coat several inches and wiped sweat from her forehead. "It feels like..." Her heavy breaths chopped her sentence into pieces. "Like we're doing the devil's work."

Bev struck the ground harder. "The devil..." *Whack...*"wants to separate..." *Whack...*"me from my daughter."

A half chuckle tumbled from Susan's mouth. "He's doing a damn good job."

Bev struck the ground again. "Fuck you, Susan. Fuck the devil, too."

"Melvin to the shed," said Cooper, a wheeze in his voice. "Then we'll get Clint."

"I can't help with the grave," said Susan.

Cooper coughed, then spat. "Help me move the bodies. Then you can wait in the cabin. Melt some more snow. Pluck the turkey."

"I hate blood."

"Plucking won't make it bleed."

"I don't care. I'll do the water."

The gray light of day was dimming. Cooper and Susan picked up the ropes again. Like oxen pulling a wagon, they dug their boots into the snow and resumed the final leg of Melvin's journey. Bev paused for a sip of water. She removed the parka's hood from her sweat-damp hair, rotated her neck both directions, and loosened more of the already loose soil. At this phase, Tanya had the harder task, shoveling away dirt, but soon Bev would be hacking deeper and wider into the hole. When her mind and her arms questioned the number of swings that remained in her capacity, she pushed the thought and the feeling aside. It didn't matter. If she had strength for five minutes but the deed required forty, it was forty that she had to give.

"This is for you, Sandra," she murmured, pulling up loose dirt with the mattock blade.

"What'd you say?" Tanya had removed her cap, and the tip of her nose glistened.

"I said…I'm feeling strong." Another thrust to the soil, another pulling up, another hack, another pull, a shuffle step left. "We're going to make it."

"Oh, Bev. I needed to hear that. I have so much on my mind." She threw dirt and scooped up more. "You… Why didn't Cooper, you know…shoot Clint?"

"I don't know. He was right in front of him. He had his gun out. But he couldn't do it."

"So you shot him?"

"Clint tried to take away the gun. I couldn't let him do that."

"So it was his own gun that killed him."

Bev loosened dirt, and Tanya tossed. Loosen dirt, toss.

"I'll never get over this," said Tanya. "We'd all be fine if I hadn't told Clint."

That's okay—those were the words Tanya sought.

And Bev would not say them, the same way she

wouldn't console Cooper in the shed after she'd shot Clint—because it wasn't okay. It would never be okay.

Luck seemed to be in short supply on this trip, but she'd need a lot of it to get away with what she'd done. Thanks to Clint. Thanks to Tanya's big mouth. The only good part of this whole grave-digging business would be when she threw the first shovelful of dirt on that asshole's head down at the bottom of the hole— and what a crazy thought that was, so removed, so foreign to what her mind had been three days ago.

Who had she become? Who would she be?

Let it go. Dig. That's all there was to do.

Cooper came back, dragging Clint inside his rag of a tent. Bev leaned on the mattock handle, gifting herself a pause. Her eyelids fell and the world blinked dark, but she caught herself before her sleeping body tottered to the ground.

She couldn't afford to close her eyes.

Later, after night had fallen, when they finally lowered Will and Clint into the grave, Bev's arms quivered not only from exhaustion. With each scrape of dirt onto the pair of bodies, she was perpetrating a horribly, cosmically unjust act—a murderer and his victim interred in a macabre embrace for all of eternity.

On the way back, it began to sprinkle, night clouds begrudging one drop at a time. Her arms had devolved into two aching appendages, useless except for balance. There was no way she could dig another grave, let alone two.

Chapter Thirty-Five

In the cabin, two votive candles provided the only light. Bev lifted the lid of the stockpot and found it one-fifth full, the water melted and warm.

"Christ, Susan. You said you'd take care of the water."

Susan set down a partial deck of cards. "Who gives a shit? We need to get out now. Can't you see it's raining?"

"It's barely sprinkling," said Cooper, lighting a Chesterfield. "We're not burning at night."

"No one's going to see it," said Susan. "It's too far out in the sticks. Doesn't matter if it's night."

"Don't push me, Susan. I don't need any of this. I don't need to help you hide the bodies. I'm going to disappear anyway. I could walk out of here right now. Leave you the keys to the van. Good luck getting out."

Still wearing his coat, he walked to the door. "Now if you'll excuse me, I've got a bird to take care of."

Bev picked up the stockpot and followed him out of the cabin.

"She's a pain in the ass," said Bev. "But would you really leave us?"

Cooper grabbed the bird by the neck. "I wouldn't leave you, Bev. Or Tanya." He yanked out a feather. "Guess I wouldn't leave her, either. Might put a gag in her mouth, though."

"That's something I'd gladly help you do." Her stomach rumbled with hunger while she watched Cooper pluck feathers. It had grown warmer outside, but not enough for snow to melt. She filled the pot and returned to the cabin.

Susan sat at the table, a cigarette in her mouth. On the sofa, still wearing her coat and boots, Tanya had fallen asleep.

Bev put the pot on the stove and sat across from Susan. "I want out of here, too," she said, "but I don't want anyone to ever guess any of us were ever here."

Susan gestured toward Tanya. "Why'd you take her side?"

"You want to know whose side I'm on? Mine. That's it. And my side depends on all of us pitching in. For example, our water supply."

"You believe that sweetness act of hers? All her '*Oh, Andy*' bullshit?"

"As a matter of fact, I do."

Susan turned a card face up, but she had no play. "We need to watch her night and day. Just because Clint did her dirty work before, it doesn't mean she can't do it on her own. Who do you think she'll get next?"

"If I were her, you're the one I'd feel the least affection for."

"I think it'll be one of us. She'll try to make it look like one of us did something to the other one. Then Cooper will have to get rid of whichever one of us is left. She'll save Cooper for last. Two hundred thousand dollars. Don't let her fool you. She wants it all."

Bev held back an urge to sweep all the cards off the table. "I feel horrible about what happened to Will," she said after pointing to a play Susan had missed. "And now he's going to just…disappear. But I think Tanya feels…"

"Terrible," said Tanya from the sofa. She was awake, her head leaned back the same way it was when it looked like she was asleep.

"But I'm not a thief," she continued. "I don't want the money. I just want this to go away. I want to wake up in my bed and let this all be a horrible dream. I should hate you, Susan, the way you're treating me. But I can't. Because it is my fault."

She leaned her face into her hands and covered her eyes.

Susan hadn't looked up or paused from the game. "There," she said. "See what I mean? A great actress."

Bev swept her arm across the table, scooping away Susan's cards. The rage behind Susan's eyes made her happy. *Go ahead,* Bev thought. *Take a poke.*

"Sorry," she said. "I need the table. Let's inventory our food and set something aside to go with that turkey."

The food they gathered filled half the table. It included Bev's leftover gorp and freeze-dried lasagna as well as a C-Ration kit featuring *Pork, sliced, with juices* from Jim's pack and four pre-rolled doobies from the suitcase. Susan added Clint's beef jerky and smashed mini-donuts as well as her own two cherry Pop-Tarts and two red ropes of licorice.

"Let's set you up with one of the packs," Bev said to Susan. "Jim's or Clint's? Tanya and I will help you adjust the straps."

Exhaling smoke, Susan eyed Bev uneasily, and then she picked up Jim's brown external frame pack.

"Let Susan have Will's share of the money," said Tanya. "That's only fair. We can divide Jim's three ways."

Three ways. Until it was two. And then one. Bev looked up at her parka, draped over the rail. She remembered the weight of the pistol and Cooper's warning to never let it out of her sight.

But there was no danger, not from these others. Clint was dead.

Another thought crept into her mind. She had enough bullets to end all the tension. What were three more bodies? The world wouldn't mourn their loss.

The idea staggered her already weak legs. God, what a thought.

Had a similar notion leaked its poison into Cooper's brain? Was that why he insisted she keep the gun?

There was another way she could end the tension. She could use the gun on herself. The others would hide her body, just like the other bodies. Sandra would never see her mommy again, but she'd never have to see her mommy in jail, disgraced, a pariah. Everyone would think the storm had claimed her, and they would be right, except it would be a different kind of storm than what they assumed.

She picked up Jim's pack and set it on the table.

She wouldn't betray Sandra that way. She wanted to live. She wanted to fight.

She retrieved bundles of cash from the main compartment, divided them, and placed her share with the rest of her money in an outside pocket of her pack. The other two women took their portions, leaving Cooper's on the table.

Afterward, she clustered uneasily with Susan and Tanya to look out the window at Cooper. He'd built a small fire. Hunks of bird cooked on a grill from the shed. When he noticed the women, he motioned for them to come outside.

It was hard to wait while the meat sizzled and the aroma seduced her body. Her mouth watered with animal craving. Droplets from light rain trickled down her forehead and cheeks, but she could not pull herself from the fire to retrieve her parka.

When finally Cooper gave the cue to eat, Bev picked up a leg from the grill. It was chewy, scalding on the outside and undercooked inside, more gamey than the turkey her mother set out on their table in what seemed like another world only days ago. She forced herself to chew slowly, completely. She took a spoon of fruit cocktail and passed the can to Tanya, who took a bite and passed it on, as though it were a doobie. The bottle of Old Crow whiskey trailed the fruit cocktail, but after one swig Bev declined further invitations.

An owl hooted somewhere to her right. In the fire, damp wood snapped. It was quiet enough to hear herself and the others chewing, the tap of the spoon against the metal can, the swish of liquid in the upturned bottle, small sounds, amazing after the siege of wind.

Eyes darting, calculating, they licked bird grease from their fingers and smacked their lips—Bev the same as the others. They had done evil things together—*evil* was the right word, wasn't it?

She never wanted to see their faces again.

Chapter Thirty-Six

Bev opened her eyes. How long had she slept? It was a miracle she'd slept at all.

Shadowy details took shape—the steep slant of ceiling planks, small black knots in the wood, pale white walls, the top of the ladder at the edge of the loft. Light wobbled. It had to come from a candle downstairs.

Susan's spot on the outside half of the bed was vacant, her sleeping bag absent, her new backpack no longer leaning against the wall. Bev bolted upright and looked to her parka. She couldn't see if the pistol remained in its pocket, but she interpreted the fact that she was still alive as evidence that neither Susan nor Tanya had gotten hold of it. She brought her pack downstairs and stuffed the parka between it and a wall.

Cooper and Tanya lay close in mummy bags on the sofa-bed, Cooper on his back lightly snoring, Tanya on her side facing him, awake. On the table, a candle burned. The door opened, and Susan stepped in with the stockpot full of snow. She set it on the stove and stepped to the window, where Bev stood searching for a glimmer of dawn.

Though oil and sweat had darkened her hair, Susan had brushed out the frizzes and clumps so that it hung full-bodied and straight. "I poured the water into the pan," she whispered.

Bev nodded. It wasn't light enough outside to see the sheds or the trees. She didn't see stars when she looked up, but raindrops had not collected on the window, nor had she heard any pattering on the roof in the loft.

"I've been a real bitch," said Susan. "That's what I said to Tanya when I saw she was awake. I just…" She closed her eyes and sighed. "I'm not going to be that way anymore."

"You've been through hell," said Bev.

"So has everyone else. But you've been solid. I've been thinking—I can do that, too. Help the group."

She stepped away from Bev, opened the stove door, repositioned the wood. Bev could see that she'd already put in a fresh piece. A moment later, Susan hunched next to Tanya and whispered something that made the waitress smile.

If the California girl could continue this new demeanor, Bev thought she might warm up to her.

Still in her sleeping bag, Tanya propped herself on an elbow and kissed Cooper's forehead. His eyes opened. He reached up and caressed her hair, then noticed Bev and Susan.

"Morning, lover boy," said Susan without a trace of sarcasm. "Cold outside, but hot in here. Would you like Bev and me to go upstairs so you can have some privacy?"

"What the hell?" he mumbled. It was too dark to see details, but Bev imagined his eyebrows rising. He sat while still inside his bag. "No, I'm good. You might want to look the other way while I get dressed."

He groaned, put a hand on each side of his head and squeezed. "Fucking Old Crow. That shit's nasty."

When he unzipped the bag, Bev turned toward the window, but Susan didn't.

"I've been thinking about this cabin," said Susan. "I hope you'll forgive me, but I still can't deal with…with bodies. But what I can do is scout around to make sure there aren't any neighbors. I'll look for tracks to the trailer, and I'll push through some of that snow the other direction to see if there are any more driveways."

"That's helpful," said Cooper. "Jesus. I thought you weren't looking."

"You said I *might* want to look away. That implies I might not."

After eating a handful of gorp and a piece of jerky, Susan left.

"Seems like Old Crow did her some good," said Cooper.

Bev, Cooper, and Tanya each smoked a Chesterfield. When they'd finished, she blew out the candle. They glanced at each other, and it felt as though they shared the same thought: have another cigarette, and another after that. None of them wanted what came next.

Bev pulled herself up onto her sore legs. If they didn't waste time, chances were good that she'd be home this very night. She could almost feel Sandra's tight hug.

She donned her parka, felt the weight of the pistol. As far as she knew, Tanya and Susan assumed Cooper had both guns. She vowed to keep it that way.

Outside, cold oozing up from the snow prompted Bev to zip the parka to her neck. They tromped across old tracks to the shed and brought back Melvin first.

His nylon-shrouded body was the straightest of all the corpses. Inside the A-frame, Cooper pulled him by the shoulders almost to the back wall.

"Shouldn't we take him out of the tent?" said Bev. "Isn't it some kind of fire-resistant material?"

"Maybe you're right," said Cooper.

Firewood stacked next to the stove caught Bev's attention. "You know what we need to do?" she said. Without waiting for either Cooper or Tanya to guess, she picked up two pieces and set them in the middle of the floor, between the table and the folded-up sofa-bed. She pivoted again and added more, starting a pile.

"Oh." Cooper's voice showed recognition.

"I hate to say this," said Bev. "God, I hate it. But the ideal outcome is total incineration. Nothing left but bones, ash, pots and pans. The stove. Broken cups. When it cools, if we're lucky, coyotes will carry bones back to their dens."

Tanya stood at the doorway, biting down on her lower lip.

"Bring some more wood," said Bev. "Kindling, too. We have to do this."

Tanya nodded and did exactly that while Cooper and Bev retrieved Jim's body. The under-ager. He'd been the best one of them all. He'd have made a hell of a lot better father than she'd been a mother—so far. Because when she got back, if she got back, God willing, Sandra would become her number one priority, even more than she already was.

They spent twenty minutes building the indoor pyres, dousing each with gasoline, pouring more of the fuel on the outside walls. Susan returned and told them there was no one nearby. Cooper lit the first match and tossed it onto Melvin's pile. Bev did the same for Jim's, and the living backed out the door.

Flames rose, embracing both corpses, exuding gaseous fumes. They stared through the doorway, watched the wood piles catch, gain heat, blaze as high as the loft. Cooper nodded, and Bev walked to the right side while Tanya and Susan took the other sides and Cooper stayed in front. When he shouted a cue, they all threw matches onto piles of kindling and wood tucked against the outside walls.

From the nearly depleted woodshed, Bev and the others watched the fire take hold. Even if months went by, whoever discovered the remains of the cabin would also find unburned pieces of kindling and firewood. Authorities would detect the residue of fuel. Theoretically, one of the men whose skeletons would be found under the open sky could have set the fire and thrown himself on a pyre. More likely, they'd conclude a murderer had also committed arson.

A wave of nausea seized her, and she turned away.

The morning bloomed dark gray and damp. Inside the woods, Bev trailed the others on the well-trodden path, carrying a shovel and pulling the sled. They'd wrapped a tarp around three tents and four sleeping bags in their stuff sacks and tied it to the sled, but the packs on their backs did carry the extra weight of an additional two thousand dollars apiece. Jim's share. Susan had an additional eight-thousand-plus, Will's share.

Cooper didn't stop when they reached the clearcut, but when he stepped below the line of the trees, he sank in snow over the top of his knees. He pulled his leg out the hole, lifted it, transferred his weight forward—and sank again. Bev and the others stayed motionless atop their spots in the snow.

"Shit!" he called.

Rain began to fall.

He extended his arms to the sky. "Thank you, gods! I suppose you think we deserve this!"

Tanya took a dainty step forward, and another, approaching Cooper on his right. "If you take soft steps…" she said, before her right leg sank through almost to mid-thigh.

"We don't have any choice," said Susan, "and it's not going to get any better."

"We might have a choice," said Cooper. "Let's go back into the woods. We'll walk near the edge, parallel to the clear-cut. Be on the lookout for a gap in the trees at the bottom of the hill."

"At least we can see the other side," said Tanya.

But Cooper sank just as much in the fringe of the forest as he did outside it.

"Maybe we can take turns in front," suggested Susan. Apparently, last night's Old Crow was still improving her demeanor.

"I'll lead," said Cooper.

"You get tired just as easily as the rest of us," said Susan.

Bev looked at her watch—9:12 a.m. "Ten minutes and we switch," she called. "Front person goes to the back. We used to do a relay like this in high school cross country."

They pushed forward, staying in the woods because the snow was slightly less deep. They progressed slowly, one tree to the next. It reminded Bev of another high school drill, this one overseen by a whistle-blowing track-and-field coach. High knees, he called it. She would extend her arms waist high, palms down, and churn her knees up to her hands. The memory of how that exercise taxed every muscle in her legs pushed into her mind, because that's how it felt right then.

Her gloves grew wet and her fingers ached from the cold. Snowfall would have been better.

Susan was in the lead when Cooper called a halt.

"Donut break?" asked Bev.

"Coffee," said Susan. "I hear there's a McDonalds around the corner."

Cooper raised Clint's binoculars to his eyes and looked down the sloping clear-cut.

"We're not going to be able to drive through this, are we?" said Tanya.

"With chains we might," said Susan.

"Have you ever driven in snow?" asked Bev.

"No," said Susan.

To their left, half a dozen crows rose, cawing, from the tops of snow-draped firs. They flapped their wings at each other before settling back down out of sight. Four of their brethren emerged from the trees downslope. They flew up the hill in the stillness of the morning, their wings sounding like flags flapping in a breeze. Melting snow rained from the trees. Moss and evergreen scents tinged the saturated cold.

At ten o'clock Cooper turned on the radio while everyone smoked a cigarette. Nixon was still at Camp David reorganizing his administration. White and black youths fought each other at a high school in Michigan. South Vietnamese President Nguyen Van Thieu insisted that a peace agreement would have to include a withdrawal of North Vietnamese troops.

Cooper swung his arm as though to hurl the radio into the ground, but he stopped himself. "Fucking crooks. They don't give a shit about their people." He held his cigarette tip down next to his leg to keep the rain from extinguishing it. He looked at Bev.

"No government does. That's why I did this. Best not to trust anyone."

Bev exhaled smoke. "Tell you what, Cooper. You're Exhibit A."

Cooper opened his mouth but decided not to reply.

"The weather," said Tanya.

...moderate rain should arrive sometime this afternoon in the Portland Metro area and settle in for the next two days...

Bev could think of nothing except to laugh. The others joined her, until a coughing jag throttled Cooper's sense of humor.

A light whoof sounded. Bev looked up just in time to receive a clump of falling snow. She removed a bent cigarette from her mouth, spat frozen particles from her lips, wiped a hand across her eyes and forehead. Another clump fell, this one to the left of Susan.

"Maybe we should get out of the woods," said Tanya.

Cooper looked downslope with the binoculars again and then pointed. "I think that's our road down there. Not sure, but we've got to cross that clear-cut sooner or later. Might as well do it now."

After twenty steps descending from the woods, it was Bev's turn to take the lead. She used her shovel as a walking stick. Rain had packed the snow, but not enough to keep her from falling through. Each step felt like a sudden drop. Lifting each leg out of its hole, forward and down into a new hole, required determination. She paused a few seconds to hold her throbbing fingers in her armpits, then thought *Sandra. Tonight.* She dropped her arms and kept going.

At this rate, to walk a mile would take a couple of hours, at least.

Cooper's turn repeated before they reached the bottom.

"Look at that." Tanya pointed toward the trees. Their trunks had shed the snow that the blizzard wind had smeared onto them. One of them bore a blotch of blue spray paint. Clint had marked the path.

It took forty minutes to get down the overgrown logging road and another forty minutes to reach the van. High-pitched wheezes accompanied Cooper's breaths. Bev felt so achy, so tired, she wanted to weep.

Clint had parked a white Chevy pickup forward against the front of the van, but they would have to back up only a little bit to get around it. Bev felt a hundred pounds lighter when she put the pack inside. Each of them either shoveled or scraped snow away from the tires, and then Cooper spread a set of chains next to each one.

"This is a one-person job," he said, handing the keys to Bev. "Why don't you ladies sit inside? Get yourselves warm, get the van warmed up."

Susan took the middle seat and Tanya the back. In the driver's seat, Bev looked into a windshield cloaked with snow. Rain dripped from her hood, and her ski pants left the upholstery wet, but she didn't care. If the chains worked the way they were supposed to work, she was going home.

She turned the key. The engine cranked and cranked. For an instant it sounded as though it would start, but then it coughed and sputtered and turned asthmatic again. She switched the key off. Unlike the engine, the rage inside her fired up and roared, an explosive bile she could have driven all the way to Portland if it only had wheels.

Chapter Thirty-Seven

Bev slammed the base of her hand against the steering wheel. The wound in her palm reasserted its presence with pain that shot up the length of her arm and into her neck.

"Fuckin' Clint!" shouted Susan from the middle seat. "He fucked up the engine. Remember what he said at the cabin?"

"Oh, god, I don't want to walk," said Tanya.

Bev glanced at the rearview mirror just as Susan whirled around at Tanya. "Fuck you, bitch! None of this would be happening if you hadn't opened your fat fucking mouth!"

Apparently, the Old Crow effects had disappeared.

Tanya closed her eyes, and her head drooped down.

The wrath in Bev aimed at Susan. It was horrible how she treated Tanya, and yet her own anger at the waitress seized her nearly to paralysis. Maybe that was good, because otherwise she might jump them both, kick and punch them, throw them out of the van and stomp them into the snow. She'd never felt such fury, not even when she was told Billy was dead.

She turned the key again and hoped for a miracle. The engine cranked like an old man who couldn't get out of his chair.

Cooper opened the driver's door, his eyes seething.

"Let me try," he said, as though he had a special talent for turning keys that a woman could never hope to attain.

"Go for it," she said, moving to the passenger seat.

The result was the same—cranking, an almost-start, cranking. He pushed down the gas pedal, turned the key again.

Whrr-whrr-whrr-whrr. Nothing except a whiff of gas fumes.

"Where's your boyfriend, Tanya?" Susan taunted.

A shriek rose up and the van rocked on its wheels. Bev turned around to find Tanya swinging her fists and arms at Susan, who wrapped her own arms around her head to protect herself. Bev sprang out of her seat, leaped over the console, pivoted around the middle, and tackled Tanya onto the seat.

Tanya's body went limp. "Okay, okay," she said, breathing hard.

"She tried to kill me!" yelled Susan, and as one voice Bev and Cooper shouted at her to shut the fuck up.

They waited a moment, and then Tanya rose from the back and hurried out into the rain.

"I swear to God," Cooper said to Susan, "I'm this close to banishing you from the group and letting you find your own way back to town."

Susan opened her mouth, but before she could say anything, Cooper grabbed the front of her coat and yanked her halfway over the console. She raised her arms in a gesture of surrender and fell back into her seat when Cooper let her go. They were quiet for a moment while rain plopped onto the padding of snow.

He turned on the headlights. The instrument panel

glowed. He got out and a moment later from behind the snow-shrouded windshield she heard him moving snow off the front of the van.

"Headlights are fine," he called. "You can turn them off."

So the battery worked.

Bev and Susan got out and followed Cooper to the pickup. He unlocked it, took the driver's seat, turned the key in the ignition.

Whrr-whrr-whrr-whrr.

"Fuck you, Clint!" Bev shouted loud enough to stir the little runt from the bottom of his grave. She'd done nothing to deserve this. The universe had gone haywire.

She staggered back inside the van and leaned her head down into her hands, rocking a little. No way could she walk home, not the way she felt, not in the wet cement snow—hell, not another hundred yards, let alone a dozen miles to the Washougal River Road.

She didn't know much about engines, but she knew enough from watching her brother Jesse that all Clint had needed to do was pull loose a spark plug wire, but that would be too easy to fix. Maybe he'd removed a spark plug, but he wasn't carrying one when he knocked on the A-frame door.

She uncovered her eyes and leaned farther down to examine the bolt in the floorboard that helped hold the engine cover in place between the driver and passenger seats. She remembered Jesse talking one time about how he'd never get one of these vans, because it was a pain in the ass to get to the engine and why the hell did they have to shove it into the front compartment anyway?

The bolt was missing.

That bastard Clint must have had the tools to break into the van. He'd removed the engine cover and sabotaged something.

She stepped back into the rain, finding Susan and Tanya on opposite sides of the pickup gaping inside at whatever Cooper was doing. When she reached the door, he was leaned over, pulling out papers, napkins, and tape cassettes from the glovebox.

"You thinking what I'm thinking?" she said.

"I'm going to find out," he said, tossing a tire pressure gauge onto the seat. "There's nothing in here."

"It looks like he removed the engine cover inside the van. The bolts are missing."

Cooper rose to a sitting position. "He's got tools somewhere. Could you step aside, ladies?"

He got out, looked behind the seat, and pulled out first a box of chains and then a small black toolkit. After everyone helped clear snow off the pickup hood, he unlatched it.

"Son of a bitch," he said, before he finished propping it up.

Bev noticed it right away, too. A single spark plug wire, dangling away from the engine block. A round hole where a spark plug should be.

Cooper spun around and glared at Tanya. "Any more doubts about what kind of man your little bar customer was?"

"No. But you hate me anyway." She hung her head, as though God and all the universe had rejected her.

"Let's look under the seat," said Bev. She found an empty Styrofoam cup and a brown paper bag. She put it on the seat and opened it.

"Bingo," she said, taking out two spark plugs. There were bolts, too, that looked like they might fit the van's engine cover.

"He thought he'd be here, didn't he?" said Susan, wiping rain off the end of her nose. "Like we wouldn't do anything to the little fucker."

Bev felt her spirit skyrocket through the clouds. They had two vehicles. Surely one of them could make it to the river road. She was done sleeping out in these creepy woods, done interacting with these creepy people.

"I'm getting out of this rain," announced Susan, heading to the van. Tanya watched her go by, then scooted into the pickup from the driver's side to the passenger side.

Cooper replaced the pickup's spark plug and started the engine. He left it running, with Tanya still in the cab, and he and Bev returned to the van, where Bev joined Susan in the middle seat.

Cooper lifted and pulled back the engine cover. Bev rose up to watch. It was cold, almost freezing, enough for fog to mark their breaths.

"Good Lord," he said, staring at the engine. "How'd he get that spark plug out? No way I can fit a socket wrench in there."

He sighed and bent down on his knees in front of the engine, as though it were a holy thing. He blew a warm breath on his reddened fingers and with the tips gripped the spark plug before snaking his hand between wires out of Bev's vision. He had to twist his body so that he peered up at an angle toward the roof of the van, navigating the plug's journey by feel, until there was the sound of a metallic clatter.

"I dropped the damn thing!" he exclaimed. "Bev, can you come up here? See if your hand's small enough to reach through that gap and feel for the plug. I can't even see it."

She switched places with Cooper and pushed her bare hand through a gap among the metal and the wires, until she touched flat steel. She twisted her wrist and groped at metal and air.

They needed that plug.

She pushed her arm farther until the back of her hand lay flat on the bottom plate, bending her wrist painfully, so she could feel a wider arc. Metallic edging scraped the knuckle of her middle finger.

Nothing.

She scraped the same knuckle while withdrawing her arm, then noticed a small piece of missing skin.

"I reached as far as I could," she said. "Maybe it fell through onto the snow."

"Shit," said Cooper.

Susan got out to help Bev and Cooper remove snow that wind had crammed beneath the van. As they neared the engine block, Bev lay on her side and carefully excavated a fistful at a time. It was like being stuck on a shelf in a frozen morgue, all for a damn little plug. When that effort produced no results, she shined a flashlight while Cooper jammed his hand up through various gaps in the plate. He found nothing.

He slid out and blew on his fingers. He, too, had scraped skin off his knuckles. Cold rain spattered the white earth and rolled off the hood of Bev's parka. Across the road, a fir released a cascade of snow.

"Fuck this," said Cooper, standing up. "I wasn't going to return this van anyway, but I thought I'd at least get it out of the woods. There's not enough room in the truck."

"I'll ride in back," said Bev. "Let's get going."

"We need to keep the snow in the pickup bed. The extra weight will help."

"I'll stand."

"We'll be bumping around. Slipping and sliding."

"I don't care. Let's go."

"You'd leave me with Susan and Tanya? How am I going to stop them from strangling each other and drive at the same time?"

"I'll leave her alone," said Susan. "I'm trying to be nice to her. Admit it—if you were in my spot, that wouldn't be easy."

Cooper went to work getting chains on the pickup, while from the van Susan took both her backpack and Tanya's and Bev carried hers plus Cooper's. When Susan reached the passenger door of the pickup, she stopped and knocked on the window. The waitress rolled it halfway down, her eyes like those of a child facing a scolding. If Susan dished out more shit, Bev didn't know how she'd stop it, but she'd do something.

"I'm sorry for being mean again," said Susan. "I'm frustrated, but it's not right to take it out on you. I don't really think you knew he'd mess up the van."

Tanya closed her eyes and tensed her lips, as though fighting tears. "I didn't know any of this would happen. I'm so sorry about Will."

"I am, too. But he's gone now, and I just have to accept it."

Fifteen minutes later, Bev stood in the pickup bed with her gloved hands on top of the cab while Cooper backed up before moving forward, backed it farther, moved forward, backed farther again, and finally turned around in front of the van.

Home. Tonight. Sandra. Her parents. Oh, they'd be upset with her, but she'd be humble. She needed to be humble. She'd screwed up, worse than any time in her life, worse than most people ever in their lives.

Something hard banged against the undercarriage. The pickup stopped.

Rocks. Maybe the same damn one they'd hit with the van.

Whatever it was, it scraped against the bottom as Cooper reversed. He turned the wheels and moved forward at a different angle. Behind them, almost as big as a toaster oven, the reddish rock lay exposed in the mowed-down snow.

Standing in the rain, Bev had a great view. A wide expanse of debris-littered snow lay before them—too wide. What part was the road, and what was not the road?

Chapter Thirty-Eight

Bev leaned left and looked over the side of the truck. They hadn't gone thirty seconds and already they were stuck again, though this time without the sickening sound of chassis screeching across stone.

Despite the chains, the tires spun in a slick, icy groove. She'd driven through enough snow to appreciate that Cooper didn't try to force their rig forward. He backed up a foot, shifted into first, and rolled forward across the tire-dug dip. Bev closed her eyes and breathed easier.

Fifty feet farther, they were stuck again, and Bev braced her legs for more back-and-forth. She'd already swept two feet of snow off the top of the cab, and now she leaned onto the metal roof for balance, her hands in wet gloves, cold and tense.

After three feet in reverse, the pickup bolted forward, dropped into the depressions the tires had made, and again spun in place. Yet again they reversed, but this time Cooper turned the wheels slightly to cut a new path, and it worked, but only for twenty yards. Still tight against the cab, Bev turned her neck to look behind them. They'd progressed little more than seventy yards from the disabled van.

Reverse, forward. Reverse again, forward.

At this rate her shins and ankles and toes would be ice cubes by the time they descended out of the snow or reached Washougal River Road, whichever came first. Bev kicked snow away from her legs, hoping to spare her toes from frostbite. When they were walking, although her legs felt garbed in concrete, they'd made quicker progress than the pickup, but she couldn't imagine hoofing it for unknown miles, sinking in the snow with a pack on her back.

A flash of movement, dark on the white snow, caught her peripheral vision, and she glanced toward the trees on her right. A solitary coyote with mottled gray fur paused to study the herky-jerk motions of the alien box invading the silent woods. *Well, Mr. Coyote,* she thought, *no point in alerting your pals. We'll be out of here soon.*

Except for the four they'd left behind. Had this coyote already visited the burning A-frame? And within that triangle in the woods, were the graves dug deep enough?

I killed a man, I killed a man, I...

She wanted to bang a fist onto the top of the cab. Why couldn't her brain shut the fuck up?

Backward and forward, backward and forward, five yards, ten, the engine whining, straining in a pit of slushy cement, until something in the geometry of land grabbed a wheel and yanked the pickup sideways. Bev tensed the rubbery weak muscles of her legs and squeezed her arms over the top of the cab to keep from tumbling off the driver's side. Leaned at an angle, the truck burrowed ahead five yards until Cooper let up on the gas.

Was it a ditch? She pressed against the cab as Cooper put them in reverse. They moved back a foot, and then the whole left side slid down. It had to be a damn ditch. How the hell were they going to get out?

They wouldn't. They couldn't. They'd have to walk.

But Cooper switched to first gear and flicked the wheels right, and thank God they gripped enough ground to pull out of whatever the hell it was that slanted them over like that.

If they were on a highway, they'd be going fast enough that she could sit low behind the cab and the rain would fly overhead and not hit her like it was now. If they were on a highway, they could get to a phone booth and she could call home and her family would stop worrying. She looked behind again. The trees came closer to the truck as the passage narrowed, but they were still within sight of the van, not even a hundred yards total. Her watch showed 12:17 p.m.—eleven minutes to go maybe eighty yards. If Jim were there, he could calculate how long at that rate it would take to go twelve miles—maybe a hundred yards in fifteen minutes, a quarter mile in an hour, four hours for a mile, forty-eight hours to go twelve.

The snow wouldn't be this thick or this heavy all the way down, would it?

They lurched forward, stopped, backed up, forward, repeat, repeat. The smell of gas mingled with evergreen trees and rain.

It was cold. She'd have been better off if it were snowing. If it did take forty-eight hours to go twelve measly miles, she thought she might be dead by then.

She was hungry, too, though she was getting used to the feeling. They hadn't bothered to eat back at the van. She just wanted to get the hell out. She'd eat at home that night. Probably all the leftover turkey was gone, but a bag of corn chips would substitute quite well.

I killed a man, I killed a man...

Shut up. Shut up, stupid brain.

When they reached civilization, how would she hold her chin up like she was someone normal, when she was no longer normal and never would be again? It didn't matter that she'd *had* to do it.

An elite club, yes? Humans who killed.

The pickup fishtailed, paused, then shot forward.

She lowered herself to her knees, pulled her pack off its bed of snow, and sat on it. The money bundles pressed against her butt. A sudden bounce knocked the back of her head against the rear window, and she repressed a cry of pain. To keep her skull from ending up like Will's, she scooted away from the cab.

Will. He deserved better than that.

There was something about Will, though, something about the way he died. A puzzle gnawed at her, but her mind went numb, her thoughts mushy as baby food, one death like another—too many, too much. Whatever it was about Will, it probably amounted to nothing, just her mind playing games.

Strangely smooth, they moved forward, a hundred yards, two hundred, maybe five miles per hour, better than what they had been doing. Trees moved by steadily, if slowly. Maybe she would be home that night. Maybe it would be only a matter of hours.

Then a snowdrift stopped them, not like a brick wall, more like a net. Cooper idled the engine, tried a nudge back, a nudge forward, but the wheels spun, locked in place.

The driver's door opened and the smell of

cigarettes wafted back. She stood and watched Cooper examine the wells he'd dug with the wheels. He sighed without cursing.

In front of them, the snowdrift had pushed through a gap in the trees and left a pile like a frozen swell higher than the hood of the truck. Yesterday, before the rain had compressed what had been a fluffy texture, they might have been able to plow right through it. But not now.

She picked up a mattock, handed it to Cooper, and climbed out with a shovel in her hands. He high-kneed it to the cab and called the others out.

It took half an hour to dig a thirty-yard path wide enough for the pickup, leaving Bev in heavy-breathing mode, thirsty despite all the frozen liquid surrounding her. She eyed Susan, then Tanya, but both of them looked away—sympathetic, it seemed, though not enough to take a turn in the back.

If they needed more than a day to nurse their jalopy back to pavement, there was no way in hell she'd be riding in the back tomorrow. She'd yank one of them by the hair, out of the cab. Probably Tanya—atonement for being a blabbermouth. At least the rain had slowed while they labored, falling now as a mist, cold but light. Bev lit a cigarette, hauled her weary legs over the tailgate, settled near the cab, and braced herself for another segment of Mr. Toad's Wild Ride.

For thirty-five minutes, they crept forward, reversing a handful of times. She wasn't great at judging distances, but Bev guessed they'd gone a mile before they stopped again. This time the wheels weren't spinning and the engine didn't whine. How nice it would be if it were a stop sign, with pavement on the other side, but of course that was a stupid thought. They hadn't gone nearly far enough.

She stood and looked ahead.

A massive tree at least four feet in diameter lay across the road.

Chapter Thirty-Nine

Around the campfire that evening, no one said much, not with ten miles of struggling through snow awaiting them. They split Bev's lasagna, the can of creamed corn, and six peanuts apiece from Jim's old stash. The rain had ceased, but the night sky remained starless. Through the neck of her parka, a pungent smell from her body drifted up. She sat smoking a Chesterfield on a portion of tarp extending out from her tent.

"Here's to Jim," said Cooper, breaking the silence. "Leaving us peanuts and cotton balls to build a fire."

"He should be here," said Tanya.

Bev had nothing to add, and neither did anyone else. From the trees a screech broke the stillness, paused, repeated, and repeated again—a barn owl, but there were no barns, at least none that she knew about.

"Smoke a joint?" Susan asked, an offer Bev knew could only be directed at her, unless the other two changed their minds about dope.

She nodded. "Yeah, thanks." Maybe she'd sleep better.

"Not here. Back up the road."

Illuminated by the fire, Susan's face looked gaunt compared to what it was when they'd begun the expedition. Weather had scoured her skin raw, while dirt smudged her cheeks and forehead.

If Bev could see her own face, what would it look like? When she reached civilization, would her eyes be capable of hiding what she'd witnessed and done?

She climbed over the tree that blocked the road, and the two of them trudged through snow the pickup had shaved flat. Susan took out a little pin-joint, not a fat momma like the ones Will rolled, and she held her hit a long while before passing it to Bev.

The first toke softened the muscles of her neck and face, then drifted up into her head and loosened the coils of her brain.

Susan took another hit, held it, and exhaled a slow steady cloud. "Nothing's happened since you took care of Clint, but that doesn't mean we're safe. She's got a bigger stash now. I think she likes it. Now she's got a bonus night, and she's going to want even more. She's going to try to kill someone. I can see the greed in her eyes. I can sense it. Maybe she'll try to kill all of us. She'll get hold of Cooper's gun, or Clint's. She scares the hell out of me."

Bev took a short toke. So much for mellow.

Paranoid Susan. But on this trip, paranoia was an asset.

"What the hell," said Bev. "All right. I'll be careful."

That night in her sleeping bag, her legs felt like punching bags. How they'd hold her up and haul her through all that snow tomorrow, she had no idea.

Her bladder woke her, like it always did. She tugged on her boots and trudged up the path the pickup had carved. No way was she stepping off into the woods.

After taking care of business, she turned around,

her flashlight still off. Twenty yards in front of her, bundled like a laundry cart, headlamp pointed straight down, Tanya crept toward her.

She wielded a shovel upside down, the head of it poised to smash.

She stopped, whirled a hundred eighty degrees, swung the shovel hard—hard enough to crush a skull.

Bev hadn't fastened her jeans yet. She swallowed and waddled back a step.

Outside her circle of light, perhaps Tanya had not seen Bev.

Or perhaps she had. The swing had been a practice swing. The next one…

Tanya advanced, her eyes pointed down to spotlight her steps. She stopped, cocked the shovel, glanced behind her.

Fear almost froze Bev. Almost. Because she knew she'd fight. She could run, too, probably faster than Tanya, but she wouldn't do that. She'd put a stop to this.

She snapped her jeans, flicked on her flashlight, pointed the beam directly into Tanya's eyes.

The waitress screamed, dropped the shovel, fell back on her butt. Then she scrambled up.

"Jesus, Bev. Why didn't you tell me you were here?"

Bev strode to Tanya, seized the shovel. Like a cop working a suspect, she pushed her flashlight in front of Tanya's eyes. Enough light filtered past the waitress's head for Bev to see both Cooper and Susan emerge from their tents.

"What the hell are you doing with this?" she demanded, gesturing with the shovel.

"It's dangerous."

"Really? Who's dangerous?"

"Everyone! Animals. Ghosts. I don't know. I'm scared."

Susan reached them before Cooper. "You caught her. She had the shovel, huh? I told you, didn't I?"

Bev handed the shovel to Tanya. "It's nothing," she said. "We just…frightened each other."

Chapter Forty

In the morning, Bev crawled out of her tent into a fog cloud. Cold dew saturated the air and beaded on her tent. Not one needle moved on the torpid firs.

And yet, despite the moisture that soaked every surface, they lacked water to drink. Among them, Bev had the most—a quarter-full canteen. She took a micro-sip, swished it in her mouth, held it in a puddle on her curled tongue. When she swallowed, she noticed the others gaping at her.

"We started with the same amount," she said. "I rationed mine."

"I don't want your water," said Susan. "Besides, wasn't there a creek next to this road on the way up?"

"Not this far up," said Cooper. All I remember up here are chuck holes and mud puddles."

"Then it's down the road," said Tanya. "We'll listen for it."

They packed and walked. Second in line, Bev focused on each step—lift her leg high, reach her boot forward across the top of the snow, step into the next hole that Cooper had created, a hole deeper than the top of her knee. When it was her fifteen-minute turn to lead, it seemed like the snow had suction cups to clutch her feet at the bottom of every hole. She leaned hard on her mattock to pull out her foot and advance. Her hamstrings tightened, sharp little pains that caught her breath and prevented her from going faster than Cooper did when he was in the lead. At least her ankle didn't bother her much.

She opened her mouth, dry like hardened paste, and tried to swallow the airborne dew. It didn't work.

Closer to the side of the road, especially where the trees grew thicker, an icy sheen covered the snow. Although more slippery than the middle of the road, for five or six steps at a stretch it held her up. She imagined herself as a ballerina, pattering soft steps on an icy stage. The others behind her sometimes plunged through the snow, but that was their problem.

Then she'd sink through and pull herself out with the aid of the mattock. The pattern continued—a whole lot of sinking, interspersed with a few blessed glides across an iced-over surface.

When her turn was done, half an hour since they'd begun, she felt ready to call it a day. She thought of Sandra and kept moving.

Five minutes into Tanya's lead, Cooper dropped like he'd been shot. He grabbed his leg, panted through gritted teeth. His face contorted with pain.

"Cramp," he gasped.

Bev knelt beside him and put a hand on his shoulder. At least it wasn't a heart attack. For a minute he lay on his side, panting, massaging his calf. After it subsided, he sat on the snow with his knees bent up, regaining his breath and rubbing the calf.

"Damn it," he said. "We should have melted snow when we had the fire last night."

"We should melt it right now," said Bev. "Seems like we're a long way from the creek."

"What? Build a fire?" asked Susan.

Bev took off her pack. "No. I've got a backpack stove. And a mess kit."

While Bev tended her Svea stove, Cooper turned on the radio. A Japan Airlines jet had crashed on a runway in Moscow, killing over sixty. An assistant professor at Harvard University was released after a week in jail. He had refused to disclose information to a grand jury investigating the Pentagon Papers. Defense Secretary Melvin Laird claimed that at most only ten thousand men would be drafted before the military switched to an all-volunteer force.

The weather forecast called for continued rain.

In an hour Bev melted enough snow to fill four one-quart canteens. They set out once more, Tanya in the lead and Susan second. The gray day dripped like a bloated bag filled with ice water. Even after the additional fluids, Bev's hamstrings felt as though someone were twisting augers into them. Whimpering now and then, Tanya crept forward, even when she hit iced-over stretches where she didn't sink. She reminded Bev of one of those octogenarians in downtown Portland who took what seemed like fifteen minutes to cross the street.

Cooper sank in every kind of snow. Whenever Tanya was able to soft-step across the top, Bev veered around the holes that Cooper gouged. More often than not, she sank, too.

After ten minutes, Tanya fell sideways in slow motion. She landed partially encased by snow and scrambled to rise, one hand slipping on the shovel handle, the other hand pushing through the snow.

"Here." Susan held out a hand. Tanya hesitated before grasping it and allowing Susan to pull her up.

"Give me a minute," said Tanya, panting lightly.

"No," said Susan. "See that tree? Kind of bent out of the ground? Go that far."

Tanya nodded and trudged ahead. Cooper, in front of Bev, breathed harder than Tanya, with the addition of a wheeze. They reached the bent tree in under two minutes. On fresh legs without the snow, Bev could have done it in ten seconds.

"Now see that dead tree without any needles?" said Susan. "That one's next. Keep going."

Tanya mumbled something and high-stepped forward, mumbled again, advanced. Bev realized the waitress was praying. "I can do all things through Christ, which strengtheneth me." Bev hadn't heard that prayer in a long time, not since... When was it?

She glanced ahead and saw they were halfway to the dead tree, where Susan would take the lead.

Billy's funeral. That's when she heard it—the last time she'd been inside a church. Since then, nearly every week, Bev's parents brought Sandra to St. Rose Catholic Church in Gresham, providing Mommy a two-hour break before she began her work week at the *Chronicle.*

She pictured herself sitting in a pew, wearing her blush-colored dress, her thigh against Sandra's squirmy leg, Mom and Dad seated on the other side of their granddaughter. Kneeling for prayers. Standing for hymns. A warm place out of the wilderness. Next Sunday she'd go, just to feel Sandra at her side.

By then, she might be unemployed.

Every slow step increased the odds that someone else would be sitting at her desk by the time she returned to civilization. When Susan took her turn in front, the pace didn't quicken. They weren't going to make it home until tomorrow. They'd be overdue by four days.

****

They pitched their tents that night where the sound of a creek played a melody in the dark. Cooper cleared a circle in the snow so they could build a fire. Susan held out a lighter for Tanya's Chesterfield. "Have you ever painted snow scenes?" she asked.

"It's hard," said Tanya. The smoke she exhaled flattened in the cloud of dew through which they'd trudged all day. "It's all different shades of white and black. I like color. You know, you don't have to be nice to me."

"Who says I'm being nice to you?"

The snow outside the circle was only about a foot high, maybe less, a decreased depth that helped them cover a mile and a half on their final hour of hiking. They'd dropped in elevation, enough so that when Bev sank, the snow reached only halfway up her calves—and she sank less often, too. Even Cooper managed to walk sections without falling through.

Bev used a match to light her Chesterfield.

"I thought you still had Salems," said Susan.

"I'm saving them for when we hit civilization. Tomorrow, for sure. Maybe you'll only end up missing three days of classes."

"I'll miss more than that. I'm done."

"But you're a senior," said Tanya. "You should finish."

"Maybe someday. But I'm going to do a disappearing act. Take my inspiration from Mr. Cooper here."

Cooper set a mattock against his tent. "You think it's easy to disappear? What are you going to use for money?"

"Don't worry. I won't go spending your twenties. I have my ways. I know how to get money."

"Where do you think you'll go?" asked Tanya.

"It wouldn't be disappearing if I told anyone, would it?"

Bev used her foot to stir gravel that Cooper's labor had exposed. Both her legs felt like mush, with a big ache stirred in. "I'll get wood if someone else gets the water," she said.

"I'll get water," said Tanya. "Give me your canteens, and I'll take my pack."

"I'll help with the wood," said Susan.

"And I'll look for a rabbit," said Cooper, still wheezing.

Tanya disappeared into the descending woods, a mix of conifers and hardwoods at their new elevation. While Cooper backtracked the way they'd come, Bev and Susan took a few steps down the road. They extinguished their cigarettes and put them back in their packages.

"It's nice to be able to walk on top of the snow," said Susan.

"Sometimes I thought I'd never be able to pull my foot out," said Bev.

"Why don't you take the right side of road and I'll take the left."

"Works for me."

Susan put a hand on Bev's shoulder. "Watch out she doesn't circle back and whack you with a shovel, like they did to Will."

Bev recalled how hard Tanya had swung the shovel last night. But she'd frightened Tanya more than Tanya had frightened her.

"I thought you said you were going to be nice."

"Nice doesn't mean stupid. Remember what I said about a bonus night? This'll be her last chance. I'm more worried about Cooper. He's the one with the guns, and he's a lot weaker. She'll go after him first."

Clint's pistol weighed down Bev's pocket, but she didn't correct Susan's belief about who had it.

"If she jumps him, she'll have both guns, and where's that leave us?" continued Susan. "She's probably thinking only one of us needs to walk out of here tomorrow with all that dough."

More paranoia. It made Bev want to shimmy inside her sleeping bag, sleep, wake up, and get the hell away from these people.

But if Susan was right...

She moved Susan's hand off her shoulder. "I'll watch her," she said.

Susan crossed the road and descended out of sight.

Bev stepped into the forest and found a small tree encased by snow lying across a stump. She kicked a branch. Snow dropped loose, but the branch was too thick to break away. Or she was too weak. A few days ago she could have done it.

Around a small snag she cleared snow and gathered a handful of match-sized sticks. From the dead tree she broke off a thin bare branch and tried without success to break it over her knee. If she had a hatchet...

Jim popped into her mind. Then Clint, sitting in his sleeping bag, the hatchet abandoned on the path that led to the cabin.

She let go of the branch and stood stunned.

How could she have missed it?

But there was no time to answer that question. The danger was not hypothetical. It was right now, real, and if she didn't act immediately, somebody else was going to die.

Chapter Forty-One

"Cooper!"

Bev stood in the middle of the road, peering the direction Cooper had gone. He didn't call back and he didn't walk into view.

Three tents, green and blue and apricot, were pitched over brown plastic tarps on a clearing of gravel and mud. The air smelled moist. Among the tools, a shovel was missing.

She shouted again and listened, but there was no reply.

Her legs ached with fatigue. It would have been nice to crawl into her sleeping bag, to wait and hope, but she couldn't do that. Every second she delayed increased the likelihood of another death. She grabbed a flashlight, picked up a mattock, and trotted across the snow down the road until, off to the left side, boot prints penetrated the snow like post holes. She veered off the road and sank to her hips.

Maybe that was a message. Maybe God had piled up the snow to slow her down, to consider the risks. She could go back, grab her pack, get away, walk through the night and into the morning until she reached the bigger road. A car would go by, and she could get a ride to the nearest phone, where she could call the cops and they'd deal with whatever the scene was down at the creek.

Except she could never call the cops. Not about this. Not about anything remotely related to the whole damned trip.

She straightened her back and pushed the mattock like a cane against the ground. It might already be too late. She plowed through the snow until she merged into a groove cut by the humans farther downslope. A few yards farther, now in the dark thicket of woods, snow depth decreased. She moved faster, pointing the flashlight down in front of her feet.

A sound like the beeper of a reversing truck froze her in place.

How could it be?

Then she remembered the Northern saw-whet owl had that exact call. The creek seemed closer, but the sound of running water had tricked her before, its decibels magnified by the surrounding terrain.

Her legs threatened rebellion, not so much from fatigue as from fear. The last time she'd fought through this kind of fear, it ended with her pulling a trigger.

I killed a man, I killed a man…

And he was innocent.

She'd buried him, too. She was a murderer. She belonged in prison.

But she didn't have time. All this analysis was just another way to surrender to fear.

She forced herself down the hill. The pistol in her pocket flopped against the bone of her hip. The water sound grew louder and louder. She stepped out from the edge of forest and for the first time saw the stream, a ribbon in the night lined with scrub willows, curving between mountains. Thirst urged her forward. Fear pushed her back.

Her next step made no mark on the suddenly slick surface, and both legs flew out from beneath her. She slid, ten feet, twenty, not stopping until creek water engulfed her boots and pant legs. Her ankle yelped. During the plunge she'd dropped the flashlight, and she watched its beam flow away in the rush of water until it lodged against a rock and bobbed like a miniature buoy on a turbulent sea. She lunged forward and grabbed it, wetting her coat sleeves in the process. She scampered out, slipped again on the steep hard snow, and skidded back into the stream. Standing in the water, she placed the mattock behind a willow, grabbed a branch, and pulled herself out.

She looked for footprints but found none—had they gone upstream or down?

She chose downstream. With the flashlight under her arm and the mattock in one hand, she used the other hand to grab the bare branches of willows to keep her balance. She stepped on a rock mid-creek, then felt herself slipping. Instinctively, she grasped a spindly branch with both hands, keeping her feet but once again dropping the flashlight. This time it bounced off another rock with a sickening plink, and the light was gone.

Where was it? If only there were a few stars or a crescent moon, illumination to cast a glimmer on the metal casing. She held onto a willow and listened. Her eyes adjusted. The black meander of creek split through the pale white of snow, rushing, gurgling.

A voice blended into the aria of dashing water. Was it human, or did it belong to the chorale of the creek?

On her knees, she made a last effort to find the

flashlight, staring for something cylindrical among the shapes of rocks in the shadow creek. She removed her already-wet gloves, groped inside the tumbling flow, and felt nothing of human origin.

Perhaps it would be better to sneak up, with no light, on that voice. It was solitary, without a second voice replying—that meant something. Something bad.

Her heart raced like the creek, and dread dug its fingers into her shoulders. She put on her wet gloves, clutched a willow, advanced.

The voice amplified. It had the quality of a mother patiently explaining something, a mild rebuke in her tone.

Another tree. Another step. A rock tucked against the bank—she hunched down to make sure that's what it was. Another step.

There—beyond the weave of jagged branches, a human shape in an ivory white coat faded gray in the night. Sitting or squatting. Hair draped to the shoulders—Susan, facing away, talking to someone Bev couldn't see. Maybe Tanya was okay. Bev stopped and listened, her feet and legs shivering wet and cold.

"No more schemes," Susan said. In the dark gloom, the college student tensed her shoulders and pushed down, like someone stuffing clothes into a suitcase. "Not from you. Not from anyone. No one's going to touch me. I won't allow it."

There was a sound of something being lifted out of water.

"Gone so soon?" said Susan. "Then we'll meet in hell."

Bev gripped the mattock with both hands. She burst forward, slipped on the ice, and slammed onto her butt. Her head hit the ground hard and a wave of pain nearly knocked her out.

Where was the mattock? Flat on her back, Bev groped with both hands, felt nothing, saw nothing, not until a dark silhouette whirled and grabbed Bev's leg above the ankle. She kicked herself free, rose enough to crawl backward like a crab. Desperate to stand upright, she pushed down the soles of her boots, but her feet kept slipping on the steep slope draped with icy snow. Susan, tall and looming, dropped knee-first onto Bev's chest.

Pain shot through her body. Inhale, exhale—she could do neither. Her breath was knocked out, and terror took its place. She twisted left and right, tried to scoot backward, thrust her hips, all without air. Susan pressed her knee down, leaned until she faced Bev eye to eye, then put both hands around Bev's throat and squeezed.

Bev twisted side to side, kicked her legs, and tried to rise. While seconds dripped in slow motion, her body weakened. She swung up her arm, rapped Susan on the side of her head, but it was a bad angle and did no damage. She swung again, the speed of her arm slow, her fist loose, the punch ineffectual. On the edge of losing consciousness, she glimpsed Tanya nearby, lying on her belly, torso and legs on land, head face-down in the water, bobbing with the flow of the creek.

Chapter Forty-Two

"Let's join your sister, shall we?" Susan rose, grabbed Bev's hair, and dragged her down to the stream.

Get up! Run! Bev's brain beseeched her, but her body had no strength. She hadn't inhaled for ten seconds or fifteen, or was it a couple of hours?

At the water's edge, Susan flipped Bev as though she weighed no more than Styrofoam, dunked her face in the water, and pulled it out.

"Why am I doing this?" Susan's voice lacked emotion, as though she were explaining why she did laundry a certain way and not another.

Another dunk. Another pull out of the water.

Still no breath. Locked throat. Locked chest. Her arms flailed, though she felt no connection to them.

"Bev Wikowski. You're a reporter, aren't you? I was sure I knew that name."

Another dunk. Another pull. She felt her diaphragm easing, breath on the brink of restoration— as long as her head was out of the water.

"But I couldn't place the name until today. Walking through all that lovely snow, I remembered— the *Morning Chronicle.* I've read your stories."

This time Susan held her head underwater, five seconds, ten seconds. Life was leaking away. She couldn't fight; she could only wiggle like a fish too long in the sun.

Tanya's lifeless head bumped against her own.

Susan pulled Bev's head out.

"And I thought: She's been lying to us. She's going to tell our story. She'll be famous, and we'll rot in jail."

Bev's chest loosened, and she sucked back a loud gulp of wondrous air. Susan slammed her face into the streaming depth, then jammed a knee into her back, like a log weighing her down. In the renewed terror of no breath, Bev pushed her head up against Susan's hand, but she lacked leverage. She reached back her arms but failed to reach her adversary.

Ten seconds. Fifteen. Twenty. Susan pinned her down hard.

Twenty-five seconds, thirty. Where was Cooper? Where was God? Where was justice?

And then a yank from the water. Air. Weak, so weak.

"Kill or be killed." Susan's voice was calm. "It's nothing personal, Bev."

Water again. Cold. Ice. No breath.

The magic carpet came. Hello, Billy. His body glowed. His hand reached for her. *Take it. Take it.*

No.

Billy disappeared.

Sandra now. Bright day. Rolling down a grassy hill. *Mommy!*

Rolling.

Roll.

Out of her deepest reserves, energy surged. She reached back, slapped a hand over the hand holding her head, and she spun, a steel dynamo, whirl-blur and power. And she was up out of the water, gulping air,

Susan beneath her, but strong, stronger than Bev. Susan broke free. With ice-cold water dribbling down to her ankles, Bev stood facing Susan, poised like a wrestler.

Susan lunged at the same time Bev swung her leg up hard. Her foot thumped against gut, but Susan's forward momentum threw Bev onto her back into the creek. She tried to rise.

Susan smacked the base of her palm onto Bev's forehead, stunned her with pain and dizziness. She grabbed both sides of Bev's head and pushed it toward the water. Bev punched once, twice, the second time smashing hard against jaw, loosening Susan's grip enough to yank free and rise to a crouch.

Susan charged again, hunched to launch into Bev. Bev raked her fingers across Susan's eye. While the college student cried out and covered a hand over her wounded eye, Bev ducked low and scrambled onto the snowy embankment. She reached into her parka, took out the pistol, gripped her wrist to steady her quivering hand.

Susan raised a hand to show surrender. She pressed her other hand over her eye and moaned with pain. Bev could barely hold the gun. It felt as though it might slip through her fingers and into the creek. Susan could reach out and snatch it from her hand and Bev wouldn't have the strength to stop her. Was the safety on? She slid a finger, touched the safety. Down. Off. Ready to fire, if she could pull the trigger.

"Out of the creek." Bev rasped as though stricken with asthma. Her throat felt constricted, bruised where Susan had squeezed it. Mindful of her footing, she moved sideways on the edge of the creek to keep distance between them.

Susan lifted a foot out of the water. "She tried to kill me first."

"I should just…"—Bev couldn't breathe through a full sentence—"shoot you." She couldn't stop the damn gun from shaking. Susan had to notice—would she attack?

Susan put her other foot on land. "She wanted me dead. She wanted all of us dead. Can't you see?"

"What I see is that you've murdered someone else."

"It was her or me."

Bev calculated that Susan was close enough to dive at her. Thick brush blocked her from backing farther away. If she kept both hands on the pistol and retreated upslope, she'd slip, fall, and slide back into the creek.

"Get Tanya out of the water."

"Sure. Whatever you say." As Susan knelt to grasp Tanya by the boots and drag her onto the bank, Bev grabbed a branch for leverage and pulled herself farther up. She kicked a foothold in the hardened snow and waited while Susan dragged Tanya's body to the narrow shore. Still kneeling, arms at her sides, Susan turned toward Bev.

Bev tightened her grip on the pistol. "Stay where you are. Sit down."

Susan didn't move. "You don't believe me, do you? But you should. She and Clint…"

"Sit down. Now."

"Okay."

"Now."

Susan sat. A shovel lay between her and Tanya. Bev darted her eyes side to side and spotted her mattock, obscured by darkness, half beneath a thicket.

Her breaths came hoarse and weak, but she stared at Susan and put steel into her voice. "How'd you know?" she demanded.

"Know what?"

"What happened to Will."

"Clint killed him. Tanya helped."

"Bullshit. You know how he died. Nobody told you."

"I know *who*, not *how*."

The gun was heavy. "You know how, because you did it. Back on the road, you said to watch out. I might get it in the back of the head, just like Will."

"That was just a guess." It was too dark to see alarm flash in Susan's eyes, but Bev heard it in her voice and sensed her adversary's body tightening.

"Bullshit. Put your hands together, like you're praying. Don't even think about grabbing the shovel."

Susan complied. She sat with her knees raised.

Wet and cold, Bev's whole body shook. "When we planned what to do with the bodies, you said Jim's and Melvin's skeletons would be the only ones not to show damage. How did you know that?"

"I never said that. You're imagining things. The stress is getting to you."

"Bullshit. I didn't understand the implication then, but I do now. You knew what happened to Will, because you did it. You killed your own boyfriend."

"You're batshit crazy. I wouldn't do that."

"And then you killed Jim. You went back toward the old fire, the only place where Clint could have gone, and you dropped the hatchet on the trail to frame him."

"Yeah, right. In the middle of a blizzard."

"Yes, in the middle of a blizzard—you, with your

eagle eyes. You caused me to kill an innocent man."

Susan nodded her head toward Tanya's body. "She's the only person I've killed. Clint's accomplice. And she attacked me first."

"Then why did you try to kill me?"

"You attacked me, too. What was I supposed to do?"

"You told me why. Because I'm a reporter."

Susan took a long breath. "Everyone wants me dead. You proved it when you attacked me. You're proving it now. After we found the money, I could see it in all your eyes. Greed. Murderous greed. It might be dark, but I can see it in your eyes right now. I can feel it thick around your soul."

"I'll be the one to worry about my soul. What are we going to do with you, Susan?"

"If you think I'm guilty, bring me to the police. They'll let me go. All I've done is defend myself."

Bev couldn't extend her arms any longer. Keeping the pistol pointed at Susan, she brought her hands back to her body. Quivering hands vibrated against her shivering midsection.

"If I hand you over to the cops, I'm handing myself over, too. I'm not going to do that. I won't flush my life down the toilet."

"So let me go. I can keep quiet. I'll leave you alone."

Something dark, darker than the night, took possession of Bev. It submerged her, hot like lava, cold as liquid nitrogen.

She knew what she had to do.

With the little strength she had left, she focused on her arms, on her finger against the trigger. She let the dark wave immerse her, so that the woman sitting before her became something less than human, something evil, something needing extermination. She extended her arms, aimed a downward angle above Susan's knees to the center of her chest.

"Beyond a reasonable doubt," she said. "That's the standard, isn't it?"

A whimper escaped Susan's lips. "You're better than this, Bev. You're a good person."

"I have no doubts. You implicated yourself in Will's death. You just killed Tanya. You tried to kill me."

"It was self-defense." Susan's plea barely rose above the sound of the creek.

"Bullshit," said Bev.

She pulled the trigger.

Chapter Forty-Three

The noise of the blast stunned her. It took a moment to realize she had done what Cooper told her she might do. Anticipating the pistol's kickback, she'd flinched. She missed the center of Susan's chest.

Susan shrieked. She put her hand near the shoulder of her white coat, but it was too dark for Bev to see exactly where.

"You bitch, you bitch!" Susan hunched over, her face barely above the ground, her breath panting, staccato.

Her lungs still smoldering, her body like a bruise, Bev took a cold, steady breath, braced her wrist, willed her hands to stillness. At the end of an exhalation, no different than if she'd been holding a camera with a telephoto lens, she squeezed the trigger.

Her ears rang from the thunderous concussion.

Susan's body spasmed, quivered a moment, then slumped to the ground. Next to her, the creek rustled by as though nothing had happened. The damp air held the scent of gunpowder.

She wanted to throw down the damn pistol and never touch it again, or any of its brethren, but she held onto it.

Where the hell was Cooper? Why hadn't he come when she called for him?

He didn't shoot Clint. Was it because he

understood Clint was innocent? Or at least had doubt?

It didn't make sense, but Bev wasn't going to take a chance. Cooper was a threat. Eliminate Bev, and there would be no one breathing who could ever tell the final chapter of DB Cooper's loot. If he hadn't thought about that before, surely he'd see the opportunity now. He was human, subject to temptations.

She put the pistol back in her pocket. Four bullets left.

"Cooper!" She had her breath back, finally, and she threw all of it into the shout.

"Bev!"

The bastard had ears after all. If he'd answered earlier, if he'd come down the hill with her, Susan could never have put Bev within seconds of never breathing again.

"Down here!" she called.

Through the darkness of the trees, a light wobbled. It grew closer, flashed across brown trunks of willows next to the creek. Wheezing announced his presence before he came into view. His headlamp blinded her until he pointed it at the ground.

Under the spotlight of the lamp, a red and gelatinous gap showed on the back of Susan's blonde head just above her neck. She had fallen forward onto Tanya's feet. The waitress lay flat and still, her head resting on snow at the edge of the stream.

Backlit, Cooper's eyes showed alarm. He pivoted, then reached for his hip. Bev took out her pistol and aimed.

"Don't," she said.

"You killed them."

"No, I killed her." She nodded toward Susan.

"I heard two shots."

"Both of them for Susan. She killed Tanya. She tried to kill me."

"Then why are you pointing..." He paused. "Oh, yeah. I was reaching for my gun."

"Yes, about that gun. I want you to take off your coat, your shirt, and your harness. Then toss the harness over to me. You make a fast move, I'll shoot."

"I don't mean you harm."

"Just do what I say."

When the harness landed at her feet, Bev took out the revolver and put it in her pocket. "Don't get close to me," she said. "I'm dangerous."

"All this time I could have killed everyone, and I didn't. Why would I do that now?"

"Maybe it's because Susan was doing the work for you."

"The hell you say. What's the proof?"

"She fucked up. Before we went to get wood and water, she warned me that Tanya might bash me in the back of my head with a shovel, the same as what happened to Will. Did you ever tell Susan what happened to Will?"

"No."

"Then how did she know? And when we were deciding who to burn and who to bury—"

Cooper cut her off. "She said Jim and Melvin would have the only unmarked skeletons. That also meant she knew what happened to Will. Damn. Why didn't I see that?"

Droplets sprinkled Bev on her forehead and nose.

"So what's that mean, Cooper?"

"She's fucking crazy."

"What else?"

He stood quietly. She couldn't tell if he understood.

"It means I murdered a man. You couldn't do it, so I did. He was innocent. He was telling the truth."

The wheezing left his breath, but there was a quiver in his voice. "We didn't know."

"If they catch us, I'm going to prison."

"If they catch *you*. They won't catch me."

"Good for you."

"Clint put himself in this. Who knows what he had planned? He should have stayed home."

"We all should have stayed home."

She wondered why she didn't feel abhorrence at herself. She had done a terrible thing, broken a commandment, committed a capital offense.

By far the greater feeling was a thirst to get home to Sandra, to stay home and never be caught. She was cold to everything else. It was like she'd shut off the light to a certain room in her being.

She looked down at the dead women. "Where are we going to bury these bodies?" she asked.

Chapter Forty-Four

It was past midnight when Bev crawled into her tent. After burying the bodies in a shallow grave, she and Cooper had staggered back to camp. They agreed to sleep until six in the morning.

She peeled off her parka and rain pants, soaked and heavy from the battle in the creek and the mist that fell afterward. Garbed in the same jeans, underwear, bra, and sweatshirt she'd worn for five days, she tucked her legs inside the sleeping bag. Rashes burned beneath her breasts and buttocks. She shined Cooper's headlamp onto her hands, wrinkled and puffy from moisture. On her right hand, a blister beneath her thumb oozed pus under a flap of skin. An open blister glistened just below her middle finger, while the same spots by her other fingers were red and raw. More blisters bubbled at the fingers on her left hand.

She closed her eyes, then opened them. Fatigue smothered her emotions. Slowly, she folded her aching fingers into fists, and the sting of it reminded her she was still alive. She wouldn't be defeated, not when she'd come this far.

From her first-aid kit, she took antibacterial ointment and rubbed it into her palms. Then she rolled up her wet parka and used it as a pillow beneath her sleeping bag. To the left of her bag lay Cooper's shoulder harness and gun. To her right, a hand-grab away, lay the pistol with four bullets in the clip.

****

When she woke, she wondered if she had died and drifted to the white light that near-death survivors experienced before life yanked them back to earth. Morning beamed as bright as klieg lights. Birds chirped. The creek—a place of death now—called from a distance.

Her watch said 8:36. Cooper's gun and harness were gone.

She sat abruptly. He'd been in her tent and she hadn't woken.

Stupid reporter forfeits gun.

He could have killed her and she would never have known. Months later someone would have found her tent on the road, looked inside, seen dried remnants of her brain and blood splatted against the floor and sides.

It would have been an easier way to die than drowning.

She strained her ears for sound, but except for the birds and the distant creek and the soft wavering of boughs, she heard nothing.

"Cooper?" she called.

The birds paused, then resumed their chatter. What would they eat, with snow piled up everywhere?

"Cooper?" Louder this time.

Her clothes just as damp as when she'd gone to sleep, she unzipped the tent, raised herself on her knees, and peered in every direction. Cooper's tent—gone. Susan's and Tanya's packs—gone. Only the sled remained.

"Fuck you, Cooper!" She retreated into her tent. "Hear that, you bastard? Or is your sorry ass too far away?"

Her legs were sore, the same as her shoulders and arms and hands. It felt as though a mountain goat had rammed her lower back. She considered going back to sleep, but she crammed her bag into its stuff sack. She'd probably be just as sore tomorrow as today, maybe more.

She dragged everything out, broke down the tent, strapped it to her pack, and set the pack next to the sled. For breakfast she planned to limit herself to a third of her leftover gorp, but when she opened the main compartment of her pack, she found an additional can of Spam, the Pop-Tarts, fruit cocktail, a full pack of Chesterfields, the transistor radio, and, in a plastic baggie, the four doobies Susan had salvaged from the suitcase.

In addition to the food, something else increased the bulk of the main compartment. Money—much more than her share. She guessed it added up to fifty thousand dollars.

She looked down the road where Cooper had gone.

"You think this makes up for anything? Fuck you. I never wanted the money. I only wanted a story."

Minutes later, she had lashed everything onto the sled. She sat on it, lumpy bundles of twenties inside the pack pressing against her butt. A syrupy smell tantalized as she spooned fruit cocktail from its can.

She looked down the road she'd be walking. "Damn right, Cooper. You fucked up my life. Yeah, yeah, I know. Nobody forced me to do this. But you know what? You're still an asshole."

On the radio she found a station that broadcast local news and almost spat out a maraschino cherry when she heard her own name.

Several days after a brutal and unexpected blizzard struck the Cascade Mountains, authorities have no new information about the fate of Portland Morning Chronicle *reporter Beverly Wikowski, who was reported overdue Saturday night from a mushrooming expedition. Authorities have been hampered by a lack of information about exactly where Mrs. Wikowski ventured into the mountains. They believe she was accompanied by one or more companions, but no specific information about them is available. Farther north, Jim Rossi of Longview, Washington, has not returned from a turkey-hunting trip. The two cases are believed to be unrelated. Authorities are advising Northwest residents to be especially cautious when traveling in the mountains during inclement weather and to always leave specific travel itineraries with family members and friends.*

Bev turned off the radio. She used her tongue to push the cherry right to left and back again along her lower gums. Of course her parents would have reported her missing. Every day would have increased their dread that they would never see their daughter again. And what would they be telling Sandra? Would they tell her that her mommy was lost in the mountains, or would they try to hide that from her?

But she wasn't lost—at least not physically. She chewed up the cherry and swallowed it. She took the last bite of fruit cocktail and tipped the can back like a cup to her lips.

This would be her last day walking. Nothing would stop her, not even the dark—she'd get home, and that was all there was to it.

But what about the others? Why hadn't the radio mentioned them?

Ted or Melvin or whoever he was—he was a phony and probably a loner. No one would miss him.

How long would it be before someone at Willamette University informed the parents of Will and Tanya that they hadn't attended their classes? Even then, no one would ever know how they'd disappeared. Maybe they had gone to a commune—lots of people did.

As for Tanya, what would people think when a barmaid disappeared at the same time as one of her customers? Clint and Tanya—running off together. Sometime in the spring someone would find Clint's pickup. What would people think then? A weird spot for adultery, yes?

The hunter would find his cabin, but whatever was left of the skeletons wouldn't match those two lovers. Someone would figure out an arsonist had started the fire, most certainly to burn the bodies. Animals would find and scatter the bones, but even if authorities figured out one of them belonged to Jim, what would be the conclusion?

Tanya took off with Jim instead of Clint? Or with both men in Clint's truck? A damned love triangle off in the boonies, ending with murder and arson. Strange times, these days, yes?

One certainty—Bev would have to claim her outing took place far the hell away from here. Assuming she did make it to civilization on this day— and she damn well was going to—the first thing she'd have to do is get her VW out of Kelso, if people hadn't already figured out it was hers.

What if she'd parked her car by the Spar Pole Saloon? She wouldn't have a prayer, then.

Whatever she said, she was going to have to play stupid. No, she didn't know the full names of the people she was with. No, she didn't know exactly where they were when the blizzard hit. Her story would stink to high heaven of deceit. No one would like it, but that's just the way it would have to be.

She put the empty fruit cocktail can in a garbage sack.

She grasped the rope and plodded down the road, pulling the sled and avoiding the scrambled snow last night's back-and-forth had stirred up. Though she had at most only twenty pounds to pull, the sled still felt as though it were piled with iron. In less than fifty yards only Cooper's footprints disturbed the soggy calf-high snow. She avoided the indentations he'd made, as if they were cracks in a sidewalk, potent with bad luck.

At least one deer, perhaps two, had walked the road. Farther down, the forked prints of a family of turkeys went crossways left to right. Steller's jays squawked like loud drunks. Beneath the feeble warmth of sun, evergreens released their last clumps of snow.

After ninety minutes, snow barely covered her ankles. She brushed snow off a stump and sat down. If she were covering a mile per hour, she still had six or seven miles to go. It would be dark when she reached the road. She might catch someone driving home from work, if any houses existed past the point where they'd left pavement last Friday.

"Guess I need to practice," she said, still sitting on the stump. She lit a cigarette.

"Hi, Pops. Hi, Mom. I'm home!"

Except she'd do better to call from a pay phone. They wouldn't mind a collect call. They'd be grateful for it.

First get the hell out of Kelso. Make the call from Castle Rock.

"No, no. I can drive. I'll be home in ninety minutes, two hours tops."

What an amazing time frame—two hours. The length of a movie. Imagine that. In a warm building, wearing dry clothes. Popcorn.

Her vision turned inward and placed her a third of the way back in a movie theater. She was a teenager again. Billy sat next to her, his arm around her shoulders, his fingers caressing her neck above the collarbone. She sensed the lust steaming from him, and it gave her a thrill to know she was doing that to him— well, she and Raquel Welch, who was playing some cavewoman bimbo on the screen. His hand found her knee and rubbed the flesh, and she knew where that hand wanted to go, and maybe this time she'd let him. Sweet Jesus—when were they going to get married?

A voice—her own voice on the theater's intercom, announced that Bev and Billy had already been married. He was dead now, and it was time to leave the theater.

Her eyes looked out at the ankle-high snow and the sled in front of her. How much time had gone by? Had she slept while sitting on the stump, or was she hallucinating?

She pushed herself up. Her legs went weak, and she fell to her knees. She laughed because it was ridiculous to collapse like that, ridiculous and deadly. She gathered energy from every corner of her body, sent it to her legs, rose, and wobbled. She took the rope and walked.

"It's okay," she said. "I can drive."

She counted out twenty steps.

"I don't know where we were. I wasn't paying attention. Somewhere around Mt. St. Helens."

She noticed her father and mother walking alongside her.

Where am I from?

Goofy Town.

She felt a moment of panic—where was Sandra? But she turned to look behind her and let out a breath of relief when she saw her daughter riding on the backpack on the sled, the same place she'd been all day. They stayed with her while she trudged ahead.

Directly in front of her, walking backward as smoothly as if he were going forward, a cop who looked like Rod Steiger from *In the Heat of the Night* stared her down.

"I'm sorry," she said. "I don't know why I don't know their last names. It just never came up. No, we never talked about where we were from, or anything about our families."

The cop shot a look through her heart.

"Yes, I was in Kelso, but I never went to any saloon. Why would I do that? I was there for a story on a basketball player, and that was it. I'm sorry about those people, but I don't know anything about them. I hope they find their way out of the mountains like my friends and I did."

Friends?

"I mean, not friends, just the people I was with."

Practice. Oh boy, did she need to practice.

"I don't know what you're talking about, Officer. I told you I was never in a saloon. That's not my style."

The hell with him—this cop walking backward in front of her. He wouldn't be able to prove a damn thing.

Except for Cooper, all the witnesses were dead.

Behaving like a proper hallucination, the cop faded into nothingness—only to have Clint replace him, gliding backward also, the same pace as Bev. Like a worm tunnel, a hole had been bored through his neck, a little off center, crusted black around the circumference.

Bev fought an urge to look away. "You shouldn't have been here," she said. "You shouldn't have lied."

He spoke, although she heard no words.

"I buried you. Go back to your hole."

He refused.

So she looked through him, to the road ahead of her, snow thinning to an inch or two, both sides thick with conifers. She pretended she didn't see him. Deprived of sustenance, Clint faded and then disappeared.

She decided to keep her family, Pops on her left, Mom on her right, Sandra on the sled. Time grew numb. At some point, in open stretches of road, puddles and mud replaced snow, although she hardly noticed it. Iced snow, hard like a skating rink, remained where trees crowded the lane. She had to creep flat-footed to stay upright, cursing the ice for slowing her pace, while the sun snuck toward the woods on her right. Perhaps two hours of daylight remained. She had no idea how far she'd come and how far she had to go. It felt as though a whole football team had spent an hour punching her thighs and quads and calves.

By the time the sun fled behind a curtain of firs and

alders, Billy joined them, walking slightly ahead on the opposite side of the road. She sensed his frustration toward her for not telling the truth, but at least he and her parents had the good sense to keep quiet about it.

When she stopped to retrieve the tin of Spam, her daughter rose off the sled to give her access to the pack. Because Sandra and the others were only hallucinations, she didn't have to share. She ate the Spam while walking, holding the tin with the same hand that held the rope and using a pocket knife in her other hand to cut and spear small chunks of meat. Chewing slowly, she made it last until dusk, stopping afterward to add the empty tin to the trash bag. She retrieved the headlamp Cooper had left in her pack, put it around her forehead, but didn't yet switch it on.

Around the next curve, she found everyone at work in the *Chronicle* newsroom. Frank, the managing editor, stepped away from his desk and approached her. His cheeks appeared more caved than usual, his head half bald, his teeth nicotine yellow. Rod Steiger in his cop uniform stepped out of the woods and joined her boss.

"I won't write a story about this," she told them in a voice that forbade contradiction. "It's too personal, too painful. Maybe in a few months. Can't you see? I'm almost dead."

She watched the various reporters—several on phones, typing or jotting notes while they spoke, several intent upon their writing, and it looked like Arnie was sketching a page layout for the sports section. They gave her short glances as she walked through the newsroom and out the other side onto the road.

****

It had been dark for two hours when she reached the main road. A swollen half-moon peeked above the trees, casting a milky stream across the gray asphalt. To her right, close but not visible, the Washougal River clamored from around a bend, frantic to reach the Columbia.

She couldn't recall any homes this far out of Washougal, but on the way up it had been difficult to notice anything with Melvin ranting in the back of the van. She could barely walk, and the harder surface magnified the soreness of her legs. She imagined herself cloaked inside the sleeping bag in a hidden spot near the river, and her legs cried out, *Yes! Yes!*

Her mother and father gave her sidelong glances, but they didn't say anything. Neither did Billy or Sandra.

She kept moving.

Not five minutes after she hit pavement, a brand-new luxury car, its exterior of pomegranate red gleaming in the light of the moon, passed by without slowing. Fifty yards down the road, the brake lights showed, and then the car reversed.

She had never hitchhiked. Too many bad things could happen.

But she had her pistol. She guessed she probably stank so badly that even Sasquatch wouldn't attack her.

When the car drew even it stopped and the passenger door opened. Bev looked left and right, ahead and behind her—her family was gone. In the car, a middle-aged man wearing a blue shirt and a black tie leaned down from the driver's seat, peering at her. He looked tall and thin, dark-haired—like Cooper, without the beard, after a long bath. She moved back a step—

Jesus, it couldn't be him, could it?

"What the blazes are you doing out here this time of night?" he asked, his voice gravelly, as though he'd damaged his vocal cords from a life spent shouting.

She bent low so he could see her. "Thank you, sir. I was out looking for mushrooms, and I got caught in the blizzard."

"What blizzard? What kind of mushrooms? I've heard about you young people."

"Up in the mountains. It was bad."

"The blizzard or the mushrooms?"

"We never found any mushrooms."

"Who's *we*? You've got somebody else with you?"

She pressed her lips together. Damn. She'd have to be careful about which pronouns she used. "He left," she said.

"What kind of man leaves a woman stranded like this in the middle of nowhere?"

"Good question," she said. "I suppose I've been stupid."

Chapter Forty-Five

It was drizzling when the cab driver let Bev out at a gas station down the street from her vehicle. There were no signs on her car, no cops waiting to see if she'd show up. She couldn't resist a quick drive-by past the Spar Pole and the grassy lot across the road from the hotel. Jim's pickup was gone. Maybe his parents had an extra key. She couldn't remember the kind of vehicle Tanya owned, only that it was lime green. It was gone, too.

She drove ten miles north to Castle Rock, stopped in front of a phone booth at a Chevron, and once more rehearsed her replies. When she stepped out, her legs buckled and she fell to the ground. She rose to her knees, grasped the door handle, and pulled herself up just as a squat thirty-something man with buzz-cut rust-colored hair dashed out from the service station.

"You okay, ma'am?"

"I'm sorry," she said. "I don't know what happened, but I'm okay."

He eyed her up and down. "You don't look okay. Can I help you? Do you need me to call anyone?"

"No. I've had a long drive from Seattle, flat tire along the way, but I'm okay."

Disappointment washed over his face—no damsel in distress for him. He turned to go back to the station, then whirled around.

"Wait a second," he said. "You're that missing woman from Gresham. I saw your picture on the news."

Her heart raced. "No, I'm not. I know I look like her. I saw the picture, too. I couldn't believe it. But I'm not her."

"They said she was driving a white Volkswagen."

"Yeah. Isn't that freaky?"

"I won't say anything if you don't want to be found. But I'll still help you. You can trust me."

"Damn it, I'm not her. You're the second person who's said that. You can go back inside. I've never been lost in my life."

"What happened to your hands?"

"I…it was hard to change the flat."

He nodded slowly.

"They said you went looking for mushrooms, but you never told anyone where."

"I'm not her."

"I pay attention to those kinds of things. Ever since they built this new freeway, all kinds of people stop here. So I study things, like those FBI posters."

"There's no convincing you, is there? Who else is missing?"

"Kid from Kelso. Went hunting and hasn't come back. That's been on the news, too. A young lady showed up two days ago with a handful of posters with his picture, wanting to hang one here, but we don't put up those sorts of things."

She looked down, held back a sob.

"You know him?"

"No. Why would I? I'm from Eugene."

"You've got a long ways to go."

"Yes, I do. Now if you'll excuse me."

She stepped toward the phone booth, hoping she wouldn't collapse. She made it inside, put a hand on the metal shelf, took a breath. Nobody was going to like her answers. Her parents would know she wasn't telling the whole story. When she picked up the receiver, her fingers shook. It did no good to remind herself how ecstatic she should be to finally call home, to finally go home. But her nerves gyrated, and her breath was tight. It was the same kind of fear she'd felt out in the woods, when someone was killing her companions.

Her mother answered the phone.

"Collect call from Bev Wikowski," said the operator. "Do you accept the charges?"

"Oh, God," gasped her mother. "Yes. Yes, I accept them."

"Mom." She thought she'd be able to hold back the tears, but a stream dribbled out her eyes and wet her cheeks. That man in the gas station was staring at her, so she turned away. "I'm okay. There was a blizzard."

"I know. Felix! Get Sandra out of bed! Bev's on the phone! Oh, Bev, we thought you'd...never mind what we thought. You're alive."

Bev felt a grin break loose, the salt of tears dripping off her lips. Her legs went weak again, but she stayed upright by leaning back against the booth.

"Say something," said her mother. "Say something, or I'll think it's a dream."

"I'm here. It's real. I'm coming home."

"Mommy!"

"Oh, Sandra." She felt her heart might burst. "Yes, it's Mommy."

"Where have you been?"

"A bad storm with lots of snow and wind made me

get stuck in the mountains."

"Good to hear your voice, Beverly." Her father. She pictured the three of them, jamming their ears together while her mother held the phone.

"It's good to hear yours, too."

"I'll come get you," he said. "Where are you?"

"I'm in Castle Rock. We were in the mountains near Mt. St. Helens. Somewhere out of Toutle Lake. We had to walk out. But my car's still here, and I've got a full tank of gas. I should be home in ninety minutes. Will you keep Sandra up for me?"

"Will we ever," said her mother. "You know, we've been saving a leftover slice of pumpkin pie. I can't think of a better sight than to see you home eating it."

"Mom, it'll be a week old."

"Don't worry. It's wrapped in cellophane in the fridge. I'll scrape off the whipped cream."

"Can I have a bite, too?" asked Sandra.

"Yes," said Bev. "We'll use the same fork."

"I'll notify Deputy Samuels," said her father. "He gave me his home phone number. Got a lot of people concerned about you."

"A lot of people are going to be very happy," said her mother. "We'll call your brothers, too."

"Thanks, Mom."

"You be careful," continued her mother. "I'll be worried sick the whole time. Are you sure you feel up to it? Your father will come get you."

"No, I'm okay. I don't want to leave my car."

"He can bring Justin, you know. Justin can drive your car back."

"Take me, too," said Sandra.

"We'll all come," said her mother.

"I just…I just want to come home," said Bev. She wiped her face with the sleeve of her jacket.

"Mommy, are you crying?" asked Sandra.

"No, Little Goose. Well, maybe a little, because I'm so happy."

"Grandma's crying, too. Are you happy, Grandma?"

"Think about it," said her father. "She's survived a blizzard. She can drive a car."

"Thanks, Pops. This call's going to cost you a fortune. I still need to call work to let them know I'm okay. I hope they haven't fired me."

"What do you mean?" said her father. "They ran a front-page story on you. *Chronicle reporter missing, feared lost in blizzard.* Jesus, the whole city's been worried. They're not going to fire you."

"We'll call them, dear," said her mother. "How are you going to call them from a phone booth? Are they going to accept a collect call?"

Bev glanced back inside the station. The little blimp was still watching her. The hell with him. He asked how he could help—he could exchange some quarters for a few bucks.

"I'm at a gas station. I'll get change. Mom, let me call them. I'm the employee."

"All right, dear. We'll get off the phone. You just be careful."

****

On a Wednesday evening in May the next year, Bev sat at a bare metal table, working through police reports at the East Precinct Station, her cigarette propped on a glass ashtray. She was on her third week working the crime beat.

A dog at large. A complaint about loud music. A minor collision in a parking lot—no injuries, so no story. A liquor store holdup—that was newsworthy.

She'd begun copying the particulars when Sergeant Lucroy turned his chair away from his desk to face her. He was tall, with a jaw that would bust marbles if his yellowed teeth could take it. His face had grown puffy from what it had probably been in his younger days, and what hair he had left was a dark gray. He set down a greasy sandwich half wrapped in wax paper and rubbed the back of his hand across his mouth.

"Hey, Wikowski."

"Yeah."

"You the one survived that fuckin' blizzard?"

"Some others did, too."

"And some didn't."

Bev stopped writing and forced herself to make eye contact. Perhaps the cops hadn't given up on her, after all. Perhaps they'd spoken to the Kelso cops.

Keep an eye on this woman. See if you can get her to slip up.

She had nothing to say to Sergeant Lucroy. She picked up her cigarette and smoked.

Lucroy probed his tongue along his cheek, fishing for bits of sandwich. "Deputies across the river got a call from some guy whose cabin burned down during the winter, a few miles from where those loggers found an abandoned truck a few weeks ago. That's not the real story, though. Real story's they found human remains. Two people. Pretty fucked up, from what they say. Busted-up skeletons, half the bones missing. Thought maybe one of them could've been the pickup owner, but the coroner says the height doesn't match. Deputies don't have a fuckin' clue. Speculation is somehow they holed up, maybe during the blizzard, maybe blew themselves to smithereens, propane, something like that, because that cabin is nothing but fuckin' powder now."

"Jesus," she said. "That sounds awful."

"No shit. You think you're safe, you've found some shelter, and you blow yourselves the fuck up. Anyway, they don't really know if it happened during the blizzard. But that's what they're thinking."

"I wish I'd found a cabin," said Bev.

"How'd you survive?"

"We had tents. It wasn't very comfortable."

He picked up the sandwich and took a large bite. When he turned back to his desk, Bev started copying again from the report. Her heart was racing, and she didn't comprehend what she was reading or writing.

Lucroy spun in her direction again.

"The papers said you were looking for mushrooms," he said while chewing. "The cooking kind, some kind of fancy name."

"Chanterelles."

"Sure. Whatever. You're not going to fuckin' fool me."

Her heart rate increased to a full gallop. "Pardon?" she asked.

Look natural. No fear.

"Had to be magic mushrooms. No one risks their asses for chanterbells, or whatever you want to call them, with a big storm barreling in. Jesus, people your age. Why can't you stick with keggers, the way we used to? We'd get blitzed, but at least it was legal. Maybe underage, but we wouldn't go to prison for it. We weren't so fuckin' desperate we'd tromp through the woods with snow pounding our faces."

Bev's heartbeat moved out of the fast lane. They didn't know.

When they found the truck and traced it to Clinton Roscoe, they'd concluded what she thought they might—he'd run off with the barmaid, and for some reason they must have had Jim Rossi with them. In none of the three states on the Pacific Coast had a man named Melvin been reported missing. Four months ago, she'd found the name *William Garfield* on the Oregon State Police Missing Persons Report, which she'd been checking weekly. Afterward, *Susan Taylor* appeared on the California Department of Justice list. Neither report mentioned the town of Kelso.

For now, Lucroy's suspicions called for an enigmatic smile and a casual exhalation of smoke, which she did her best to supply.

"You can think whatever you want," she said.

A word about the author...

Rick E. George is also the author of *Vengeance Burns Hot.* He has been a sportswriter, a hotshot firefighter, and an educator. He lives in the Cascade Mountains of Washington. Visit him at:
http://rickegeorge.com
Like him at:
https://www.facebook.com/rickegeorge/
He welcomes reviews on Amazon and Goodreads.

Thank you for purchasing
this publication of The Wild Rose Press, Inc.

For questions or more information
contact us at
info@thewildrosepress.com.

The Wild Rose Press, Inc.
www.thewildrosepress.com

To visit with authors of
The Wild Rose Press, Inc.
join our yahoo loop at
http://groups.yahoo.com/group/thewildrosepress/